# SMOKED MEAT

D0540344

# SMOKED MEAT

Rowena Macdonald

FlambardPress

First published in Great Britain in 2011 by Flambard Press
Holy Jesus Hospital, City Road, Newcastle upon Tyne NE1 2AS
www.flambardpress.co.uk

Typeset by BookType
Cover Design by Gainford Design Associates
Cover image 'White Chevy, Red Trailer' © John Salt, used by kind permission of John Salt and Birmingham Museum and Art Gallery
Printed in Great Britain by Bell & Bain, Glasgow

A CIP catalogue record for this book is available from the British Library.

ISBN: 9781906601331

Copyright © Rowena Macdonald 2011
All rights reserved.
Rowena Macdonald has exerted her moral rights in accordance with
the Copyright, Designs and Patents Act of 1988.

'We Will Rock You' Words and Music by Brian May © 1977,
reproduced by permission of EMI Music Publishing/Queen Music Limited,
London W8 5SW

'Montreal' by August Kleinzahler from *The Strange Hours Travelers
Keep* (Faber & Faber Ltd, 2004), reproduced by kind permission of
August Kleinzahler

'Brian, McMurphy & Sally Too' was first published in *Little Roasts*
(Roast Books, 2009)

Flambard Press wishes to thank Arts Council England
for its financial support.

Supported by
ARTS COUNCIL
ENGLAND

Flambard Press is a member of Inpress.

The paper used for this book is FSC accredited.

*for Chloé and Mark*

# Contents

*Corinna of the milky thighs*
*unfastened her wrapper and drew a bath*
*so that she might wash, dream,*
*then wash herself again*
*that warm spring night in the fragrant room.*

'Montreal', August Kleinzahler

# Brian, McMurphy & Sally Too

'Brian's sort of classically ugly,' Sally pointed out, not long after she had met him. Though McMurphy had never really thought about it before he could see she was right. Like Disney's version of the Hunchback of Notre Dame, Brian's ugliness was so cartoonish it was almost cute – he was short and fat; his face was round and chinless; he had jug ears, a banana nose, and a buck-toothed grin. The finishing touch was a large port-wine stain splashed across his left cheek.

McMurphy meanwhile was handsome: tall and blond with sexily brutal Germanic features that belied his Irish roots. He wasn't conceited about his appearance and maintained (mainly to himself) that such things didn't matter, but equally he never looked in a mirror without feeling pretty pleased. He could not imagine how it felt to be disappointed by your reflection; indeed, he had never tried.

Brian & McMurphy were a ubiquitous and inseparable fixture on Montreal's underground scene. They lived together in an eight thousand square foot loft on the seventh floor of a decrepit warehouse on Rue Ontario, round the corner from the red-light district. There they made art, ran life-drawing classes, held huge parties and plotted their eventual conquest of New York City. Brian painted portraits of local waitresses, bar tenders, shop girls and pizza-delivery drivers. McMurphy focused on traffic signs, telegraph poles, road markings and street lamps. They wanted to show the beauty in everyday life, though they never explained this as such. If you collared them at a *vernissage* they would simply mumble, 'Uh . . . yeah . . . it's Jimmy from the *dépanneur* on Clark' or 'That stop sign is on Sherbrooke. I liked the look of it.'

People often remarked on what an odd pair they made, implying that McMurphy ought to hang out with someone better looking. In fact McMurphy was loyally bonded to Brian by a long shared history. They had grown up together in Gimli, a deadbeat town on the outskirts of Winnipeg where the biggest thrills were shooting-up horse tranquilisers and playing chicken on the railroad track that ran across the main street. The only shops were Jake's Bait Shack, which did a brisk trade in lugworms, a hardware store where you could get your ice skates sharpened along with your knives, and the Food Mart, which sold every kind of Kraft dinner but no vegetables.

The first time McMurphy saw Brian he was drawing a penis on the Gents sign outside the boys' toilet block at Gimli Junior High. When McMurphy suggested amending the Ladies sign too, Brian scrawled breasts, a vagina and a pair of devil's horns onto it with casual haste. Though Brian was an obvious bullies' target and McMurphy was an obvious bully, McMurphy liked Brian's disregard for authority. They became firm friends, sitting next to each other throughout school, nursing secret artistic ambitions and dreams of escape. At eighteen they vanished to Montreal together to pursue the same painting degree at Concordia University, both discarding the embarrassing parts of their names. Consequently, no one in Montreal knew that Brian's surname was Smellie or that McMurphy was known to his mother as Nigel. Admittedly, the name Brian was not exactly suave but it had a retro charm and, of course, the name McMurphy had thrilling overtones of insanity.

They decided to wear matching outfits at all times. Their look was classic clean-cut Americana: blue Levi's, Converse sneakers and bright T-shirts emblazoned with logos for Coca-Cola, Budweiser and Reese's Peanut Butter Cups.

Their one-word names and co-ordinated clothes were calculated to create charisma, as was the mystery surrounding their sexuality. In truth, McMurphy was vigorously straight while Brian was hopelessly gay. They slept in separate cubby-holes partitioned off from the rest of their loft by curtains.

The loft itself was part of their mythology. They ate, slept, washed and watched TV surrounded by half-finished canvases and the smell of paint and turps. The kitchen was denoted by a two-ring camping stove and a yellow chrome-trimmed fridge, the size of an upended Cadillac. It led into the silver-painted bathroom, which featured a makeshift shower and Brian's collection of Action Men. The living room was separated from the studio by walls made from old books bought in a job lot from a garage sale. These walls were often toppled during parties and had to be re-built the next morning.

The studio dominated the loft. By night it was lit

by four arc lamps stolen from a theatre. By day the sun spilled through the giant windows across the paint-spattered floorboards. A jumble of easels and donkey benches faced towards a four-by-four raised wooden block where the life models did their thing. Brian & McMurphy kept a long list of models' phone numbers stuck to the fridge with a magnet shaped like a banana. At one time the models' photographs had been stuck there too until Barb, one of the drawing students, complained it was infringing on their privacy.

'But we all get to see them in the nude anyway,' Brian pointed out.

'Yes, but that is within a designated space and time as part of an agreed contract. Sticking them up on the fridge is a breach of this contract and turns them into mere objects of public consumption.'

Barb also protested against the calendar of life-drawings Brian & McMurphy produced for sale one Christmas because it was entitled *A Year of Pin Ups*: 'It's totally pandering to the male gaze.'

'We've got men in there as well,' said Brian. 'Look: February is a man, so is June . . . September *looks* like a man . . .'


Life modelling was a lucrative business in Montreal. There were dozens of drawing classes in colleges, galleries and studios across the city. Brian & McMurphy's class was a particularly sought-after gig because Brian played records on his decks and McMurphy handed out beer during breaks. They did wacky things like make the students draw with their eyes closed or get the models to pose with a cowboy hat and a rocking horse. The whole set-up was just so *cool*.

One January morning someone banged on the door of the loft. McMurphy was out taking photographs of a lamp-post that had been knocked down by a snowplough on St Urbain. Brian was indoors building a sandwich: a masterpiece involving ham, cheese, mango chutney, alfalfa sprouts, sun-dried tomatoes, sliced banana and two halves of a raisin-and-cinnamon bagel. Parliament's 'Give Up The Funk (Tear The Roof Off The Sucker)' was thumping from the stereo. In the tiny gap between this track and 'Aqua Boogie (A Psychoalphadiscobetabioaquadoloop)' Brian heard the banging.

'Yes?' he shouted.

In the doorway stood a tiny girl dwarfed by an enormous Puffa coat and a huge Cossack hat.

'I knew there was someone in!' she shouted back.

'I had my music on.' Brian loped across the studio and turned the volume down slightly. When he turned round the girl had come in and was sizing up his sandwich.

'Can I help you?' He sat down and swung his sneakers up onto the dining table.

'Are you Brian McMurphy?'

'Brian.' He folded his arms.

'Brian McMurphy?'

'Just Brian.'

'Oh.' The girl took a scrap of paper from her pocket

15

and peered at it.' I was told your name was Brian McMurphy.'

'I'm Brian. McMurphy is my partner.'

'Partner?'

'Colleague. Co-worker. Roommate. Business partner. Partner in crime. Whatever.'

'You don't sleep together then?'

Brian swung his feet back onto the floor and frowned. 'No, we don't. Excuse me, what is this? I'm just having breakfast here, so . . .'

'I'm sorry to interrupt. I was told you run life-drawing classes and you might be looking for models. I was wondering whether I could leave my number with you and maybe you could use me sometime?'

'Do you have any experience of life modelling?'

'No.'

'What makes you think you would be able to life model?'

'I've got a good body.'

'OK. Do you have any photographs?'

A Polaroid was produced from another pocket. It was out-of-focus but there was no mistaking that the girl reclining along one hip on a green linoleum floor was the girl standing before Brian. Though he wasn't moved by the sight he could see what she said was true.

'If I write my number on the back, will you call me?'

'We do have a long list of models and we are booked up for the next two months, but if anyone drops out then I might give you a call.'

'I'd really appreciate that, Brian.'

Brian watched as she leaned against the wall and

scrawled *Sally – tel: 514 931 0457* on the back of the Polaroid in metallic pink ink.

'Sally.'

'That's right.'

'Where are you from, Sally?'

'Honey Harbour. Ontario.'

'Honey Harbour, huh? That sounds nice.'

'It's not that nice. Not in winter, anyhow.'

'Where is, in Canada?'

'I guess.' She goggled at the loft as if she had only just noticed it. 'Wow! Do you live here all the time?'

'Yes I do. All the time. Me and McMurphy.'

'You *and* McMurphy. Brian *and* McMurphy.' She stressed the and. 'Hey, that's a cool fridge. In both senses of the word.'

'Thanks.'

She strolled up to the fridge and inspected the models' list.

'Are these all your models?'

'Yes they are.'

'It's a long list.'

'Yes it is.'

Dropping the list, she looked up and fixed him with wide eyes. 'Brian. I really am desperate for work. I've been in Montreal a month and I've tried everywhere asking for jobs but the place is dead. Everyone's saying, "Wait till spring," but I have absolutely no money and I really need a job, so please, if you would consider me as a model, I would be so, so grateful.' The tilt of her face grew more plaintive as she spoke.

Brian nodded. 'I'll see what I can do.' He pulled his sandwich towards him.

'Thank you. I'm sorry to interrupt your breakfast.' She withdrew into the hall and closed the door.

Normally, Brian would have left the Polaroid out for McMurphy to peruse when he returned. That day, however, he shoved it into the back pocket of his jeans and slowly ploughed through the sandwich, frowning over the interruption to his morning. He had a mind to tear Sally's picture into very small pieces but an innate respect towards the medium of photography stopped him. The better part of his character sympathised with her plight but something about her struck him with an ominous chill; something about the assertiveness with which she had used his name: '*Brian. I really am desperate . . .*'

'Hey, did you eat all the sun-dried tomatoes?' McMurphy had returned with a full roll of mangled lampposts.

'Sorry Mac, I was really hungry.'

'Anybody call?'

'No, nobody important.'

\*

A few days later McMurphy stepped over Brian's legs and hunched over the coffee table. 'I'm two dollars short for some smokes. Brian, you got two bucks?'

Brian was stretched out on the old Buick seat, watching TV with the sound turned down and singing along to Betty Harris' 'I'm Evil Tonight'. He patted all his pockets and found seventy-five cents. 'Have a look in my other jeans.'

'Where are they?'

'In the bathroom, on the floor.'

McMurphy returned, waving the battered Polaroid. 'Sally, huh? Who the hell is *Sally*?'

'Some girl that came round the other day.'

'She wanted to model?'

'Yeah.' Brian drummed his fingers.

'You never told me about her.'

'I forgot.'

McMurphy raised his eyebrows and stuck Sally's picture to the fridge.

'Barb won't like that,' said Brian.

'Fuck Barb.'

\*

'I'm sorry I don't have a dressing gown.' Sally's tone was not apologetic.

She was standing in the centre of the four-by-four block in Brian & McMurphy's studio, naked except for her Puffa coat and surrounded by a circle of students, all waiting with pencils poised.

'I think I might have something you can wear.' McMurphy retrieved a towelling robe from his bedroom and laid it at her feet.

It was the moment they had all been waiting for. Brian, who could stand the suspense no longer, clapped his hands, 'OK everybody. Let's go.'

Sally shrugged the coat from her shoulders and raised her arms aloft. Nothing was said. There were no gasps of surprise or delight but the atmosphere in the room was as taut as a freshly stretched canvas. She shimmered before them, a vision of perfection, every curve and angle corresponding with the classical ideal as if she had been composed by a draughtsman with an expert eye. The arc of her bottom and her high round breasts cried out to be cupped in the palm of a hand. Her nipples were pinkish-brown, well defined from her creamy skin, which had a density like liquid marble. Her thick black hair was pulled up with a rubber band, all the better to see the graceful length of her neck. The only distraction from the clean lines of her figure was a tattoo of a turtle crawling around her left ankle.

First off were five-minute warm-up exercises to prime the students. When Brian said, 'Change!' Sally rearranged herself and remained motionless until the next 'Change!' She posed with a feather boa, a piece of rope, her Cossack hat and two full-length mirrors, so the students had to draw an infinity of Sallys leading into nowhere. Each new position was strong and fluid; she sat, stood, curled, crouched, stretched, twisted and even, at one point, balanced elegantly on one leg.


During the break she sat in a corner picking at her feet and swigged from a bottle of Molson that McMurphy gave her. The students kept a respectful distance, the way they always did with the models. They felt awkward making small talk with someone they had just seen naked. McMurphy watched Sally stand and shuffle around the easels in his robe. Brian watched McMurphy sidle across the studio to join her.

'Hey,' said McMurphy.

'Hey,' said Sally.

'What do you think?'

They surveyed a drawing of her profile.

'What do *you* think?'

'I would say it's a good drawing but it's not a good portrait.'

'I wish I looked like that.'

'You don't like the way you look?'

'I wish my nose was that straight.'

Sally's nose was small and *retroussé*. McMurphy suspected she secretly liked it.

'You've got a cute nose.'

'Well, thank you.'

'Want a cigarette?'

'Sure.' She ducked her head to catch the flame and smiled as she veiled herself in a ring of smoke.


After the class was over she disappeared into the bathroom to get dressed. Brian was in the kitchen opening a can of soup when she poked her head out and asked if she could take a shower.

'Of course you can. No problem,' McMurphy chirruped from the other side of the studio.

'Thank you so much. Thing is, where I'm staying at the moment, the water is really cold, so I have to grab a shower whenever I see a nice one.'


'So, where are you staying at the moment?' McMurphy asked, when she reappeared with wet hair and all her

21

clothes on.

'In a rooming house, down in Little Burgundy.' She wrinkled her cute nose.

'Is it horrible?'

'It's full of really gross old men. I can hear them all coughing at night.'

'Not exactly the Ritz then . . .'

'Not exactly.' She gathered up her bag and edged towards the door. 'I guess I ought to let you get on with your dinner.' She nodded towards their soup.

'You're welcome to stay. We got enough, haven't we, Bri?'

Brian dropped his spoon with a clatter.

Sally inched further towards the door. 'Don't worry. I'll get something on the way back . . .'

McMurphy pulled out the empty chair for her. 'Relax. Stay.'

'OK.'

'You're easily persuaded,' said McMurphy.

'That's what they all say,' said Sally.

By one in the morning she had consumed two bowls of tomato soup (Campbell's – bought for the label, naturally), one grilled cheese-and-ham sandwich, one chocolate-chip muffin (Betty Crocker's), one bowl of ice-cream (Ben & Jerry's Chunky Monkey) with three spoonfuls of Dulce de Leche sauce, two glasses of cola (Coca-Cola), three bottles of Molson, three joints (a third of each), half a bag of lychees and two shots of moonshine from an old Courvoisier bottle (brewed from excess cattle crop by McMurphy's father).

By two in the morning Brian had slunk into his cubicle. When he woke the next day Sally's coat and boots and bag were scattered about the kitchen. He was not surprised when she emerged from McMurphy's cubicle wearing nothing but McMurphy's Butterkist T-shirt, followed a little later by McMurphy himself.

A strained breakfast ensued – strained for Brian & McMurphy at least. Sally seemed impervious to the atmosphere and helped herself to two bowls of Cheerios, a bagel with peanut butter and cream cheese, three cups of coffee and one glass of grape juice, while maintaining a stream of chatter about the biker wars back in Honey Harbour, the tattoos she was planning to acquire, the bad attitudes of French-Canadian waitresses and the time she tried to pierce her nipples with safety pins. This was the first morning in two years of living with McMurphy that Brian had been forced to share with a stranger. Certainly, McMurphy had zipped through his fair share of Montreal women, disappearing for nights on end and returning with bags under his eyes and a swagger to his step, but he had never brought them home. He tacitly understood that introducing a female into the microcosm of the loft would upset its delicately balanced ecosystem.

'I don't think you should get any more tattoos, Sally,' McMurphy said, while Brian stared blackly into his coffee.

'Nigel doesn't like my terrapin,' Sally explained to Brian.

'What?' Brian jolted.

'Yeah, Nigel doesn't like the terrapin I've got on my ankle.'

McMurphy seemed completely unfazed by Sally's use of his first name. He was pointing at Sally's foot,

'It's that turtle thing she's got tattooed on her ankle – it's a terrapin. Sally's really into terrapins – she's got one in her rooming house . . .'

'Yeah, I really ought to get back and feed him actually. René's gonna be missing me . . .'

'. . . her terrapin's called René – isn't that just the greatest . . .'

'. . . after René Descartes. I used to have two others called Søren and Jean-Paul, but they died . . .'

'. . . René, Søren and Jean-Paul – that's just hilarious . . .' Brian observed with distaste as McMurphy convulsed into paroxysms of mirth. 'I'm going for a walk,' he said.


When he got back many hours later he found a large fish tank bubbling in the middle of the coffee table. Between a tangle of pond weed he detected a small turtle-shaped creature with a face like a very old man. DO NOT TOUCH RENÉ!!! screamed a note in pink metallic capitals.

'Don't worry, René, I'm not even tempted,' he muttered.

For supper, he ate a cold frankfurter slapped between two crusts of bread, washed down with slugs of vodka straight from the bottle, his forehead pressed against the cold glass which separated him from the traffic winding towards Place des Arts.

He went to bed early to avoid Sally and McMurphy when they got home. Sleep refused to rescue him from his misery. He tossed and turned, worrying about the implications of Sally. The way she had McMurphy running around her like a slobbering dog sickened him. Bile rose in his throat as he pictured them together and he had to stay motionless for some time before it quelled. He was still awake when they crashed through the loft after midnight, laughing loudly at things that weren't funny. Though Brian was desperate for a pee he remained trapped behind his partition, listening in eyeball horror to their cries of passion and the Buick seat squeaking up and down. It was a long night.

The following morning he waited until their goodbye kisses had petered out and the front door had banged shut before venturing from his bed. McMurphy was bouncing about the kitchen cooking eggs, wearing nothing but an apron with the body of a naked woman on the front. 'Want some breakfast?'

Brian shouldered past him to the bathroom.

'No.' Brian peed long and loud, drowning out the sound of McMurphy's reply. He flushed the toilet and stared into the mirror above the sink. His eyes and mouth looked like they had been dragged down by long fingers and his birthmark was as livid as a sharp slap. He arranged his face into an expression of sardonic indifference.

'No breakfast? That's not like you, Bri,' said McMurphy, when Brian reappeared.

'I don't feel hungry.'

'Why not?'

'Because the sight of you in that stupid apron makes me feel nauseous.'

'I thought you thought this apron was funny. You were the one that bought it.'

'It doesn't amuse me anymore.' Brian wrenched the kettle from its socket and filled it with water, turning the tap full blast.

'It amused Sally.'

'Yeah, well, that's the kind of thing that would amuse her.' Brian slammed the kettle onto the counter.

'Meaning?'

'Meaning it's simple minded, puerile and crude.'

They paused. McMurphy flipped his eggs while Brian concentrated on his coffee spoon.

'You don't like Sally, do you?'

'What makes you think that?'

'Come on, Brian . . .'

Brian gritted his teeth. 'I don't *mind* her but –'

'– well, that's good. I'm glad you don't *mind* her –'

'Why?'

'– because she asked me if she could stay for a little while until she finds a place of her own –'

'What!'

'She asked me if –'

'What did you say?'

'I said she could. She's gone to fetch her things now.'

They faced each other in deadly silence. Brian calculated he had a certain psychological advantage over McMurphy by virtue of the fact he was fully dressed and not wearing a naked-woman apron.

'I don't get any say in the matter?'

'Brian. It won't be for very long. She's living in a rooming house in Little Burgundy, for Christ's sake. She doesn't know anyone here and she needs somewhere to stay. We've got so much space. She won't be any trouble. She'll clean, she'll cook; soon as she gets a job she'll find another place and pay us back some rent. Brian, please, she likes you.'

'Does she?' The pleading repetition of his name made Brian bristle with irritation. 'What if I say no?'

'Well, then, I guess I'll have to reassess a few things.'

'Reassess what?'

'Our friendship, our working relationship, our living scenario.'

'You mean, you'd move out?'

'Like I said, I would have to reassess.'

'What about New York?'

'Like I said . . .'

'. . . OK, OK, she can stay. One thing though . . .'

'What?'

'Don't fuck on the Buick . . .'

'Right.'

'. . . or the kitchen table . . .'

'OK.'

'. . . or the modelling block, or the donkeys, or in the shower . . .' Brian scanned the loft wildly for other potential surfaces. '. . . or any place that isn't within your designated bedroom partition. That's not too much to ask, is it?'

'No, it's not. Thank you, Brian. You've been very kind.'


It was no surprise to Brian that Sally turned out to be wilfully undomestic, more like a boy in the way she scattered her dirty underwear, her ashtrays, her vampire and alien magazines and her greasy Chinese-takeout cartons throughout the loft. She had no regard for other people's things, blithely wearing whatever clothes were lying around and helping herself and her terrapin to whatever took her fancy in the fridge. He was riled by the death-metal CDs she played at full tilt on his stereo and he hated the sight of René squinting blearily at him through his glass box. Her contraceptive pills and Lady Schick razors littered the bathroom. Her used Tampax blocked up the toilet and her hair got stuck to the soap. Girls' ablutions were so public, their excretions seemed to ooze and make far more mess than men's, Brian found. And for someone so small, Sally's presence filled whatever room she was in.

She was utterly confident in all her views, made them known in her deep, booming voice and laughed with her head thrown back so you could see the back of her throat. All her gestures swung with energy and she was interested in everything and everyone, hungry for information and experience. She quizzed Brian & McMurphy in detail about their backgrounds and told them all about hers. She had run away from home four times trying to escape from her insane alcoholic mother. At fourteen she was seduced by her best friend's father, who continued an affair with her while his wife took their daughter to gymnastics. At fifteen she fell pregnant and had an abortion. At sixteen she screwed her way through a biker gang before settling on a Hell's Angel named Melvin who took her on a motorcycle trip to Vancouver. They split up somewhere along the Trans-Canada Highway and she hitchhiked all the way home. After two years making cardboard boxes in a cardboard-box-making factory, she was convinced there had to be more to life and set out alone for Montreal to find it.

McMurphy listened to these high jinks with loving admiration – 'God, what a woman! What a force of nature!' Brian found Sally's stories exhausting. He was affronted by her vigour: it made him feel sickly and ill designed. She slept soundly and ate heartily, her bowel movements were regular, she had no allergies and she never got spots or hangovers, even after downing a bottle of vodka. When they all ate bad shrimps in Chinatown, she was the only one who didn't get sick, and she barely noticed when she cut herself with a penknife, trying to open a can of smoked clams for René. She emerged unscathed from taking liberties with her appearance that other girls wouldn't dare: piercing her eyebrow with a sewing needle; dyeing her hair cerise; getting a tattoo of a pig on a skateboard on her left arm.

She was indefatigably cheery towards Brian, a cheeriness that masked a deep dislike, he was sure. Trying to force a cosy intimacy, she took a concerned yet prurient interest in his sexuality, analysing his formative years with psychological theories she had read in the problem pages of *Cosmopolitan*. To begin with, she wouldn't let up on her heavy flirtation routine. She gazed deep into his eyes and allowed her T-shirt to fall off her shoulder as she told him how everyone had gay tendencies, how even she had French-kissed her best friend and fantasised about having sex with Angelina Jolie. On hearing this, Brian had shrugged while McMurphy instantly dragged her behind his bedroom partition. Gradually, she realised that Brian wasn't stirred by the sight of her cleavage as she leaned forward to ask him about his relationship with his mother. Slowly, she understood there was no point in uncrossing her legs to reveal her lack of underwear as she dissected his recurring dream which featured Keanu Reeves and a swimming pool filled with kiwi fruit. As it became clear that her charms held no power over him, she became dismissive and irritable.

She still had no regular job and made no efforts towards finding one. McMurphy cancelled all the models booked up for their drawing classes and employed Sally every week. When Brian objected, McMurphy said, 'The thing you seem to be forgetting is that Sally is an exceptional model.'

Brian had to admit that she did have a great talent for standing around naked.

Through their classes she picked up some work posing for Martin, a cartoonist who had been working for years on a pop-up history of the world, but had become fixated on the Stone Age as it allowed him to indulge his penchant for drawing naked women. Martin was a faltering loner whom Sally enjoyed taunting. In front of the other students she slunk up to him, let McMurphy's dirty robe fall open, and whispered, 'So, Martin, would you like to see me alone again this week?'

'Uh . . . yes . . . if you're free . . . sure,' he stuttered, trying to keep his eyes on his pencil.

'I won't be free, Martin, but you'll get your money's worth.'

Everybody dissolved into laughter; everybody except Brian, who disapproved of such public humiliation and Barb, who just generally disapproved.

The effect of Sally's arrival rippled far and wide. Coming in one day after a half-hour of escapism in the chocolatier round the corner, Brian was accosted by the Haitian guy who owned the clothes shop on the ground floor.

'*Vous avez une fille chez vous, maintenant, ouais?*'

'*Oui.*'

'Lucky guys, eh? *Vous la partagez?*'

Brian had to make clear that no, he and McMurphy did not share Sally but yes, she was a fine piece of work. While the guy elaborated on the fineness of Sally's finer points, the Saturday salesgirl showed up with an unlit cigarette and eyed Brian's bags of chocolate and Turkish delight so greedily he felt obliged to give her some.

But, as they were constantly reminded, Sally was not just a pretty face: 'I'm totally obsessed with the life of the mind. I want the mind.' With this aim she went to every *vernissage*, book launch and first night she heard about. McMurphy gave her the run of his art materials and she spent hours creating faux naïf pictures of the mess on the coffee table or René in his tank.

'Isn't he gorgeous?' She would hold the terrapin aloft with his limbs flailing and plant a kiss on his wrinkled nose. 'My handsome boy.' Brian had a vague idea you could catch salmonella from terrapins, but Sally petted René all the time, typically with no ill effects. The fridge was stacked with Tupperware boxes of fresh steak, shrimps and crab, labelled 'RENÉ'S FOOD – VERBOTEN' in sparkly pink. She would pick out choice morsels and drop them into his sad little mouth, while crooning slow numbers by Slipknot into his tiny ears. Twice a week she put him in a casserole dish of water while she cleaned his tank with bleach and Q-tips. Brian reckoned you could eat your dinner out of it, she kept it so uncharacteristically pristine.

As well as painting René, she also wrote poetry: mildly amusing doggerel, which she declaimed to anyone who would listen.

One afternoon she breezed in with a flyer for a poetry slam at Blizart's on St Laurent.

'*"If you're a poet and you know it, get your ass down here and show it."* Hey that's me, I'm getting my ass down there. The prize is half the money they get from the door.'

'That'll be at least three dollars then,' said Brian.

'Three dollars fifty if you come.'

'Fine. Perhaps you can donate it towards your rent.'

Brian was secretly itching to see Sally being savaged by the Blizart culture vultures, though he affected reluctance as he accompanied Sally and McMurphy up to the event.

'I can't wait to share my work with a wider audience,' yelped Sally, as they trudged through the dirty snow.

'I'm sure your wider audience can barely contain their excitement,' said Brian.

Blizart's was bathed in dark red light and crammed with the usual Plateau crowd – all complicated hairdos and casual poses. Sally zigzagged about saying hello to those who knew her, most of whom had first seen her naked. At the back of the bar was a makeshift stage and a microphone. On one side six stony-faced judges sat on tall bar stools. A manic girl with scarecrow hair leapt up and introduced herself as the compère for the evening.

'Let's hear it for our first poet – or should I say poetess? – the one, the only, the dreamy, the steamy, the very creamy . . . Cheryl Cheesecake!'

Cheryl Cheesecake had a severe black bob, wire-rimmed spectacles and a pin-striped suit. 'I'm a poet *not* a poetess,' she declared, before reading out her poem from the side of a shampoo bottle. It began with the lines,

*For a noticeably softer, shinier and more manage-
    able girl,*
*Wash three times a week,*
*Massage well to create a thick lather,*
*Rinse thoroughly,*
*Repeat as necessary and towel dry.*
*The result: your girl is noticeably more supple and
    will have less irritations . . .*

The audience clapped weakly. The judges held up six squares of cardboard marked with twos as if she was an ice skater.

A dishevelled man wearing dungarees appeared next. He turned out to be English.

*Oh man alive*
*I'm just twenty-five*
*and I haven't had sex for six months.*
*If anyone's willing*
*I'll slip them a shilling*
*for a flash of their tits*
*and a cunt.*

Nervous laughter fluttered through the crowd, then a man shouted, 'I'm willing. You wanna come and see me later?'

'You don't sound like you've got tits.'

'No, but my girlfriend has.'

Everyone cheered as the English guy left the stage. The judges held up three sixes and three fours.

Next came a pop-eyed boy with blond curls and a burgeoning beer belly.

'I went down on her SIX TIMES,' he bellowed, jumping off the stage and sweeping through the smirking audience with a preacher's zeal.

*Not once, not twice but SIX TIMES I went down on*
*    her,*
*was she GRATEFUL?*
*HELL no!*
*Montreal was EMPTY but it didn't MATTER.*
*And I said to the Lord . . . LORD: WHY HAVE YOU*
*    DONE THIS?*

'Yeah, Lord, why the fuck?' muttered Sally.

The judges didn't agree with her and gave him four sixes and two fives.

A baby-faced French boy read a poem, which mixed political commentary with ice-hockey metaphors. The subject only became apparent when the compère said, 'Only in Canada would you get political commentary mixed with ice-hockey metaphors. OK, next up . . . we have the very delightful, the very insightful, the not at all frightful . . . SALLY!'

Sally leapt onto the stage and stood with her heavy-booted feet planted wide apart and her arms akimbo.

'This poem is called "Gripped by a Frantic Pervert".'

A few titters of suspense drifted from the crowd. Sally did not smile.

*Every night I am molested.*
*Gripped*
*by a frantic pervert,*
*offered no conversation,*
*used for sexual gratification,*
*drunkenly wrangled by a monkey.*
*Oh what a life.*

Of the entire crowd, Brian laughed the loudest. 'Was that about you, Mac?'

McMurphy looked faintly appalled. 'I don't think so.'

When it came to the judging, Sally lost out to the religious cunnilingus freak.

'No way,' she said as they debriefed in the harem bar of Nantha's Cuisine afterwards. 'There's no way that pop-eyed loser should have won. My poem was way better.'

'You should have gone down on the judges SIX TIMES,' said Brian, who was feeling quite warm to Sally in her defeat.

'What should I have done?'

'GONE DOWN ON THEM SIX TIMES . . .'


Brian & McMurphy's next exhibition opened in the bar of Chez Nanigans, a pub in the Old Port managed by their friend Zoë. Brian had met Zoë while working as a busboy at Gibby's one summer. He had painted her in the Gibby's serving wench uniform, the first in a series of waitress pictures for which McMurphy produced accompanying canvases of pepper grinders, cutlery and napkins folded into water lilies, swans and boats. When Zoë got a job at Chez Nanigans she promised they could use the bar as a gallery.

It took a whole day to hang the show. Sally milled about, passing screwdrivers and scrounging free pints of Guinness.

'So what do you do, Sally?' Leila, the other barmaid, inquired, as they contemplated a painting of the rude German waitress from Dusty's Diner.

'In terms of work?'

'Yes. Do you have a job?'

'Only job I've got right now is taking off my clothes.'

'You're a stripper?'

'No, I'm a life model.'

'You mean like . . . art?'

'Yeah.'

'Don't you feel embarrassed?'

'No.'

'God, I could never do that . . .'

'It's good money.'

'Yeah, but you have to take your clothes off.'

'You get used to it.'

The two girls huddled into a corner to discuss the financial potential of Sally's line of work. They were interrupted by Brian yelling, 'What is this!'

He had unwrapped a six-by-six canvas depicting a girl wielding a frying pan wearing a naked-woman apron. The girl bore a slight resemblance to Sally.

'I was going to tell you about that,' said McMurphy.

'This isn't part of the exhibition,' said Brian.

'That's what I was going to tell you: I think it should be.'

'Is it Sally?'

'Yes. Can't you tell?'

'Not really.'

'I was trying to subvert the idea of domesticity.'

'Well, that sounds about right – Sally certainly subverts my idea of domesticity.'

'Oh for Chrissakes . . .'

'This picture doesn't fit with the rest: Sally's not a waitress. Anyway, I'm the one who does the waitresses.'

'That's another thing I was going to tell you . . .'

'Nigel wants to do pictures of people,' Sally chipped in.

'*I* do people. McMurphy does inanimate objects.'

'Nigel doesn't want to do inanimate objects any more.' Sally moved into their space, hands on hips.

'But he's terrible at people. I mean, this barely looks like you. That's why we divided up the subjects when we first started. And stop calling him Nigel.'

'That's my name, Brian,' said McMurphy.

'No, it's not: it's not our name. Brian & Nigel McMurphy: it doesn't sound right. What if I started calling myself Brian Smellie?'

There were a few sniggers from behind the bar.

'I wouldn't have a problem if that's what you wanted to call yourself.'

'You wouldn't have a problem with Brian Smellie & McMurphy? It sounds terrible. It's not us.'

'No, it's not us.'


The painting of Sally stayed up. Everyone else liked it. Brian went to the *vernissage* in a green Dr Pepper T-shirt and a black mood. Sally and McMurphy said they would follow on later.

At ten o'clock when everyone who was anyone had arrived and the pub was a cacophony of canapés and chatter, the door swung open and Sally and McMurphy strode in. Brian stood aghast at the far end of the bar. They were both dressed in identical outfits: blue Levi's, white Converse boots and red Coca-Cola T-shirts, one of which belonged to Brian. Sally had cropped all the pink from her hair so it was as short as McMurphy's. They made a stunning pair, him so blond and her so dark. The guests swarmed around them pressing drinks into their hands and heaping praise onto their brimming egos. Brian overheard Sally announce that Nigel had 'enough charisma and looks and talent to make it as a really big star on his own in New York City' and was devastated to see Jess, an art-school friend whose judgment he had always respected, nod in agreement. He shrunk into the shadows, next to Crazy Davy, Chez Nanigans' resident lunatic, and decided that he would get horribly drunk.

*

He staggered home alone and unnoticed, tormented by the unfairness of life. At the corner of Rue Ontario, he slipped on the hard snow and shrieked. He lay in a heap, trembling with panic. He felt as if he were disintegrating into his surroundings, his edges bleeding like the print on the poetry-slam flyer that he found crumpled in his pocket when he searched for a tissue to wipe the graze on his hand. The dirty sky wheeled overhead and the city echoed with the screams of the modern world.

The loft was in disarray, strewn clothes, scattered bottles and, to Brian's disgust, locks of shorn pink hair all over the kitchen floor. The worktop was silted with broken Ritz biscuits and bits of cheese and the stove was splashed with chicken-noodle soup. The half-empty soup pan had been dumped on the dining table where it had burnt a black halo into the blue Formica. The yellow fridge – still 'cool in both senses of the word' – was entirely devoid of beer, the Molson stockpiled for the drawing classes gone. Howling like a wounded animal, Brian staggered through the studio, an empty bottle in his hand. He wanted to break something, smash something, fuck something up. His blubbery face lurched up to greet him as he tripped and fell into one of the mirrors. Swinging the bottle like a baseball bat, he smashed his reflection into smithereens. Shards rained in every direction. He picked up another bottle and flung it. Glass and water erupted with shocking force. It took Brian a moment to realize the fish tank had exploded. In horror, he picked through the debris, and found René slowly painting a trail of blood and guts across the floor. Grabbing a pair of barbecue tongs from the kitchen, he grasped René by one leg and made for the sink in the hope he would be able to mend him somehow. Briefly, their pained expressions matched. René's sudden piercing mewl made Brian drop him in fright. Flinging the tongs aside, he tried to pick René up with his bare hands instead, but the clammy mess of flesh and shell was so repellent that he tossed the terrapin blindly across the room. With a splash René landed in the soup pan. He let out a choked gurgle as he sank beneath the noodles. Brian began to cry.

# The New Chef

It was eleven thirty. The hacks from *La Presse* who made up the lunchtime crowd had yet to show. The new chef was in the kitchen, making Irish stew.

When Zoë turned up for her shift that morning, the man had been sitting in darkness at the far end of the bar with his head in his hands; a skinny, pale figure dressed entirely in black.

He looked up as she stomped the slush off her boots.

'Are you . . . did Bobby let you in . . . ?' She approached him tentatively, shaking snowflakes from her hair. Close to, she saw a cigarillo dangling from his fingers, a half-drunk pint of Guinness at his elbow and the *Globe and Mail* open in front of him. He was reading the small ads.

'I'm not a customer.' His voice was low and Zoë detected an Irish accent.

'Oh?'

'I'm the new chef.'

'The new chef . . . ?'

'Sean.' He clamped the cigarillo into his mouth and shook her hand. 'You must be Zoë – Bobby told me about you.'

'Bobby never said we were getting a new chef . . . What happened to Max?'

'Max?' Sean shrugged.

'The Russian.'

'No idea. Bobby didn't say.' He ran his hands through his hair. Zoë reckoned she could see the grease glaze his fingers.

'What about Franco?'

'Franco who?'

'The other chef. The Italian. He does Wednesdays, Thursdays and Fridays.'

'Not anymore he doesn't.'

Zoë took off her jacket, her scarf, her mittens, her woollen sweater and her cotton shirt until she was left standing in jeans and a red halterneck, worn in anticipation of Max. She switched on the lights. Sean looked her up and down. His eyes were the kind he would probably describe as 'smiling'.

\*

'You talked to him yet?' Leila was rotating a tea towel round a brandy glass. She hung the glass from the ceiling rack, knocked the long ash from her cigarette and took a deep drag.

'He told me he was from Ireland.' Zoë peered at her reflection in the mirror behind the bar. Her face was framed by the words 'Guinness is good for you'.

'Yeah, he told me that too.'

'Dublin "to be precoise".' Zoë tried out a come-hither look in the mirror. 'The special today is gonna be Irish stew.'

'Kinda cliché.' Leila laughed lazily.

'Some chef, huh?' Zoë turned to see Leila's expression.

Leila regarded her with benign inscrutability. 'Some chef.'

'I think Bobby might have taken me on to try and bring a little authenticity to Chez Nanigans, you know,' said Sean. ''Stead of all these Eye-ties and Ruskies . . .'

They were in the basement, where the paltry remains of the stock were kept. Zoë was giving him a tour of the premises.

'I tink you moight be roight. After all, neither me or Leila has an ounce of Irish in us . . .'

'Would you like some?' He winked.

'Jeez, you're a smooth operator, aren't you?' She rolled her eyes and hauled a barrel aside, partly to reach a box of peanuts and partly to show him she was strong. 'There's all the bar snacks . . . there's where we keep the ketchup and shit . . . Where the hell is Bobby anyway?' She shook her head as Sean held out a thin tin of cigarillos.

'He went to see a man about a dog.' Sean lit up and slid the tin into his back pocket. 'Don't bother to show me the ropes . . . I've found my way round dozens of stock rooms . . . You haven't heard about the place where I worked in London . . .'

She soon had – how the kitchen was three times the size of Chez Nanigans and the restaurant over-looked Trafalgar Square and had a four-hundred-room hotel attached, in which Sean had slept on a circular waterbed in the penthouse suite with a view of Buckingham Palace.

'Wow,' Zoë's eyes were shining. 'I would so much love to go to London.'

*

'So Sean . . . you been in Montreal long?' asked Leila, after the lunch rush was over. She, Sean and Zoë were huddled at one end of the bar eating the leftovers, as far away as possible from the sole remaining customer, Crazy Davy, who sat staring into space at the other end of the bar.

'Three months. I'm living downtown.' He ran his fingers through his hair.

'Oh yeah?'

'Yeah. In a 3½, just off McGill. Gorgeous place. I'll have to have a housewarming sometime. Nothing compared to the apartment I had in Paris though . . .'

'Oh yeah?'

'Yeah. Just near the Notre Dame it was – I could see the Eiffel Tower from my window. Amazing. That's where I did my training mostly, in Paris . . . you know, the old Cordon Bleu.'

Zoë dug into the rough-hewn Irish stew and frowned.

'*Bleu, bleu, qu'est-ce que tu dis? Donnez-moi un Bleu.*' Davy banged his empty glass on the counter. He began crooning 'Blue Moon' in a cracked accent, swooning towards them, his eyes wandering across the ceiling.

'Oh God, you've activated Davy,' said Zoë. 'He's not allowed any more after this.'

'*C'est la dernière, ouais?*' Sean spoke in perfect Joual, shifting behind the bar to pour Davy a pint of Molson Blue. Over his shoulder he continued, 'Yeah, Paris is beautiful. Beats Montreal any day. There's real class there, real civilisation, you know? When it gets to spring I might head back out there . . .'

'God, I would so much love to go to Paris,' said Leila.

*

'Pour us another one before I get started, sweetheart.' Sean waved his empty glass at Zoë as she took off her coat.

The new chef had said this to her every day for a month; a month in which it had snowed ceaselessly, turning the Old Port into an empty stage set of raking angles and dark façades as the other store owners locked their shutters and headed for Florida. The neon Guinness harp outside Chez Nanigans was one of the few lights still burning along Rue St Jacques. Bobby now disappeared for days on end and the stock had dwindled along with the drinkers. In his absence, Zoë began to go to the pub even when she wasn't working, treating it like her own glorified drinks cabinet.

Whatever time she turned up, Sean was always there, always in the same black outfit, which had got dirtier and dirtier as the days progressed. His desert boots were now looped with tidemarks from the side-walk salt.

'How come you never wear an apron?' she asked, leaning into the kitchen hatch, watching him chop carrots into haphazard chunks. Irish stew was now dish of the day every day.

'I couldn't find one here – the last chef must have walked out with it.'

'You could buy one.'

'Yeah, I could.'

'How come you don't?'

'Because I can't be arsed.'

He cooked absentmindedly, one eye scouring the small ads, one hand reaching for the cigarillo he'd propped on the nearest saucer, tomato-can lid or dessert spoon.

'What is it you're always looking for in there? In the paper?'

'Oh, you know – stuff.'

'What kind of stuff?'

'Just stuff . . . what is this – twenty questions? For fuck's sake . . .' He dropped the knife and ran his fingers through his hair. 'You're very nosey, for a wait-ress.'

'What do you mean – "For a waitress"? I am at college as well, you know . . .'

'Studying what? The Spanish Inquisition?'

'Modern European languages actually.'

*

'*Donnez-moi un Bleu.*'

'*Plus de Bleu*, Davy.' Zoë pulled a splutter of air from the pump to show she wasn't lying. '*Tu veux un* Guinness?'

'God, is that all we got left now?' asked Leila.

'Got a couple of barrels of Rousse, three Blonde and four Noire but Guinness we got the most of.' She poured Davy a pint with a shamrock etched in the creamy head.

'Cool,' said Leila. 'Chef show you how to do that?'

Zoë nodded. Leila smirked: 'You and the new chef, huh? Like that.' She held up crossed fingers.

'No.' Zoë held the fizzy-drinks pump aloft and squirted a stream of Coke straight into her mouth.

'Bobby'd go crazy if he saw you doing that,' said Leila.

'Good job he's not here then.'

'Can you show me how to do that clover thing sometime?'

'Shamrock.'

'What?'

'It's a shamrock not a clover. National flower of Ireland, according to Sean.'

'"According to Sean . . ."'

According to Sean, the cream in Irish coffees had to be poured over the back of a spoon to create a perfect spiral. According to Sean, Martinis should be stirred not shaken. According to Sean, Bloody Marys had to contain celery salt, Tabasco *and* Worcester Sauce.

Last week he'd shown them how to light a match on their teeth and the day before, he'd taught Zoë how to throw a knife.

'Hold it at the tip horizontally then just flick it vertically so it tumbles,' he explained, tossing a paring knife into the bull's-eye of the dartboard. 'Now, you have a go.'

Zoë's first knife skidded across the wire numbers and clattered to the floor. 'I don't think it's sharp enough . . . there's a sharpener in the kitchen. Shall I sharpen it?' She dashed away.

Sean watched her through the kitchen hatch as she zipped the knife across the sharpener with swift smooth strokes. 'A woman with a sharp knife is not to be trusted.'

'Is that some kind of olde oirish proverb?' She repositioned herself in front of the dartboard.

'No, it's just . . . I don't know, you looked sort of dangerous . . .' He winced as she pressed the point of the blade into the pad of her thumb. 'Here, shall I show you again?' He stood behind her with his chin almost touching her shoulder and his face so close to hers that his stubble grazed her cheek. His skin was warm and carried a distilled scent of the pub, not entirely clean but not entirely unpleasant. His fingers closed around hers, adjusting her grip on the knife.

'What are you two up to?'

Sean and Zoë started in unison. Leila was standing in the doorway.

'Sean's teaching me how to throw knives.'

'How very useful. Where'd you learn that, Sean – the circus?'

'I used to be in a biker gang.'

'Whereabouts?'

'At home. In Ireland.'

'Right.'

*

It was the morning of Jean Chrétien's birthday. CBC had announced it while Zoë was dressing for work.

'And we'd just like to wish the President a very happy birthday . . .'

The President was a Capricorn. A characteristically cynical star sign for a politician who probably didn't believe in such nonsense, thought Zoë, as she peeled on her red halter top. She wondered what Sean's star sign was – Scorpio, perhaps: mysterious, secretive and very compatible with Geminis like herself.

The pub was pitch black when she arrived at work. Even the neon harp was dead. Zigzagging around, flicking on lights, she paused a moment to note the toothbrush and razor standing in a beer stein on the sink in the men's toilets. She slipped a Bob Marley CD on the stereo (something Bobby wouldn't have allowed because it wasn't Irish), poured a Tia Maria (she and Leila were working their way through the unpopular drinks) and pulled out the copy of *War and Peace* which she kept under *The Bartender's Bible* for quiet moments.

Sean crashed through the door no sooner than she was settled. His face was puffy with bruises and blood gushed from a cut on his chin.

'Oh my God. Help me.' In his panic he sounded more Canadian than Irish.

Zoë ministered to him with a beer cloth soaked in soda water and a quadruple Glenfiddich, which he knocked back in one.

'What happened?'

'Got in a fight.' Sean screwed up his eyes.

'A fight? Who with?'

'Nobody.'

'It must have been somebody.'

'Pour me another one.' He pointed to the whisky.

'Not until you tell me who you were fighting with.'

'It was a tramp. A fucking tramp punched me. He asked me for a dollar and I told him to fuck off.'

As she swabbed his chin and applied a Band-Aid from the dusty First Aid box, he squeezed her free hand and told her she was a 'good girl'. She could have sworn she detected perfume beneath his regular odour of smoke and grease.

*

'So, Sean, when are you having a housewarming in this gorgeous apartment of yours?' demanded Leila. It was late one night a few days after the tramp incident. The bar was empty and only the light above the pool table was still burning. Sean was potting the balls with offhand expertise.

'I moved out of there. Place I'm in now is too small.'

'You never told us you moved out.'

'I don't tell you everything, Leila.'

'How big is it, this new place? A 2½? A 1½?'

'Something like that.' He shot the final yellow into the far right pocket.

'Whereabouts?'

'Other side of town.' He waggled his cue eastwards.

'When's your birthday?'

'Not till November. Perhaps I'll have moved some-where bigger by then and I can have a party.'

'I knew it, I knew it – November: a Scorpio,' Zoë piped up.

'What?'

'I just knew you were a Scorpio. Scorpio is one of the best star signs, along with Gemini . . .' She caught Leila's knowing grin. '. . . yeah, and of course Aries is a really cool sign too.'

'But not quite as cool as Scorpio, right?' Sean stood up to look at Zoë. She was erasing the drinks promotions from the blackboard as the drinks on promotion had all run dry. He leaned on his cue and read aloud the words she was chalking up instead: '"To achieve harmony in poor taste is the height of elegance." Hmmm.'

'Jean Genet,' said Zoë.

'Well, I don't know about you two star-crossed intellectuals but I'm heading out.' Leila was pulling on her moon boots. 'You wanna lock up?' She threw Zoë the keys.

'Fancy a game?' asked Sean, once Leila had gone.

'You'll beat me easy.'

'I could give you some tips.' He pushed three quarters into the slots and the balls rained down with a shudder. He positioned them carefully, swiping the triangle away like a conjurer performing a trick. 'D'you wanna break?'

'You break. I can never do it right.' Zoë watched the way he leaned in low over the cue, focused his eyes to the tip and fired an explosion of red and yellow across the green.

'You're holding it all wrong,' he said, when she arranged herself to take a shot. He snuck around the table and showed her how to make a solid crutch between finger and thumb and to hold the cue lower down, sliding it in one long smooth stroke. When it came to her next turn, he hovered beside her, one arm lingering around her waist while she potted a red ball.

'Your go: you're yellow.' She turned to face him and found herself caught between his two arms. The cut on his chin had dried to a thin red line.

'How about we call it quits?' He moved closer, pressing his crotch into hers and slowly pushed her back onto the pool table.

'Why don't we get a cab and go back to yours?' suggested Zoë. The balls rolled away beneath them. 'We might screw up the baize.'

'Fuck the baize.'

*

'You did what!' Leila clutched her hand to her mouth and turned the stereo up to drown their conversation, so Van Morrison was practically roaring about his 'brown-eyed girl'. She glanced towards the kitchen hatch but Sean remained oblivious.

Zoë smirked. 'I know – I'm terrible, huh?'

'What was it like?'

'Kind of hard . . . The table I mean . . . And you know what?'

'What?'

'He only has one ball.'

'One ball!'

'Yeah: one testicle. I got a shock when I felt down there.'

'One ball, huh?' Leila glanced at the hatch again. 'Is the rest of him . . . *satisfactory*?'

'Oh yeah. *Very* satisfactory.'

'God. One ball. Was he born that way?'

'He told me he lost it in a motorbike accident.'

'Oh really? How very *macho*.' Leila perched on the edge of the pool table.

'Yeah, I know.' Zoë stared into space. 'I mean, I do kind of like deformities . . .'

'You do?'

'Yeah, it makes people more interesting.'

'I guess.' Leila lay back on the baize, testing it for comfort.

'. . . though obviously Sean's deformity is not ideal.'

They both giggled.

'Oh shit, he's coming.'

'*Don't* say anything, Leila.'

Sean appeared from the kitchen, wiping his hands on his trousers. 'What's with all the hilarity?'

Leila rose up from the table. 'Oh you know us, Sean: we're just happy in our work.' Slowly, she tossed the cue ball from one hand to the other.

# Boys an' Men

'It's only a bus ride away from Côte-Vertu,' the man had said on the phone. It was impossible to judge his age but Leila had been reassured by his friendly voice. Now, trundling through blank industrial estates and shopping malls, she felt uneasy. Night had fallen and the other passengers were all tough-faced teenagers in nylon sportswear. Their narrowed eyes bored into her, assessing her fur-trimmed coat and shaggy moonboots. The West Island was truly another world.

As instructed, she got out on the corner of St Jean and Westminster. The bus stop was on a screaming freeway overlooked by towering apartments. The building where the man lived had long low-lit corridors lined with brown-tinted mirrors, like a Soviet-bloc hotel from a Bond film. Leila ignored her anxious reflection as she paced down to the elevators. In her imagination Apartment 317 was the sound-proofed torture chamber for a gangster with a malevolent disability – a hook hand, a missing eye or a mouth full of razors. She hoped he would let her use the toilet as she was desperate for a pee.

Approaching 317, she heard a familiar voice: 'Leila, is that you?'

'Yes, where are you?'

'I'm here. The door is open. I'm sorry – I can't get up.'

A sharp tomcat smell escaped from the open door. Inside, a white-haired old man in a wheelchair was sitting at a small desk piled high with photographs of underwear models.

'I had a car accident a short while ago, so I don't get around so good,' said the old man. Leila replaced her relieved grin with a sympathetic smile. He held out his hand. 'Bob Zeller. You must be Leila. Sit yourself down over there. Just shift that stuff over.'

The smell, which was clearly stale urine and emanating from Bob Zeller himself, forced Leila to breathe through her mouth. She cleared a space among the photographs which littered the balding velour couch.

'Take a look at these. These are some of my girls.'

He tossed over picture after picture of girls with big frosted hair and big frosted lips trussed up in bits of lace: 'Gorgeous, huh? . . . Real sweet kid, that one . . . Beautiful . . . Very sexy . . .'

Leila murmured in vague approval. When the pictures kept coming she said, 'Yes, yes, yes, but obviously I don't look like an underwear model. Do you have anything for me? Is this legit?'

'Of course it is. I been in the business for thirty years. Used to have my own studio down on Ste. Catherine. We did a lot of work. All the girls came to us. I had an Oriental girl come in last week. Just off the boat. Got her an awful lot of work. Let me tell ya, Montreal's wide open for a girl like you . . . Let's see your pictures.'

Leila took out the nude snaps which Jason, her ex, had taken on holiday in Cuba. Her skin was mottled and pink like salami and her eyes shone red like an albino rabbit.

'Very nice, very nice. You got a nice figure and you're not a bad-looking girl. I know a lot of photographers that would be interested in you.' Bob took out a sheet of paper. 'Here, I made this list – I'm gonna call these guys up and say I've got a new girl they might be interested in . . . Doug – I'll ask him for twenty bucks, Lionel – he'll pay sixty bucks an hour – he's a good one, he's got a lot of contacts. Martin – he's an artist – probably won't give you more than fifteen but you might get twenty, you never know. Yep, Montreal's wide open if you're not shy and I can tell you're not shy. You got a nice figure and you're not a bad-looking girl.'

'Thanks. But what's in it for you?'

'What do you mean?'

'I mean, where do you make your money?'

'Oh I make a few bucks here and there for fixing everything up. I'm the fixer, see . . . I got contacts all over the city . . . Ask anybody in this business about Bob Zeller and they'll tell you: "Bob Zeller's the fixer . . ."'

Among the photographs on the couch was a stack of photocopies of a dark-haired girl in a cutaway bra with her head thrown back and her lips parted. Beneath her picture in a childish hand were the words, 'My name is Tina. I'm sweet sixteen and horny as hell. If you want to have a permanent hard on give me a call.'

'That's my daughter.'

'Your daughter! You're kidding!'

'Nope.'

'Oh my God! Is she really sixteen?'

'Nope. She's thirty-two. She was twenty-five when that picture was taken . . .'

'Jeez. Don't you find it . . . strange having pictures of your daughter like this?' Strange was the most neutral word she could think of.

'No, I'm just looking after them for her. She had that picture done when she was at McGill. She used to be a dancer at SuperSexe, down on Ste. Catherine. Lot of those girls in those clubs, dancing and stripping an' all – lot of them are students at McGill and Concordia. Bright girls. You'd be surprised.'

'Didn't it bother you, knowing she was doing this?'

'Aw no. Aw no. She was just making money to pay her school fees. She's got a degree in psychology . . . I'm very proud of her . . .'

'This looks like . . . more than stripping . . .'

'Aw no. Aw no . . . it's just a little bit of fun. You can have one of her pictures if you want. She's married now. Got three kids. My son, he's an actor. In LA. Been in a lot of commercials . . . a few soaps . . . *General Hospital* . . . *The Young and the Restless* . . . He's very successful.'

The need to pee, which had receded, was now overwhelming Leila.

'Uh, may I use your bathroom?'

'Sure, but you'll have to excuse me 'cos there's no door. I had to get it taken off so I could get the wheel-chair in there. I hope you don't mind. I won't peek.'

'Oh . . . OK.'

The bathroom was rank with the stench of incon-tinence. It smelled a million times worse than Bob

Zeller. The bin was filled with used Depends pads and the sink was coated in black mould. Hovering with her hand over her mouth, Leila wondered if she could contain herself until she got home but now a toilet was in sight she knew she couldn't. Holding herself above the sticky seat, she kept one eye on the empty door space and one ear cocked for the creak of Bob's wheelchair. He didn't peek. She washed her hands as thoroughly as possible. Her eyes were wide and anxious in the mirror behind the sink but the way she planned to make this situation into a story for her friends was on the tip of her tongue.

Back in the living room Bob brought out his paintings from behind the couch. All were of nudes. 'This is a little bit Cubist, kind of in the style of Picasso . . . here I'm going for Surrealism, like Salvador Dali . . . here's something Impressionistic, inspired by Monet . . . As you can see I'm quite artistic.'

He talked her through the family portraits lined up on a cabinet – 'That's me when I was five. That's me when I was twenty-five. Wouldn't believe it, would you?' The blue-eyed, wide-smiled handsome man in the photograph was unrecognisable. 'That's my mother – Ukrainian, she was. Spoke five languages. Imagine that! Five languages . . . That's Tina at her wedding. That's my son, Gary, the actor.' Gary looked exactly like his father had done at twenty-five. Leila pictured the young Bob charming the ladies at his studio, cracking corny jokes behind the camera as they dimpled in cheesecake poses. Leila felt a surge of pity for him, confined to his chair, in his piss-sodden flat, leafing through pictures of underwear models. She asked if there was anything he needed doing before she left.

'No, I'll be fine. Hey, you like rice?'

'Uh . . . yeah.'

'I got a load of rice. And some other food. You can take it. It was given to me but I'm on a special diet so I can't eat it. Some do-gooding kinda Godbotherers heard I was in a wheelchair and since then, every two weeks, they've been giving me all this food. I don't know what to do with it but I take it. I mean, if they're giving it me for free what you supposed to do? I give it away to the girls who come here. The Oriental girl I had in, she took a load of rice. Said she loved rice. I still got some left though. You want it?'

'Uh . . . well, OK.' Leila could tell Bob would be upset if she said no.

'Take the rice. Take whatever you want.'

'Are you sure?'

'Course I'm sure. Take it all. I can't eat it.'

Leila filled two carrier bags with rice, tins of crab-meat, jars of pasta sauce and boxes of pancake mix.

'See – at least you got something out of coming all the way over here,' said Bob, as they shook hands. 'And I'll fix you up with some work . . . yep, Bob Zeller'll fix you up . . . like I said, Montreal's wide open for a girl like you.'

His final words sang in her head as Leila lugged the food back to the bus stop. A group of kids were loitering there, smoking, flicking their butts a little too close for comfort and drawing on the glass in marker pen. The girls pressed up against their boyfriends, sallow and prematurely world-weary, suspicious of

Leila's secret smile. Sitting at the front of the bus, Leila eavesdropped on their twangy Joual chatter and briefly wondered about their futures before turning her mind back to her own.

*

Martin was the only one of Bob's contacts who wanted a model right away.

'I'm making an illustrated history of the world from prehistoric times,' he told Leila over the phone.

When she got to his apartment, a few blocks from her own, he showed her his sketchbooks crammed with pneumatic, tumble-haired, cartoon women with Bambi eyes.

'So, only women existed in prehistoric times?'

'I haven't gotten round to doing any men yet.' Martin gave her a thin smile.

'And women never wore clothes in prehistoric times, huh? What about during the Ice Age – I mean it must have gotten pretty chilly during the Ice Age, right?'

Martin shrugged and directed Leila into a dingy bedroom which had a dank mustiness suggestive of excessive masturbation. He explained the lounge was out-of-bounds because of his roommate.

'Would it be OK if I left the door slightly ajar?' asked Leila.

'I guess. The other girls never mind if it's closed.'

'It would make me feel more comfortable.'

He left the room while she undressed. She pondered why it was more intimate to watch people undressing than to see them fully naked. There was no mirror in which she could assess her body but, looking down, she feared it was soft and ungainly. Her breasts, belly and thighs radiated out in a series of semi-circles. The naked girls in the Polaroids on the wall were angular, with jutting hip bones and breasts that were little more than enlarged nipples. Most had unshaved armpits and riotous pubic hair; hippy types, clearly also unsuitable for modelling lingerie. Their eyes twinkled with patronising amusement. Seeing their pity for Martin made Leila bolder. She pulled on her bathrobe and glanced over the papers on his desk. With a shock of recognition, she found a black-and-white photograph of Sally taken from below; hands on hips, legs akimbo, staring into the lens in defiant challenge. Her stance was a world away from the simpering provocations of the other girls. Despite her nakedness, she had an aura of utter command.

'Find something interesting?' Martin had sidled back into the room.

Startled, Leila quickly threw a drawing of a naked cavegirl riding a woolly mammoth over Sally's photograph.

'No, no . . . I was just looking at your drawings . . . very interesting.'

'I'm glad you think so. Were you looking at the picture of Sally?'

'No . . . uh yes . . . actually, I know her – she's the one who gave me the idea to do this.'

'Best model I've ever had . . .' Martin gazed into the middle distance. 'Total fucking bitch though.'

Leila was shocked but didn't disagree. Everyone who knew Sally knew she was trouble.

The thirty seconds it took for Martin to settle behind his drawing board and find a pencil lasted a sweaty eternity but when he looked up and said, 'Ready?' Leila whipped off her robe with an flourish, determined to prove a better model than Sally and daring him to behave with impropriety.

As it turned out, he was disarmingly meek; they talked about the neighbourhood, the best bars, the best *boulangerie*, the best place for brunch; he told her about his failed career as an architect and his dream of becoming a pilot. The walls were covered with posters of jets and aeroplanes and a model bi-plane hung from a string over his bed. He did not insist on a Polaroid and the only dubious moment came when, after a long silence, he sighed with exasperation and said, 'You have very subtle nipples.'

His final picture bore little resemblance to her – he'd narrowed her waist, shortened her nose and perked up her breasts like a pair of cherry buns offered up on a tray.

He offered coffee but she pocketed his cash and declined. Racing down the front steps, she slammed into a good-looking dark boy accompanied by Corinna's boyfriend, Henry, whom she had met once before. They edged around each other in a confusion of embarrassment. Henry said he was there to pick up some books for his course. Leila said Martin was teaching her desk-top publishing, that she had met him when she was working at Chez Nanigans; he was a regular there. She sensed she was over explaining herself suspiciously but Henry seemed too distracted to notice. Walking home, she flushed with the ease of this moneymaking venture – forty dollars for two hours doing nothing with no clothes on.

*

'So how about we meet up then, Lee-la?' The voice on the other end of the receiver was ingratiatingly perky, the accent Québécois overlaid with Canadian.

'OK,' said Leila, 'whereabouts?'

'There's this great little place I know on Sherbrooke, just next to the museum. It's called Le Boisseau d'Or. Do you know it? It's very relaxed, very down to earth.'

'I know where the museum is but I don't really hang out in that area.'

'How about somewhere near you then?'

'No, Le Boisseau d'Or is fine. I'll find it. How will I know who you are?'

'Well . . . I'm in my forties, I've got black hair, I'm about five foot nine and I'm very handsome . . .'

'*Right* . . .' Leila sighed. Middle-aged men could be so wearisome.

'. . . only kidding! You'll know who I am because I'll be wearing a leather jacket and carrying a copy of the *Journal de Montréal*.'

Leila walked to their rendezvous. She needed time to psych herself up. The snow was beginning to melt, revealing dozens of deformed bicycles locked to lamp-posts. They had been destroyed by the snow trucks over the winter. This time of year always felt dirty to Leila and her boots were too heavy. She wished she'd worn more suitable shoes, some high heels perhaps.

Le Boisseau d'Or turned out to be a touristy place with a long glass counter of complicated cream cakes and bushels of gold-sprayed corn arranged in every available corner. The place was heaving with lacquered ladies waving empty forks over plates of salad. Lionel Leplastrier stuck out like a piranha in a goldfish bowl. He'd failed to mention his tinted spectacles, his unnatural tan and the fact that his black hair looked like a toupée. He rose to greet Leila, pulling out a chair and baring his teeth in an approximation of a smile.

'It's Lee-oh-nell . . . not Lie-uh-null,' he said, when she pronounced his name the English way.

'Well, I'm Lay-la, not Lee-la.'

While she studied the menu, he sat creaking gently in his expensive leather jacket and told her to order whatever she wanted.

'I'll just have an espresso *alongé*.'

'No cake? The cakes here are very excellent.'

'No, I'm fine.'

'Are you watching your weight? You really don't need to, you know. You've got a beautiful body, I can tell already, even through your clothes.'

He lit a cigarette, blowing the smoke through his nose as he rifled through her photographs. When the waitress appeared he did not bother to conceal them. She took their orders with one eyebrow cocked in amusement. Leila squirmed. The waitress was barely out of earshot when Lionel said, 'Well, Bob was right – you've got a beautiful body and I could definitely get you a lot of work. I've got a lot of contacts. I know a bunch of artists in New York who'd be falling over themselves to use you.'

'New York!'

'Yep – all expenses paid – nice hotel, nice restaurants. I'd drive you down – I go down to New York about twice a month . . .'

'I can't believe these artists would be willing to pay for all the expenses.'

'Believe me: the artists I deal with are not short of cash.'

'Surely there are plenty of life models in New York?'

'Not professional ones. Not girls who look nice and clean, like you. They trust me, the artists I work with. They know I'm going to find 'em nice-looking, professional girls who don't have a drug problem. Do you have a drug problem?'

'No.'

'I didn't think so. They trust me, my contacts. They know I'm gonna come up with the goods.' He drummed the tabletop with his gold signet ring.

'Is this legit?'

'How do you mean?' Lionel glanced around and continued drumming.

'I mean – no funny business . . .'

'Funny business?'

'I'm not doing anything . . .' As she said the word 'sexual', the waitress placed their coffees on the table with exaggerated care. Lionel lounged back in his chair, 'Well, I won't put you with the crazy ones then.'

'What do you mean – crazy?'

'You know how artists can be – a little bit crazy.'

'Explain to me the exact nature of their craziness.'

'Don't worry, I won't put you with the crazy ones if you don't want to. Most of these artists are, you know, strictly professional. I sell their work in my gallery.'

'Gallery?'

'Yeah, I've got a gallery down in Place Bonaventure. High-end stuff. You can make a lot of money in this business . . .'

'The crazy ones . . . what do they do?'

'Oh, you know – they like to party. Leila, don't be so worried about everything . . .'

'Party?'

'Yeah – have a good time . . .'

'What kind of a good time?'

But he wouldn't expand. He flicked through the pictures again, drumming his ring all the while. As they drank their coffee he asked if she had ever had a Québécois boyfriend.

'Oh yeah, dozens of them.'

*

'You have to be kidding,' said Zoë, 'This sounds *so* dodgy.'

'But an all-expenses trip to New York. It's *so* tempting,' said Leila.

They were sitting in Chez Nanigans, the bar in the Old Port where Leila had once worked. The boss, Bobby, had 'let her go' after business had dried up over the winter but she still whiled away many an afternoon there playing pool and gossiping with the last remaining barmaid, Zoë. Leila had walked from Le Boisseau d'Or, mulling over Lionel's proposal. He had left her with his embossed business card, saying he'd be in touch.

'That's the whole point – he wants you to be tempted,' said Zoë. 'This is how girls end up getting sucked into the porn industry . . .'

'But he's got an art gallery in Place Bonaventure.' She showed Zoë his card.

'*Lionel Leplastrier. Art and antiques.* Lionel – what kind of a name is Lionel?'

'It's pronounced Lee-oh-nell . . . He's French.'

'Figures.' Zoë topped up Leila's gin and tonic. When Leila fumbled for her purse she held up her hand: 'Don't worry about it – former staff privileges and all that. Bobby won't notice. He hasn't been in for ages.'

'Do you know what's happening?'

'Nah. He's running it into the ground, I guess.'

The pub was empty as usual. Zoë was more lacksadaisical about her job than ever – and hadn't bothered changing out of her snowboots and had salsa music blasting over the stereo rather than anything remotely Irish.

'So you got this job from that guy out on the West Island?'

'Well, it's not a definite job yet.'

'He liked your photos then?'

'He said he did.'

'God, it all seems like a hell of a lot of trouble to me. Why don't you just get another bar job?'

'Because everywhere's dead. No one's taking anyone on till April. Anyway, this is easy money. Sally gave me the idea.'

'You and Sally are way braver than me. I could never be naked in front of a complete stranger.'

'That's not what I've heard . . .'

'Shut *up*!' snapped Zoë, just as Sean appeared from the kitchen.

'*Laaaay-la*!' he yelled, miming an air guitar and planting a fat kiss full on Leila's lips.

'Hey, Sean.' Leila pushed him away.

'So, Leila, I hear you're pursuing a *new* career path these days . . .'

'Who told you that? Hey, Zoë . . . I thought I told you not to . . .'

Zoë shrugged and blushed, 'Sorry . . .'

'Jeez, I thought I was desperate for cash but even I wouldn't stoop to taking my kit off . . .'

'I don't think anyone would want you to,' Zoë threw over her shoulder as he disappeared back into the kitchen. *Sotto voce*, she added, 'Especially if they knew what he's got down there . . . or should I say what he *hasn't* got down there . . .'

Leila sniggered. 'That's a bit below the belt, Zo.'

'*Anyway*,' Zoë continued, when they'd both recovered straight faces, 'If this Lionel Leplasterer or whatever his name is does get you some work in New York, I think you should take me with you for protection.'

'OK. It's a deal.'

*

Lionel drove a spanking new GM Camaro with a racing stripe. Zoë sat in the back, smirking at his car, his choice of music, his slip-on shoes and the way he held the passenger door open for them. Lionel had not minded Zoë coming along. ('Of course he doesn't mind. He thinks he's getting two girls for the price of one,' said Zoë.) As they cruised down the interstate with Celine Dion warbling at the top of her voice, Leila was dazed with amazement that the trip had come to pass. Out of his many contacts, Lionel had conjured up Clarence Delancey, a 'genuwine New York Impressionist' who 'wasn't at all crazy' and who was willing to pay Leila to pose for two days at two hundred American dollars a day. He had an apartment in Chelsea, to which they had all been invited to stay.

'What kind of impressions does he do?' drawled Zoë, picking through a family pack of marshmallows. 'Bugs Bunny, Clint Eastwood, George Dubya . . . ?'

'Eh? He is an artiste.' Lionel frowned at her. 'An Impressionist artiste.'

'I thought the Impressionist movement was over in about 1905 . . .'

'He might be an Expressionist,' said Lionel.

'They didn't tend to work from the human form.'

'Impressionist, Expressionist. I don't know . . .'

'I thought you were an art dealer. I thought you knew about art – *Lionel Leplasterer – Art and Antiques*, right?'

'Lee-oh-nell Leplastr-*ee-ay*. My specialty is sales, you understand . . . Hey, Leila – your friend – does she always ask this many questions?'

Leila shrugged.

Zoë had clearly decided to ignore her pleas not to be uppity with Lionel.

'I'm just trying to get to know you, Lee-oh-nell,' said

Zoë. 'So we feel more comfortable with each other while Leila is *working*.'

'Nothing would give me more pleasure than to feel comfortable with you, Zoë,' said Lionel, happily oblivious to Leila shooting warning frowns at her friend.

At the border, an immigration officer demanded to know where they were going.

'New York City, sir,' said Lionel.

'And what is happening in New York City?'

'What's happening in New York City?' Zoë looked astonished. 'New York City is happening in New York City!'

The officer remained stoney-faced. 'Are you intending to pursue any kind of paid employment when you get to New York?'

'No, this is purely a pleasure trip,' said Lionel. 'We are in the pursuit of pleasure, isn't that right, girls?' The girls smiled and Zoë slid her arm around Lionel's waist.

'I'm a lucky guy, huh?' Lionel grinned.

The officer stamped their passports in silence.

'That was very excellent!' crowed Lionel, when they were safely over the border. He winked at Zoë in the rear-view mirror.

'Just trying to make you feel more comfortable, Lionel.' Zoë winked back.


The splendour of the city spun into view as they swooped across the George Washington Bridge. Leila's blood rushed with adrenaline. No matter how many times you saw it, the New York skyline never dulled. It sparkled with hope and ambition and success. They fell silent as Lionel navigated the hectic streets which were both strange and familiar, bursting with everything they had ever seen at the movies: yellow cabs and traffic cops and neon signs and people, people, people.

They ate a late lunch in a diner which Lionel said was 'around the corner' from Clarence's apartment. The place hummed with New Yorkers, talking fast and loud. The menu boasted fifty different sandwiches but they all ordered pastrami on rye and agreed it wasn't as good as Montreal smoked meat. During lunch Lionel went outside to use his cell phone and Leila and Zoë watched him through the window, pacing up and down.

'What's with all the flirting, Zoë?' said Leila.

'What flirting?'

'You're flirting like a total moron with Lionel.'

'No, I'm not . . . I'm being charming.'

'You're being annoying.'

Zoë turned the pepper shaker upside down to make a dusty flower on the tabletop. She jerked her head towards Lionel who was still speaking intently into his phone. 'Why doesn't he use it in here? His phone?'

'Maybe he's being polite.'

'Maybe Clarence Delancey doesn't exist.'

But he did. Clarence Delancey ushered them into his penthouse apartment on West 20th Street, with excessive bonhomie and clutched them to his cheek in an eye-watering wave of cologne. He was a dapper little man in a silk Nehru suit with the sleeves rolled up, *Miami Vice*-style. His small office-boy hands were well manicured, his goatee neatly trimmed and his white hair scraped back into a small ponytail. His shoes were very shiny. The apartment was white and minimalist and dotted with ostentatious sculptures – a black marble panther with diamond eyes strutting across the blond-wood floor; a crystal horse head; a sinuous bronze relief of a man and a woman entwined.

Leila and Zoë's overnight bags were stowed in separate bedrooms. Both rooms had brutally clinical ensuite bathrooms and were dominated by king-size double beds. Leila's had a mirrored ceiling and a six foot painting of a naked woman with her legs open, exposing a vagina like a dark and bloody tunnel. The room's décor had not been designed with a good night's sleep in mind.

'What the hell's going on?' Leila grabbed Zoë on the landing outside her door.

'What do you mean?'

'Well, where are they going to sleep? Why have they put us in separate rooms? Where the hell are they going to sleep? I don't see any other bedrooms . . .'

'Will you just chill out, Leila. This is supposed to be an adventure. It's supposed to be fun.'

'This is not my idea of fun.'

Zoë tossed her hair and sashayed down the stairs. By the time Leila had caught up with her, Clarence was bearing down on them with a pair of large martinis.

'You don't want to get to work right away, Mr Delancey?' asked Leila, as they stood admiring the view from the balcony.

'Don't worry about that. We'll get to work tomorrow. It's too late in the day to start anything now. I'm a morning person. You can call me Clarence, by the way.'

'Is your studio in the apartment, Clarence?'

'No, it's not far from here.' He gestured airily to somewhere beyond the balcony.

'Clarence is a very excellent artiste,' said Lionel.

'Why thank you, Lionel,' said Clarence.

By sunset they were heavily dosed up on martinis.

'Let's go eat,' said Clarence, 'I'll dial a cab.'

From the window of the cab, the streetlife reeled out like a silent movie. Leila and Zoë were squeezed thigh-to-thigh between Lionel and Clarence. Both men had their legs apart, as if their balls needed room to breathe. Zoë was drunk and teasing: 'Come on, Lionel, take off the rug, we know it's not real.' Lionel's hair remained attached to his head when she tugged it but she still wasn't convinced: 'It's a hair implant, isn't it? You've had it sewn in . . .' Swimmily, Leila noticed that Lionel didn't seem to mind.

At the restaurant, the wine flowed – Clarence kept waving the empty bottle and snapping his fingers – 'Come on, garçon, load us up.' Every bark of 'garçon' and finger-snap made Leila shudder. She was being meticulously polite to compensate though the waiter revealed nothing from behind his impassive professional mask.

Alcohol was the only way to cope with the horror even though Leila knew it would be wiser to keep her head. Zoë seemed unbothered that Lionel had one arm around her and one hairy, gold-ringed hand on her thigh. With slow, drink-sodden fathoming she realised how stupid it had been to bring Zoë along as her minder. This was the girl who'd had an affair with the deputy editor of *La Presse* because of his luxury chalet in the Laurentians. The girl who had screwed every single one of the chefs at Chez Nanigans, including one-balled Sean. The girl who flirted with Crazy Davy when she was bored because she could still 'glimpse the beauty' in his addled face. For a weekend of the New York high life, she would have no qualms about going to bed with a paunchy, orange-tanned, toupéed old roué. 'I just like to live other people's lives a little,' she had once told Leila, '. . . and the quickest way to live another life is through a man's cock.'

'Would you like a little carpaccio, Leila?' Clarence pushed a forkful of meat towards her lips. The bloody flesh was reminiscent of the painting in her bedroom. Clarence's hooded eyes were fixated upon her chest. 'You know what I would really like to do right now, Leila?'

Leila shook her head.

'Perhaps I don't need to explain in words.' He wheedled one finger down her throat to the top button of her shirt, while whispering, 'You have the most delicious breasts. I can't take my eyes off them, I just want to run my hands all over them and feel your nipples growing har –'

'I've gotta go to the bathroom.'

The toilet cubicle was mirrored on every side, so

you could watch yourself pissing into infinity. From some angles her reflection gazed into the middle distance as if she was having an astral projection. She had to concentrate hard on the tricksy soap dispenser and the citrus-scented soap to quell her rising panic. Returning to the restaurant, she caught the other diners regarding their table with distaste. She saw herself and Zoë through their eyes and slunk shame-faced back to the table. When Zoë got up, with a breathy, 'Excuse me gentlemen but I have to go and powder my nose,' Leila followed her.

'Are you sick?' asked Zoë. 'You went to the bathroom two minutes ago.'

'We've got to get out of here.'

'What?'

'I said, "We've got to get out of here."'

'Oh, for God's sake, stop being such a killjoy, Leila.'

'I may be a killjoy but at least I'm not a fucking whore.'

'Fuck you.'

'No, fuck you. I'm going. I'm sick of all this lowlife shit. If we go now we can stay up all night and get the bus back to Montreal at dawn.'

'I don't want to go back.'

'Fine, stay here then. Stay here on your own and get mauled by that fucking lech. I doubt he'll even be able to get it up.'

Zoë's eyes welled up with tears. She was at that stage of drunkenness where emotions flip faster than a tossed coin. 'Don't leave me. Leila, don't leave me here on my own. *Please . . .*'

'OK. Well, this is the plan.'

The plan was simple:

Leila emerged from the toilets leaning on Zoë, dabbing her mouth with a tissue.

'Leila's feeling sorta nauseous. She needs some air,' Zoë explained.

'You poor thing, you want some water?' Clarence proffered a glass.

'No, we'll just take a little walk around the block.'

A few paces out of the restaurant, they staggered into a run. Pedestrians parted as they charged along the sidewalk; cars screeched out of the way; a boy on a skateboard shouted, 'Watch where the fuck you're going'; a cabby honked his horn. Their feet pounded, their sides ached with stitch, the cocktails and Chardonnay rose in their throats but they kept going until the city swallowed them up. They collapsed to a heaving halt in Washington Square.

'Oh my God . . . I'm think I'm going to . . .' Zoë emptied the contents of her stomach, narrowly missing Leila's feet.

'Oh gross . . .' An Abstract Expressionist splattering now decorated the sidewalk.

'I'm sorry . . .' Zoë dropped to her knees.

'Are you OK?'

'Yep . . . I feel a bit better.'

'Come on, let's walk on and find somewhere to sit down. Get a Coke or something. Something non-alcoholic.' Leila hauled her up.

'What about our stuff?' said Zoë.

'You got your passport?'

'It's in my purse.'

'That's fine then.'

'Yeah, but my stuff . . .'

'Forget your stuff.'

'. . . I left my best red sweater . . .'

'Fuck your sweater.'

The streets grew darker, the bars grew seedier and the passers-by grew poorer and more downbeat as they walked. At a big intersection they turned right onto the Bowery.

'We could find a flophouse to sleep in. Like Jack Kerouac,' said Zoë.

'I am not sleeping in a flophouse.'

'What are we going to do?'

'Hey, ladies, are you coming in?' A boy in oversized jeans outside a bar handed Leila a flyer – *CBGB & OMFUG presents the Battle of the Bands*.

'CBGBs! Wow! Come on, we have to go in.'

'I never heard of it.' Leila turned her nose up at the flyer. 'CBGB . . . OMFUG? What the hell does that mean?'

'I think it stands for something like Country Blue-Grass Be-bop . . . Odd . . . Music for . . . er . . . Unusual . . . Underground . . . oh I don't know. Doesn't matter. We have to go in. This place is legendary. Everybody started out here: Blondie, the Ramones. Come on, we've gotta pay homage to Debbie Harry.'

The bar was thick with unhealthy-looking people. The floor vibrated with a thumping bass and the black walls dripped with condensed sweat. The band consisted of four skinny boys, all in badly fitting suits. Only their friends at the front were dancing. The rest of the crowd was static. Leila waited an age before a surly-faced bar girl in a Sergeant Pepper jacket noticed her. She hollered her order and the girl slammed two bottles of Coke onto the counter.

She returned to find Zoë squeezed into a corner beside a boy in a Nike hat pulled down low over his eyes.

'Don't go to the toilets!' Zoë yelled.

'Why?'

'They're really nasty.'

The boy in the hat smiled at Leila and shouted something incomprehensible. He had the kind of large nose she sometimes found attractive.

'I can't hear what you're saying.'

'I said, "Do you like the band?"'

'They're OK.'

'They're friends of mine.'

'How come you're not dancing then?'

The boy stretched over to grab a lighter from his friend. Though he was wearing a baggy T-shirt, Leila could see the tautness of his body. He pulled a cigarette from a pack of Marlboros with his mouth. She waited for him to offer her one but he didn't.

'What were you saying?' he yelled.

'I said, "How come you're not dancing?"'

'I don't believe in dancing.'

'Why not? It exists.'

'What?'

'I said . . . Oh forget it.'

'How come you're not drinking?' He had a carefully

considered smoking technique, the cigarette held between thumb and first finger like a cowboy.

'What?'

'How come you're not drinking?'

'How come we're not drinking? . . . 'Cos we're drunk already.'

'Excellent! so where are you from?'

'Montreal.'

'Montreal!' He turned to his friend, who was wearing a toilet chain around his neck, 'Hey Nate – these chicks are from Montreal.'

'Canadians!'

'Yeah!'

The boys introduced themselves as Nate and Marcel. They were from the Upper East Side and worked together in a record store.

'What do you do?'

'We're failed porn models.'

'Excuse me?'

'I said, "We're failed porn models".'

'You failed your *law modules*? Are you law students?'

'Nah . . . forget it – it's too complicated to explain.'

The four skinny boys finished their set and were replaced by another four skinny boys. Leila wove her way through the hot bodies to the toilets, which were scrawled with layers of graffiti and were almost as nasty as Bob Zeller's bathroom. She returned to find Zoë and Nate kissing. After a few minutes pretending to watch the band, Marcel grabbed Leila and forced his tongue into her mouth. The action was inevitable and she felt too drunk to object. Before long, the boys had picked up their skateboards at the coatcheck and she and Zoë had been manoeuvred out onto the street.

'So where are you ladies staying?' asked Nate.

Zoë and Leila swapped sheepish glances. 'That's the thing . . . we've had a bit of a problem tonight and we don't actually have anywhere to stay,' said Leila.

'Are we far from where you live?' asked Zoë.

'Uh . . . pretty far.'

'How long would it take us to get there?'

'Quite a long time.'

'How long?'

'Uh . . . well, the thing is it's not really convenient for you to come back to our place.'

'Why?'

'Well . . .'

Now it was Nate and Marcel's turn to look sheepish.

'Your girlfriends wouldn't like it?'

'Not exactly . . .'

'You live with your girlfriends?'

'No . . .'

'Well, then: we can stay with you . . .'

'No . . . it wouldn't be a good idea.'

'Why not – we need a place to crash. C'mon, where's your famous Yankee hospitality, huh?'

'We're from New York. We don't do hospitality. Anyway, it's not that . . .'

'What is it?'

'Actually, we live with our parents . . .'

'Both of you?'

'Yeah.'

'How old did you say you were?' asked Zoë.

'I'm *eighteen*,' said Nate, defiantly.

There was a pause. Nate bounced his skateboard up and down on the toes of his trainers as if he was trying to cut them off.

'He's fifteen,' said Marcel wearily, pulling off his hat and rubbing his head, 'And I'm going to be sixteen in August.'

'You're both still in high school!'

'Yeah.'

'Jeez. What is it with our luck tonight?' said Leila as Nate and Marcel crashed off into the darkness on their boards.

'I know. You know what though? I wouldn't have minded leading Nate into the world of womanhood.'

'Whatever turns you on, Zo. Personally, I'm not really into all that Mrs Robinson shit.'

They spent the rest of the night, white-faced and jittery, downing coffee and doughnuts in an all-night diner. Just the names 'Lionel and Clarence' or 'Nate and Marcel' kept sparking fits of caffeine-fuelled, sugar-hyped laughter.

'Are you still drunk?' asked Leila, after their third refill.

'The room's stopped spinning so I think I'm sobering up.'

'Sorry about what I said earlier.'

'When?'

'In the restaurant . . . you know . . . in the bath-room.'

'Don't worry about it. Hey, talking of whores, have you checked out those women in the corner?'

They took surreptitious peeks at a group of improbably tall prostitutes, all in improbably clichéd crotch-high skirts and killer heels.

'They're not women. They're men, I'm sure of it,' said Leila.

'Get me another doughnut, will you? I'm getting my appetite back.'

'What do you reckon Nate and Marcel are doing right now?' asked Leila, returning with a chocolate-coated sugar ring.

'Jerking off on the Upper East Side over the thought of us.'

'What about Lionel and Clarence?'

'The same, but in Chelsea.'

'Hey, what's so funny, girlfriend?' demanded one of the whores. She stalked over to them, a terrifying vision of overblown womanliness with legs so long she looked an escaped giraffe.

'Oh, nothing . . . just some boys we met . . . and some men.'

The whore snorted with amusement and flapped her wrist, jangling a waterfall of gold bangles: 'Oh, boys an' men, boys an' men – don't talk to me 'bout boys an' men.'

# Down to Rue Beaudry

It was winter when Henry first went down to Rue Beaudry. The snow hadn't arrived but the sky was low and weighty and it was already too cold to keep his hands outside his pockets. Henry stood on the college steps jangling his change, and calculated, without looking, that he was carrying ten dollars. Instead of taking his usual route, he turned right and trudged along Ste. Catherine for a long time without consciously deciding to go to Rue Beaudry. On reaching the street he walked up and down pretending not to look at himself in shop windows, before pushing open the door of a dimly lit café.

The boy behind the counter sized Henry up as he made his coffee and set the cup in front of him with exaggerated care. Henry took out his book, lit a cigarette and waited for something to happen. The other customers' intent murmurings were drowned out by the hiss of the espresso machine. Only the middle-aged man opposite, writing in a journal, glanced up. Eventually he contrived to drop his pencil at Henry's feet and darted towards it, smiling up from between Henry's knees with an eager 'Bonjour'.

'*Je ne parle pas français,*' Henry lied. The man retreated irritably and Henry felt too uncomfortable to linger.

\*

Corinna was still at work when he got home so he put Etta James on the record player and sang along to 'Blind Girl' four times in succession while making an omelette. When Corinna returned, he gave her a foot massage. She didn't appear to notice any difference in him. As usual, she was too caught up with complaining about her colleagues.

'Hilde shouted at me again about not cleaning the counter.'

'The German?'

'Yeah, miserable old bitch. I think she's got some kind of OCD about the counter.'

'Poor sweets.' Henry put his arms around her.


It was still winter the next time Henry went down to Rue Beaudry but this time the snow lay three-feet deep. It was so cold the smoke from the chimneys had stalled in the deceptive blue overhead. Corinna had gone to her parents for the weekend. Henry excused himself with an essay deadline. For the fortnight before Corinna's departure he was taut with anticipation and apprehension at what he was going to do while she was gone. He almost wished she were staying. When she set off with her rucksack of dirty laundry, all bundled up for the journey, he was filled with pity at her innocence. She looked so appealing in her rabbit-fur hat – the one she thought of as lucky because she'd been wearing it when she'd met him.

'Have a good time, sweets.' He leaned in to kiss her.

'You too, bunny. I wish you were coming.'

'I wish I was too but you know how it is.'

'Yeah, don't work too hard.'

'I won't.'

Once the door was shut he showered and shaved and carefully composed an artlessly bohemian outfit finished off with the green scarf, which brought out his eyes, according to Corinna. It was still morning, still too early so he sat at his desk and opened *The Fundamental Questions of Philosophy* by A.C. Ewing, M.A., D. Phil (Oxon). An hour passed during which he read page fifty-six about The Pragmatist Theory of Truth over and over again without taking in a word. His hand hovered above a blank sheet of paper and wrote nothing. He lit a cigarette, smoked it, stubbed it out, picked up the pen and wrote, '*My name is Henry and today I am going to . . .*' The thought of describing what he was going to do excited him but when written down it sounded trite and ridiculous. He tore the sheet into very, very small pieces.

There was nobody beneath the Angel at the park. She spread her wings beatifically over fresh virgin snow. Henry dallied, calming himself by making neat trails of footprints where no one else had trodden. The park was in the opposite direction to Rue Beaudry. He stopped and turned three hundred and sixty degrees, four times over, with his face to the cold clear sky. The snow was so pillowy he was tempted to fall backwards and make an angel imprint. Sometimes it felt like too much effort to stay upright. He knocked a cigarette out of his pack of Du Maurier's and flipped his lapels up – his Jean-Paul Belmondo look. The stone lions guarding the Angel reminded him of the previous winter when he and Corinna had sat beside them and watched a total eclipse of the moon. It had been smaller and redder than they had expected and the shadow of the earth made the moon seem as if it was suspended like a Christmas tree-bauble in the sky. They had stroked the lions and Henry had kidded Corinna that they came alive at midnight.

'Do they remind you of yourself, the lions?' she'd asked, running her fingers through his thick auburn hair.

'No, not really.'

During the summer they had danced to the beat of the tam-tam drummers who congregated beneath the Angel on Sundays. Those days they spent their whole time dancing. He'd shown her how to salsa and she'd picked it up quickly, her hips swinging smoothly with the rhythm. The merengue had been harder and she couldn't get the foot movement right – 'They look too flat,' he'd told her, titupping his own high-arched feet like a dressage pony.

'Thanks a lot.'

'There's no need to get offended.'

'It's totally insulting to tell a woman she's got flat feet.'

After that she'd refused to dance with him, claiming he made her feel unfeminine.

*

The neon sign was broken, so if you weren't looking for it, you might miss the door. The address was burned on Henry's memory though, so he scanned the empty street to make sure no one had seen him and quickly slipped inside.

'*Salut, mon beau.*' The man in the reception booth took his money, placed a folded towel in Henry's outstretched hands and dropped a locker key and a condom on top. '*Ta première fois, ouais?*' Henry nodded and the man's sly eyes glittered as he directed him down the corridor. '*Tournez à gauche et continuez tout droit.*'

Red bulbs filled the corridor with a sulphurous light and tendrils of steam curled around Henry as he walked further, his mind racing over the scenes that waited inside. The changing room reeked of feet and cheap cologne like every other changing room Henry had been in before but, unlike every other changing room, there was a hushed excitement among the other men who stared at him openly as he removed his clothes and arranged the towel around his waist. By now his heart was pumping so hard he felt it might dislodge his internal organs. With self-conscious casualness he sauntered down another dark corridor into an even darker chamber where it took a minute for his eyes to adjust and see the shiny bare flesh of a dozen other bodies. The air was opaque with steam and sweat and heady with amyl nitrate and it pressed against his mouth and nose, making only the shallowest breaths possible. Silently, the other bodies shifted to accommodate him and he squeezed into a space between two pairs of muscular thighs. Though he had never been so vulnerable, the womb-like secrecy of the place cradled him. As he luxuriated in the dripping warmth and the hot pressure of his growing erection, a large hand landed on his knee and pulled his towel open. Instantly, Henry was alert, his heart pounding again. Part of him felt oddly detached, as if he was observing the experience from afar, noting the heaviness of the hand, how different it was from a girl's. The other part was holding his breath as the hand crept up to his crotch.

A little later, Henry emerged from the chamber, light-headed and sweat-soaked. He stumbled through the labyrinth of corridors, passing doorways, some of which were shut and some of which led into small rooms where men were lying face down and naked on single beds. They looked up hopefully as he passed. An enormous bald man, cross-legged like a salacious Buddha, gestured to his erect penis with a triumphant '*Voila!*' Henry moved swiftly on. The man in the final room lifted his head, stared at Henry and lay back down without smiling. He was young and slim with haughty cheekbones and a beautiful mouth. Henry stood hesitantly in the doorway. The man beck-oned him inside. He held out his hand. Tentatively, Henry held out his own. Their fingertips touched for a second and then, roughly, the man pulled Henry towards him.

*

The freezing air was like a whiplash to their hot faces when they came outside. They had forgotten how cold it was and lost track of time. The glass buildings on the peak of the Plateau shone like slices of pure gold in the ricocheting rays of the setting sun. The storefronts on St Denis dazzled with strings of fairy lights in red, blue, pink and green.

'These are the best lights in the city,' said Alexei, as they marveled at the tiny coloured bulbs which dripped from the canopy outside La Merveille du Viêtnam. Viewed from the side they melted together in a neon Milky Way. Directly below, each light blazed crisp as a miniature firework burst. They stared up for so long the Maître d' emerged with a menu and asked if they wanted a table.

'Some other time.' Alexei pulled Henry away.


He took Henry to his room on the third floor of an apartment where the Rues St Dominique and St André crossed. On the landing, they passed a lugubrious man who looked away when he was introduced – Alexi's roommate.

'Martin's a cartoonist. He brings women back here to draw,' said Alexei, when Martin was out of earshot.

'Naked?'

'Yeah, naked. He pays them.'

'Where does he find them?'

'He advertises in *Le Miroir*.' Alexei ushered Henry into his room and disappeared to make coffee. The room was bare save for a mattress and a pile of mathematical textbooks. The view from the window was a geometric tangle of fire escapes, washing lines and telegraph poles against the snow. The windowsill was covered with manic scribblings about COKE and ANARCHY.

'That wasn't me,' said Alexei, returning with a steel coffee pot and two cups. 'I keep meaning to paint over it. The guy who lived here before wrote all that. According to Martin, he was pretty nuts.'

'I can see.'

'Yeah, he was from California. All built up. Drank high-energy drinks and lifted weights. Played hip-hop at one hundred decibels. Wrote crazy stuff all over the walls and then jumped the rent. I'm pretty normal in comparison, apparently.' He laughed so Henry could see every single one of his crooked teeth.

'And these are for your course?' Henry flicked through one of the books and gawped at the never-ending equations spinning neurotically into infinity. Alexei was studying mathematics at McGill.

'Yeah, I just drop a little acid and spend my days making pretty patterns out of numbers.'

'Cool,' said Henry. He really thought it was.


It would be easy to explain Alexei to Corinna, Henry reckoned, as he followed him through the trees. 'I'm just going round to Alexei's . . . yeah, Alexei, this guy whose just joined my class . . . yeah, he's a nice guy . . .' Henry ran through the possible lies as he tried not to slip on the frozen snow.

'This is the coolest thing in this city,' said Alexei, when they reached the foot of the illuminated cross. 'I can't wait for it to turn purple when the Pope dies. I mean, how much more kitsch can you get?'

'Not much,' agreed Henry. His eyes were ablaze with the screaming yellow light that slapped retinal imprints all over the black sky. His mind was cascading with the revelation of a wide new future. His lips murmured a silent prayer, though he had an inkling you weren't supposed to pray for yourself. 'Everyone in my writing class always says *La Croix* is a symbol of repression,' he said. 'Same with the angel. You know, religion and the colonial powers oppressing Québec and all that . . .'

'What a load of PC crap,' said Alexei. 'The masses have no sense of style.'

Henry thrilled to his arrogance. It had to be because the guy was Russian; something which also explained his bad teeth. 'My parents were dissidents,' he'd told Henry proudly. 'When I've got my doctorate I'm going back to Moscow.'

They wrote each other's name in pee in the snow (Henry only got as far as the 'x') and skidded along the moonlit paths to the plaza that fanned out in a crescent beyond the Chalet. From there the whole sparkling spread of the city was flung like jewels on a bolt of black velvet. The last time Henry had viewed this panorama was on Corinna's birthday. They had waltzed across the paved semicircle, drunk on champagne and love.

'Who were you last here with, Alexei?' he asked.

'God knows: some guy or other. Some lucky guy.' Alexei smirked over his shoulder, then pointed out the

Notre-Dame Basilica, the Jacques Cartier Bridge and the street where he lived, five blocks back from the line of red and yellow car lights inching along St Denis.

Henry counted the streets back from St Laurent and wondered what Corinna was doing at home before remembering she wasn't there.

'I think that's where I live,' he said, but Alexei was looking in the other direction. He slid his hand into Alexei's pocket and entwined their warm fingers together. Looking down, a balloon of joy swelled in his chest. He fancied he could cast himself over the balustrade and swirl like a snowflake, weightless and free, between the glittering tower blocks. At that moment he realised Corinna would have to know the truth. Even so the balloon continued to swell.

# Slow Burn

*Sunday, 14th February – Valentine's Day x ❤ x ❤ x ❤ x !!!*

*3.47 p.m. – In my room.*

*We have new nieghbors. A man and his wife. The man has hare like a lion. The lady is really pretty. She has got long yellow hare like a mermaid and she wears a hat that looks like its made of a rabbit. I dont know how old they are but definitly not as old as Mom and The Blob. I got a card today but I know it was from Mom so it dosnt count.*

It took Esmé three months to infiltrate Number 3949. The new inhabitants moved in during a blizzard on Valentine's Day, dropping a trail of shoes, CDs and saucepans through the snow as they unloaded their belongings from a taxi. The man had a mane of red hair and the lady was wearing a rabbit-fur hat. Esmé liked the look of them.

She kept up a low-level surveillance of their movements from February to April, the tiresome quarter of the year when the endless snow exhausted rather than charmed. Mornings and evenings, the lady scurried to and from her front door, her hat pulled down low.

Esmé never caught her beyond the confines of Clark Street. She once spotted the man strolling down St Laurent, with his coat lapels up and a jaunty angle to his cigarette. Another time she saw him at the foot of the Angel on Mont Royal. She was hiding in the bandstand, skiving from hockey practice. He was walking in circles with his eyes on his feet. Suddenly he halted and turned three hundred and sixty degrees, four times over, with his face to the sky. His rotations in the snow reminded Esmé of the clockwork ballerina that twirled inside the white-satin lid of her jewellery box. It was heartening to see that even grown-ups did pointless things.

When the man set off back towards Duluth, she snuck out of the bandstand and placed her boots in his footprints a hundred paces behind him across the park. She imagined herself a hunter stalking a wild animal. At the sidewalk, his footprints merged into a million others but with his red mane and his green scarf trailing like a flag, he was easy prey for Esmé, like a lion in the Arctic.

At Clark Street, she expected him to turn right and go home, but he carried on across St Laurent and St Denis and all the boy saints in between – Dominique, Christophe and André – to the corner of Parc La Fontaine, beneath the snow-laden trees, through wind-carved drifts, then down the deadbeat backwater of Rue Beaudry. Esmé kept her hood up and cleaved to the corners of shopfronts with blacked-out windows. Halfway down, the man stopped short beneath an unlit neon sign, which spelt out the word BAIN. He scanned the street, almost sniffing the air as if he could detect the scent of his pursuer. Esmé pressed herself into the doorway of what appeared to be a high-class pet shop, judging from the baroque dog collars and leashes laid out on red velvet in the window. Without warning, the door opened and she fell into a mountainous figure shrink-wrapped in black leather.

'*Tu cherches quelque chose, chérie?*' The leather mountain was topped with a head like an overblown balloon punctured by metal spikes and bolts. 'You search for something, darling?'

'*Non, non, rien.*' Esmé edged away.

Back on Rue Beaudry, the man had disappeared.

\*

*Sunday 28th February – The shortest month of the year*

*5.17 p.m. – In the bathroom.*

*Why does the man next door have to go all the way down to Rue Beaudry to have a bath? I am sure they have a bath in there apartment cos it looks like its built the same way as ours. This is a mistery. I need to investigate.*

\*

By the end of March, the snow had dissolved to cold dust in the gutters. Loads of mutilated bicycles were uncovered. They had been locked to lampposts, hidden by six-foot drifts and mangled by snow ploughs over the winter.

On April Fool's Day the sun emerged like a miracle. The air was eerily humid, the light cut with a nuclear edge and the sky tinged greyish-yellow like the yolk of a hard-boiled egg.

Esmé woke up wishing she had someone to trick. The only potential victims were her mother or stepfather, but Evangeline was out working a double shift at Café Santropol and she knew it was inadvisable to make a *Poisson d'Avril* out of Bobby. Bobby owned a pub called Chez Nanigans down in the Old Port but spent most of his time on the living room couch making mysterious phone calls involving times and numbers. Though at first sight he looked as fat and merry as Santa Claus, Bobby was always deadly serious.

Bobby was in the kitchen with his feet on the table, surrounded by the congealed remains of an extensive fry-up when Esmé finally went downstairs. Quasi, the cat, whimpered around her ankles. Bobby only ever troubled to feed himself. The sausages, bacon, eggs, hash browns and *fèves au lard* were gone and he had drunk all of his step-daughter's special purple grape juice. Esmé opened the refrigerator to see what Bobby hadn't eaten.

'How come you ain't at school?' said Bobby, without looking up from his newspaper.

'I've got a temperature. Mom said I could have the day off,' Esmé lied. By the time Evangeline got home, Bobby would be too drunk to remember that Esmé had missed school.

'Did I say you could have those waffles?' This was

thrown over his shoulder as he punched numbers into his cell phone. Esmé returned the waffles to the freezer, poured a bowl of Meow Mix for Quasi and took a piece of bread and peanut butter for herself before heading back to her room.

'I got some people coming round. Business. Important business. So I don't want you hanging round all morning, you got it?'

Out of earshot, back under her duvet, Esmé didn't bother to reply. She decided to write up her observations of the new neighbours in an out-of-date five-year diary retained for this purpose.

*Thursday 1st April – April Fools Day, Poisson d'Avril!*
*9.43 a.m. – In my bed. (I am playing hooky again today!)*

*I followed the man next door again yesterday evening. He went to an apartment on the corner of St Dominique and St Andre. I couldn't see who lived there because they just let him upstairs with the buzzer. I hung around for quite a long time but they didn't come out and I got cold so I came home. I think the lady next door might be a waitress because she always wears black pants or black skirt and white shirt. I know this cos I have seen her emptying the trash without her coat on. The Blob is being an asshole as usual.*

Once the neighbours' movements had been logged, Esmé took out the jewellery box with the twirling ballerina and sorted through her trinkets: the napkin from Gibby's where she'd gone for her first grown-up meal on her tenth birthday; the Davidoff cigar matchbox which contained nine centimetre matches; the heart-shaped stone from Îles-de-la-Madeleine; the iridescent marble that looked like a bubble; the blue china elephant given to her by a nurse when she had appendicitis; the miniature Courvoisier bottle filled with sea-washed glass; the dead butterfly with wings like peacock's feathers; the origami geisha girl brought back from Japan by her uncle and her prize possession – her grandmother's emerald ring. When Nana died, Evangeline had given her the ring 'because Esmé is short for Esmerelda, which means emerald in Spanish'.

'Was I named after emeralds?'

'No, your dad named you after *For Esmé – With Love and Squalor*. That's all we could give you then.' Esmé was disappointed. She had read the book, after finding it on a shelf with the words *Jon Bloom, Québec City, 1982* written inside the cover, but found it boring and the character of Esmé irritating. It would have been so much cooler to be named after a jewel.

Occasionally, she had flashbacks to a moustachioed man in a Davy Crockett hat, whom she had always assumed to be her father, though Evangeline eventually told her that Jon Bloom was clean-shaven and only ever wore a deerstalker. As Esmé hadn't seen him since she was four and he now lived in Tijuana with a Mexican woman and their three children, she was unlikely to verify the memory any time soon.

She arranged her trinkets neatly within the white satin of the jewellery box. One of the busboys at

Gibby's had drawn a cartoon of her on the napkin. He had scribbled it after lighting the candles on her birthday cake, given her puppy eyes, a kitten nose and a speech bubble saying 'For I'm A Jolly Good Fellow'. When she tried to return the favour on a coffee coaster, he snatched her pencil and snapped, 'Stop it. I'm not cute enough to draw,' rushing off before she had the chance to tell him she thought he was very cute, even though there was a weird mark on his cheek like someone had flicked purple ink in his face.

That day there was a new item to add to her collection: a silver hacky sack made from leather so soft it felt like a warm peach when pressed against her lips. Evangeline had bought it the week before to appease for Bobby's tantrum when Esmé had accidentally sat on his new sunglasses. It was almost too gorgeous to use but the painful significance of its origin made Esmé chary of putting it with her other treasures, which represented happy memories. She knew she would eventually forget where her precious souvenirs had come from but at that moment she knew the history of everything. The ballerina spun to the tinkle of *Für Elise* and she thought about the man next door twirling in the snow.

The doorbell rang and she heard Bobby lumbering to answer it, then voices in the hall, deep, urgent voices: Bobby's 'people' doing their 'important business'. Slipping out the front door, she glimpsed them in the living room – three thickset men in winter coats wreathed in smoke, toadying around Bobby who was reclining on the couch like the caterpillar out of *Alice in Wonderland*, his hands folded over his fat stomach.

Out in the yard, she stood in the damp dirt and threw the hacky sack in the air, beginning low and getting higher, counting the seconds between throws and catches. The neighbours' door swung open. Esmé dropped the hacky on a record six-second throw. The red-haired man appeared, spread-eagled behind an egg-shaped wicker basket chair. It was like the one on the porch of Nana's old house in Hochelaga.

'Hi.'

The man gave a slighting nod in response. Esmé blushed and turned away, before remembering she had always been hidden when she had seen him so it was little wonder he didn't recognise her. Clearly he was not in the mood for April Fool's banter but Esmé kept her eye on him while counting the seconds between throwing and catching. He was trying to suspend the chair from a hook above the porch.

'. . . one, two, three . . .' The hacky sack careened through the nuclear sky like a loose asteroid. '. . . four, five, six, seven . . . seven seconds! You see that?'

'Fuck.' The chair dropped to the ground. The man glared at her.

'Do you want some help?'

'I don't think so . . .'

'Actually, I'm really strong.' Without waiting for his reply she hopped over the low fence separating their yards. 'You want me to lift it, so you can hang it up?'

'OK.'

'Can I have a go?' said Esmé, when the chair was hung.

'A go?'

'I wanna sit in it and you twist me.'

'Twist you?' The man made a wry face. 'OK, whatever.'

She sat down, kicking out her legs as he twisted the hanging rope. When he let go she spun like a broken yo-yo and saw Clark Street flash past in split-second snatches.

'Woah . . . I feel really dizzy.' The world reeled, forcing her to lie down.

'You're not gonna puke, are you?'

'I never puke,' said Esme. 'Actually that's not exactly true: this one time I drank a whole load of milk and then about three glasses of cherry soda. It was *so* weird 'cos you'd think the puke'd come out pink but it came out *orange* . . .'

'Thanks for sharing.'

'That's OK.'

The man tugged the rope to test its strength and lowered himself into the chair.

'Comfortable, huh?' said Esmé.

'Not bad.'

'You want me to twist you? It's really fun.'

'Go on then.' The man grinned at her as she rotated him, his blue eyes translucent in the uneasy sunlight like her bubble marble.

Esmé giggled. These neighbours were way more fun than the previous yuppie couple who had escaped to Westmount after six months. She twisted the rope one more time. 'OK . . . I'm gonna . . .' Stepping back, she let the rope go. '. . . Oh shit.' In agonising slow motion that she was powerless to pause, the rope snapped and the chair dropped to the ground. The man bellowed as his forehead smashed against the doorframe.

'What the hell . . . Henry are you OK? Henry . . .' The man's wife appeared in a frilly pink apron. She knelt over his crumpled body and laid a rubber-gloved hand on his shoulder. Esmé muttered apologies through her fingers. She was thankful Bobby hadn't seen the incident.

'Don't worry, it's not your fault,' the lady reassured. She led Henry into their apartment and shut the door.

A while later she reappeared, still in the apron but minus the gloves.

'Is he OK?' Esmé had retreated to her own side of the fence.

'I think he'll survive.' The lady kicked the defunct chair aside and unlatched her gate.

'Are you going out?'

'Just to the *dépanneur*.'

'Can I come? I've got two bucks . . . I wanna get some gummy bears . . .'

'Sure.'


On the way up the street, they introduced themselves.

'Were you named after the Salinger book?'

'Yeah, how d'you know?'

'I've read it.'

'Who were you named after?'

'No one. My parents just liked the name Corinna.'

In the *dépanneur*, Esmé introduced Corinna to Jimmy, the owner.

'Hey girl, what's cookin'?'

'Excuse me?' Corinna frowned.

'You look like you dressed for cookin' baby . . . Maybe you wanna invite me round for food?'

'Maybe. Maybe not.'


On the way home, Corinna told Esmé she would introduce Henry properly if he wasn't feeling too bad.

'Is Henry your husband?'

'Husband! No! He's just my boyfriend. How old did you think we were?'

'I dunno. Thirty-seven?'

'Thirty-seven! Jeez. I better get a better moisturiser. I'm twenty-four. Henry's twenty-five.'

'Oh.' Twenty-four still sounded impossibly old to Esmé, but she thought it wise to change the subject: 'I had concussion this one time, you know. When I was eight.'

'Yeah? How'd it happen?'

'Actually, I don't remember exactly – I walked into a door or something. Doesn't the sky look really weird today?'

'Yeah, it does. Hey, how come you're not at school?'

'Oh, the teachers – they've got a training day or something. Hey, I think Jimmy liked your apron.'

'I think he did.'


Henry was lying on a big brass bed. The blinds were pulled down. Though it was hard to see the full effect of their boudoir in the gloom, Esmé vowed to emulate the atmosphere of worldly glamour in her own room.

There was a jug of dying lilies on a triple-mirrored dressing table, a candelabrum fit for a church altar, laced with gothic drips of wax, and, on the bedside chair, garish foreign banknotes tossed amid a brace of champagne flutes, containing abandoned mouthfuls of red wine. As soon as he saw Corinna, Henry sighed and clutched his brow.

'Hey, bunny. How're you feeling?' Corinna shifted the glasses, scattered the money to the floor and perched on the chair.

'Isn't it obvious I'm in extreme agony?'

'You've already met Esmé, haven't you? She wanted to make sure you were OK.' Corinna presented Esmé to Henry with a flourish as if she were a courtier paying homage to a king.

'I bought you an O Henry,' said Esmé, 'An O Henry for Henry . . .'

Henry took the chocolate bar with languid fingers and smiled weakly. 'So. Esmé. After the Salinger book?'

'You've read it too!'

'Yes, I have.' He winced. 'Look, Corinna, I think I may need to go to hospital.'

'Of course you don't need to go to hospital. Don't be such a fool.'

Esmé sensed it was the wrong moment for an April Fool quip.

'I am not being a fool. What if I have concussion? People die from concussion.'

'You're being a drama queen. As per usual.'

'No, I'm not. You never take my ailments seriously. Did you get me some lemonade?'

'Yes I did.'

'Is it pink?'
'Yes it's pink.'
'Good.'

\*

*Thursday, 1st April*
*9.31 p.m. – In bed. Again!*

*I actually talked to the new neghbors today! They are
really nice. The man is called Henry and he is twenty-
five. The lady is called Karena and she is twenty-four.
They are not married. They have a kind of chandaleer for
candles in there bedroom. It is really cool. I really want
one for my bedroom but I bet mom wont let me cos
of fire risk and everything. Mom is so boring sometimes.
The Blob ate all the apple strudel that mom bought
back from work. He is such a ~~fucking~~ greedy pig. And he
told Mom I cut school today. I hate him. Mom went
totally mad at me and sent me upstairs. And I could
hear her shouting at The Blob too cos he hadnt made
sure I went to school. Ha! Serves him right. They're
still argueing now but I think its about something else.
I wish theyd shut up. I bet the neghbors can here.*

\*

'So, you put that hand there and that hand there and
then you look into my eyes and step, step, step, step,
swing, swing, swing . . .'

Esmé tripped after Henry, her feet mirroring his,
several beats behind. It was the following week. Henry

had recovered from his ordeal and was teaching Esmé how to dance. She liked the warmth of his hands but his sharp blue eyes made her uncomfortable. Unlike Corinna's, they looked like they could see your secrets. The wound from the door was like a claw scratch through his right eyebrow.

'Don't look down. Look at me.'

'But I need to see what my feet are doing.'

'No you don't. Just feel the rhythm and move . . .'

'Corinna, do you wanna dance?' Corinna's face was poised between amusement and irritation; Esmé couldn't quite tell which but she thought it safest not leave Corinna out.

'No, I'm fine. Henry says I've got two left feet anyway.'

'I never said that!' Henry broke eye contact with Esmé and shot a look of mock-shock at Corinna.

'Yes, you did . . . or was it flat feet? You said I had flat feet.'

Corinna had finished sprinkling seeds in the flowerbeds and was nestled on the stoop with Quasi on her knee. The cat's full name was Quasimodo, though it didn't have a hunchback and was female. 'My mom thought she was a boy and then she got knocked up by a stray so we knew she wasn't,' Esmé explained.

'"Knocked up", huh?'

'Yeah, that's what Bobby said. You know, like pregnant . . . kittens.'

'You look a bit like Quasi, you know?'

'Do I?' Esmé was delighted.

'Yes,' Corinna lifted Quasi up to compare, 'Black hair, green eyes, cute noses.'

'Were you born with a tail?' asked

'Don't be silly. Of course not.'

'She acts like a cat though, doesn't

'How? How do I act like a cat?'

'You're sort of solitary and secretive. Friendly but independent.'

'Really?' Esmé basked in this description. She considered Henry and Corinna's animal characteristics: he was a lion, of course, and she had to be something graceful and elegant. A mermaid, perhaps – although a mermaid wasn't a real animal. Maybe a swan. No, a swan was too big, too slow. Corinna was a small bird, light and flitting, nervous and pretty. Esmé imagined a bluebird, though she had never seen one.

Evangeline loomed suddenly out of the gloaming in her dirty chef's whites, returning from the late shift at Café Santropol.

'Hey, Mom: look. See me doing the salsa?'

'Wonderful. Come on now, Ez. Bed. Corinna and Henry might want a little time to themselves.'

'No, don't worry. We like playing happy families,' said Corinna, 'Don't we Henry?'

*

*Saturday, 1st May – May Day! Though I don't know why I bothered to put an esclamation mark cos I did'nt do anything spesul today.*

*9.51 p.m. – In bed. Where else?!*

*Henry has been spending a lot of time at that apartment on St Dominique and St Andre. I know because*

...have been following him. I wear my baseball hat and hide behind the cars and he never sees me. I still don't know who lives there. Karena never goes with him. Mom and The Blob have been fighting a lot recintly. Yesterday The Blob did something terrible. I fucking hate him so much and I'm not even going to cross out the fucking. Thats how much I hate him.

\*

During the baseball season, Bobby rigged the TV up outside stacked on a Molson crate and sat on a deck-chair, cheering at the Expos' home runs.

'Get the fuck out of here. You're distracting me,' he yelled as Esmé sambaed around the screen with her hacky sack. She hung over the fence and was pleased to see Corinna emerge with the pink lemonade bottle full of water.

'Hey.'

'How's it going?'

'Fine.'

'Where's Henry?' Esmé reckoned she knew where he was but she wanted to check whether Corinna did.

'How should I know? Out.' The hardness to Corinna's voice startled Esmé. She watched as Corinna emptied the bottle over her flowerbeds. The seeds had sprouted and unfurled into such tender greenness they appeared to glow from within. Esmé imagined the roots and leaves curled like foetuses inside those dry specks. It was a marvel she couldn't quite explain.

'Hey, what happened to your face?' Corinna's voice

softened on noticing the graze across Esmé's cheek-bone.

Esmé glanced at Bobby but he was leaning forward, concentrating hard on the TV screen. 'Nothing. Fell over . . . Hockey practice. What will they turn into, the flowers?'

'Sweet peas, nasturtiums, marigolds and sunflowers.'

'Sunflowers!'

'Yeah, they'll probably grow even taller than you.'

'I wish I could grow sunflowers in our yard.' The only things that grew in their yard were a patch of nettles and Bobby's mountain of beer bottles.

'Well, maybe you could ask Bobby?'

Esmé shrugged. 'Nah. He won't want to.'

'He might . . . Hey Mr . . . er . . . Bobby!' Corinna shouted across to him.

'Huh?' Bobby's eyes were moving with the white arc of the baseball.

'Can Esmé grow some sunflowers in your yard?'

'No.'

Corinna touched Esmé's cheekbone, very lightly. 'You can look after mine.'

*

*Thursday, 13th May – Ascension Day – whatever that means. Big deal.*
*7.45pm – On the front step. Henry and Karena are nowhere to be seen.*

*I havn't seen Henry for ages. I have stopped following him to St Dominique Street because its getting really*

*boring just waiting for him for ages outside that apart-
ment. I really want him to carry on teaching me salsa.*

\*

As the evenings lengthened and the air warmed,
Corinna spent more time alone swinging in the resur-
rected basket chair. Esmé avoided asking after Henry
as she sensed it pissed Corinna off. She and Corinna
took to playing Crazy Eights on the stoop with a deck
of Air Canada cards. When it got dark she brought
out the candelabrum and allowed Esmé to light the
candles. Esmé practised striking the matches into her
chest like a boy. She had always loved fire. Volcanoes,
fireworks, bonfires, barbecues, candles, cigarette lighters, joss sticks – anything that burned. She heard that
Eskimos watched their campfires like televisions – a
notion she found entirely understandable.

'I asked my mom if I could have one of these in my
room but she wouldn't let me.'

'Well, it could be a bit dangerous. I expect she's
worried you'll fall asleep with it burning.'

'She says I'm a pyromaniac.'

'That's a good word.'

One of Esmé's rare bonding moments with Bobby
had been when he showed her how to make a rocket
by pouring meths into the cap of an empty soda bottle,
setting the bottle at a forty-five degree angle into the
ground and flicking a lighter at the cap. The bottle
shot into the air like a cannon ball and exploded
three metres up in a ball of flames. Evangeline was
furious with Bobby and confiscated Esmé's collection

of empty soda bottles: 'You crazy fucking pyroma-
niacs, the pair of you.' When Esmé looked the word
up in the dictionary, she was thrilled – '*pyromania* the
uncontrollable impulse and practice of setting things
on fire'. Pyromania was totally cool.

Corinna seemed to find it soothing to talk about the
trivia of Esmé's life, though sometimes her eyes glazed
over as she listened to tales of geography tests, the
physics teacher's glass eye and Janine Labelle's latest
hairstyle. Esmé was equally comforted by Corinna's
company. Unlike her parents, Corinna had a knack for
domesticity – her kitchen was scruffy but homely, with
an ever-changing aesthetic arrangement of fruit in a
blue glass bowl, a pink gardenia on the windowsill and
an enormous spiderplant nicknamed Ziggy, postcards
from friends stuck to the cupboards and interesting
food stacked within. Most evenings she poured Esmé
a glass of wine – 'I want to educate your palate so you
don't start drinking Alcopops when you're fifteen' –
and presented her with a plate of palm hearts, smoked
oysters or Spanish ham from pigs fed on acorns. Esmé
didn't relish these snacks as much as she would a
packet of Doritos or a handful of M&Ms but she glowed
to think that Corinna considered her worthy of such
grown-up luxuries. When she suggested Evangeline
buy wild boar paté instead of baloney for her packed
lunch, Bobby creased up mirthlessly and said, 'You
been hanging round that stuck-up bitch next door too
long.'

'She's not a stuck-up bitch. She's really nice.'

'She goes round like she's got a poker up her ass.
No wonder her boyfriend spends his whole time

mincing up and down St Laurent to get away from her. Actually, he'd probably like a poker up his ass. Fucking flamer . . .'

'Don't be mean about Esmé's friends, Bobby. It's nice that she gets on well with the neighbours.' Evangeline spoilt this show of allegiance by patting Esmé's head and adding, 'Don't bug Corinna too much, Ez. She might not want to spend every evening with an eleven year old.' Esmé felt enraged. To prove that she didn't bug Corinna every night, she stormed up the road with her silver hacky sack, to the basketball courts opposite the Angel, where the serious hacky sackers played every night, darting between the white slices of floodlights.

She stood on the sidelines for some time, desultorily knocking her hacky from foot to foot, too shy to join them. Five sets of shadows jerked across the tarmac in triplicate, colliding with the five silhouetted players like some new-fangled Indian spirit dance.

'You coming over?'

Esmé looked over her shoulder.

'We're talking to you. Come on over.'

At first she was a jangle of mistimed kicks and fumbled catches but eventually she caught their rhythm with a satisfying harmony reminiscent of dancing with Henry. The other players were older than her, all dressed in baggy boyish gear, even though two were girls.

During a short break, two figures caught her eye beyond the honeycomb of the fence. They were huddled together, deep in conversation, possibly holding hands. The light-footed gait of the shorter one was familiar: Henry. Henry and a friend wandering down Avenue du

Parc on a hot summer night. It was odd how people popped up when you thought about them.

'Hey! Henry!' Esmé's voice rang out in the still air. Having a grown-up friend, especially one like Henry, would increase her kudos with the other players.

The two figures stopped and appeared to disentangle from one another, though this was hard to see in the glare of the floodlights.

'Esmé? Is that you?'

'Yes. Is that Henry?'

'Yes. What are you doing?'

'Playing hacky.'

The other players resumed the game.

'Cool.' Henry ambled towards the basketball court. His friend remained by the road.

'Do you hack?' Esmé tossed the hacky in the air and counted five seconds before catching it. Henry was visible a few feet away on the other side of the fence. He was wearing a T-shirt Esmé had never seen before. It had the word TRUST across the chest in fuzzy felt letters. If she had been on the other side of the fence she would have been tempted to stroke them.

'Do I hack?' Henry smirked and cleared his throat. 'Only in the mornings.'

'Huh?'

'Doesn't matter.'

'Who's your friend?'

'Someone from my course.'

'Why doesn't he come down here?' She peered up at the strange man – it was definitely a man – and deciphered only curly hair, angular shoulders and the orange tip of a cigarette.

'He's shy.'

'Do you wanna come and play?'

'I'd love to but Alexei wants to go eat.'

'Alexei. How do you spell that?'

'A-L-E-X-E-I.'

'That's a nice name. Is it foreign?'

'Russian.'

'Russian. Cool. Is he Russian?'

'Yes.'

'Does he speak English?'

'Yes.'

'That's good.'

'Why's that?'

'Well, you don't speak Russian, do you?'

'No, I don't . . . Look, Esmé, I gotta go. Alexei's waiting.'

'OK.'

He bounded up the grassy bank to Alexei and they disappeared over the brow of the road towards the city centre, slightly further apart than before.

'Are you still playing?' asked one of the girls, kicking the hacky over to Esmé, who caught it on her toe and flipped it back.

'Yeah, I'm still playing.'

\*

*Saturday, 22nd May – There is nothing specul about this date.*

*8.32 p.m. – In the TV Room. Watching 'Friends'. Karena is like a much much prettier version of Feebee(?).*

*I swear to God Henry was holding hands with that Russian man. Alexie. (Not sure I've spelt it right.) I think it's really unfreindly that Alexie didn't come and talk to me. His name is really stupid anyway. It sounds like a girls name. Maybe The Blob is right about Henry. I wonder if Karena knows about this. I don't think she does. I wonder what she will do when Henry tells her. I hope he doesn't tell her.*

\*

The next time Esmé saw Corinna, she was kneeling on her kitchen floor, lining up black and white linoleum tiles. She asked Esmé to pass the tiles to her alternately, black, white, black, white, like a chessboard. The brown cupboards had been painted a yellow so glossy they looked like they had been dipped in egg yolks. They smelt more delicious than hot tar, creosote or even, Esmé's favourite, felt tip marker pens.

'Next thing, I'm going to make a red and white gingham cloth for the table,' said Corinna.

'Gingham.'

'Checked cotton. You'd know it if you saw it. The kind of tablecloths they have in old-style Italian restaurants.'

'I think I know what you mean,' Esmé lied.

'And I'm going to buy some blue and white crockery to go with it all.'

'Crockery.'

'Bowls and plates – china.'

'Cool.' Primary colours pleased Esmé. She was on a wavelength with Corinna's taste in interior décor – the chequered floor looked like something you would see behind the front door of a kid's drawing of a house and the crockery and tablecloth sounded straight out of Hansel and Gretel.

'Ziggy's grown heaps of babies, hasn't he?' Esmé flicked one of the tiny spiderplants which sprouted from a long trailing shoot.

'You can have one if you like,' said Corinna. She detached one of the bigger babies from the father plant and placed it in an empty anchovy jar filled with water.' Leave it for a week or so, till it grows some roots. Then you can plant it.'

'Should I name it?'

'I guess. It would be sticking with the tradition.'

'Think of something.'

'I don't know. How about Aladdin?'

'Huh?' Before Esmé could find out why she'd suggested this name, Henry appeared, padding up behind them on his dainty dancer's feet. He didn't bother to greet her though she hadn't seen him since the night at the basketball pitch.

'Jeez! Henry. You gave me a fright.' Corinna pressed her palm to her chest as if taking her heartbeat.

'You two look busy. What are you doing?' He stood on the new floor, one foot on a black tile, the other on a white, his hands in his pockets.

'What does it look like I'm doing? Would you mind not standing right there, Henry – the glue isn't dry.'

'I thought we were going to buy the tiles together. Who decided on black and white?'

'Who do you think? Me.'

'But I never said we should have black and white. I

was gonna suggest these sort of *trompe l'oeil* rippling swimming-pool effect tiles – I saw them in a magazine. It would be like we were walking on water . . .'

'Well, if you'd been around when I was choosing the tiles you would have been able to suggest that, Henry. Even though they sound totally hideous . . .'

There was a crackle in the air that Esmé had witnessed all too often between grown-ups. She edged towards the front door. 'I think I'll see you guys later.'

Neither acknowledged her departure. As she slipped out their voices rose but she didn't stick around to find out what they were saying.

Back in her own kitchen she set Aladdin on the sink and poured a glass of grape juice. Quasi made a figure-of-eight around her legs. Upstairs, she tried to encourage the cat to lie in the crook of her knees, but Quasi was in a contrary mood and kept leaping off the bed and scratching at the door.

The spying diary lay under her pillow but the idea of logging the neighbours' movements no longer held any appeal. She flicked through it – her writing, squashed together and reduced in size so it could fit into the small pages suddenly seemed obsessional and unbalanced; the way the heavy pressure of her pen had scored the paper seemed creepily avid. She was a snoop, a nosey parker, a busybody. Nobody liked a tell-tale. What if Corinna found this diary; read all about how she had followed Henry? She would think Esmé was a silly little girl, not worthy of all the grown-up attention she had lavished upon her. Esmé felt hot with shame.

*

The fireplace in the living room hadn't been used since March but it was easy to shift the dried-flower arrangement aside, screw up a stack of newspapers, hide the diary among them and light a match. Or at least it would have been easy if Esmé could find a match. Evangeline kept her matchbook collection stashed in a Chinese steamer on the top shelf of the kitchen cupboard, too high for Esmé to reach. Bobby's Zippo was kept about his person. The cooker, being electric, was ineffective as a flame provider, though Esmé had, on occasion, seen her mother bend over the hob with her hair held aloft and the end of a cigarette pressed to a hotplate. Evangeline didn't like to plunder her matchbooks. Suddenly, Esmé remembered her own Davidoff matches in their pristine white and gold box. It pained her to spoil the unused surface of the striking panel but there was no other option.

She read Zino Davidoff's romantically fountain-penned directions on the back: '*Un cigare ne doit être allumé ni trop vite ni trop lentement, mais régulière-ment, à petites bouffées.*'

The first lighting was far too *lentement* and merely wrinkled the kindling paper, leaving the diary charred but still readable in the grate. Quasi refused to stay out of the living room and kept diving into the balls of newspaper that littered the floor. As it was summer both the wood basket and coalbunker were empty. On the coffee table, among Bobby's rolling papers and tobacco, was a bottle of lighter fluid. Esmé squirted some onto the diary. The fluid soaked away so she gave the bottle another squeeze. In the circumstances, she was sure Monsieur Davidoff would have recommended a little *vitesse*.

Esmé struck another match and held it upside down. As the flame ate up the nine centimetre stick and licked at her fingers, she tossed it onto the diary. The *bouffée* that ensued was far from *petite*.

# Welcome

'Welcome, my friend,' said Ibrahim. He pointed to an empty chair with his cigarette. Josh sat down.

Ibrahim was small and had a large moustache. 'So. How do you find out about this job, Joshua?'

'I sort of know one of your waitresses.' 'Sort of' were the operative words but Josh hoped this would soon change.

'Aah! Which one? Let me guess. It is not Hilde?'

'No, it's not Hilde.'

'It is not Bradley?'

'No.'

'Of course. It cannot be. Bradley is not a wait*ress*.'

'It's Corinna. She's house-sitting for my sister.'

'Corinna! Yes!' Ibrahim crowed. 'Yes, of course. It is Corinna. Corinna, a beautiful girl. But always she is unhappy. Perhaps you can make her smile.'

'Uh, yeah, well . . . perhaps.' Josh would try his best.

'And from where do you come, my friend?'

'Er . . . do you mean like way back, or where I've come from today?'

Ibrahim made a circular backwards motion with his cigarette.

'Oh. OK. Well, my grandparents on my mom's side were originally from Newcastle, in England, and my grandparents on my dad's side were from Chicago but

I was born in Ottawa and we moved to Montreal when I was six, so I guess that means . . .'

'I am from Lebanon. Do you know where that is?'

'Uh . . . the Middle East?'

'Lebanon is situated on the Mediterranean Sea. It is situated between Syria and Israel. It is the smallest country in the Middle East but it is nevertheless an extremely vital part of the . . .' He gave a detailed explanation of Lebanon's importance on the world stage, before finally asking, '. . . and so, my friend, do you have many experiences of working in restaurants?'

Josh's only restaurant experience was three days behind a McDonald's counter at the age of sixteen. He had been sacked for improvising with the Big Mac and Quarter Pounder formats. To provide variety for the customers, he had incorporated bacon when there should have been cheese, barbecue relish when there should have been gherkin, a Filet-o-Fish when there should have been an extra burger.

Upon his dismissal the manager had yelled, 'There is no room for originality in the McDonald's enterprise, Josh.'

For Ibrahim's benefit, Josh expanded these three days into a career spanning four years, touching upon his aptitude for teamwork, his punctuality, his honesty, his hardworking attitude, his multi-tasking abilities and his high regard for rules and regulations.

Ibrahim nodded seriously. When Josh had finished he spread his hands like a plaster saint and said, 'Welcome.'

Josh guessed there would be few people wanting

to work the lunch shift in a restaurant in the middle of the Royalmount industrial estate, twenty minutes walk from De La Savane station on the furthest reaches of the orange line. Corinna had told him about the job and he needed a cover for his illegal earnings as his parents were getting suspicious. Unbeknown to them, he and his friend Phil ran a drug-dealing operation from their house, called The Prescription. Henry, Corinna's ex-boyfriend, had been a Prescription client. Josh first met Corinna when he sold Henry some hash. She had shimmied into the living room with a tray of coffee and a plate of Portuguese rice cakes wrapped in blue-and-white paper, then knelt on the floor and served them like a geisha. When she bent forward to pour the coffee, her long blonde hair curtained her face and he could see down the front of her shirt. She was wearing no bra and her breasts were the colour of cream. Henry was exactly the kind of good-looking bastard who would have a girlfriend like Corinna, so Josh was amazed and delighted when Henry left her. For a *man*. A man Josh knew in fact: Alexei, one of his classmates at McGill. There was no doubting Henry's sexual proclivities: if you wanted to leave a girl like Corinna for a man you were definitely gay.

Corinna and Hilde weren't due in till later that morning but Ibrahim presented Josh to the other staff. The chef was an amiable Bengali named Assad. His morose assistant, also from Bangladesh, was introduced as Eddie. Suhil, a huge menacing Libyan friend of Ibrahim's, was the kitchen porter. The barman was twenty-one-year-old Brad, newly arrived from Ontario. He had a simple open face and spoke very slowly.

When Josh asked if he was a student or a real person, he said, 'Nah, I'm just a hick.'

Josh smiled – in the battle for Corinna's affections, Brad would be no competition.

'What about you?' Brad asked him.

'What?'

'Are you a student?'

'Yup. McGill. I'm doing a Masters in Math.'

'So does that mean you're not real?' Brad grinned, pleased to have picked up Josh's phraseology.

'No. I'm real.'

The restaurant had changed management and chefs but retained Corinna and Hilde from the old wait staff. The name, Royalmount 2000, had stayed even though it was several years out of date. 'People, they know this name,' said Ibrahim. 'It will be bad for business to change.' He wanted to re-open the following day. As the restaurant was so ingrained with dirt from its previous incarnation, they spent the whole morning cleaning. The previous owner's purple carpet and gold Venetian blinds had remained, but Ibrahim added his own pseudo-Salvador Dali soft-porn paintings to the walls.

'You don't think these are gonna put people off their dinner, Ibrahim?' asked Josh.

'No, my friend, I think they make a nice welcome.' He pointed at an unclaimed cigarette smouldering in an ashtray: 'To whom this cigarette?'

'To me, I think,' said Josh, clamping it into his mouth.

The job they had all been avoiding was the toilets. Brad endeared himself to everyone by spending two hours scrubbing off dried-on shit with Comet. From time to time he had to rush outside and take long deep breaths of fresh air.

'You on a Comet high?' asked Josh.

'Uh, yeah, I guess.'

'I might have to try it out when you're finished.'

Brad laughed gratefully as if Josh had let him into a secret club.

Hilde promenaded queen-like through Royalmount 2000 when all the dirty work had been done. She was a German woman in her fifties, with a nipped in waist and a meringue of transparent hair teased up into a style that clearly hadn't changed since her twenties. Corinna turned up late in a fluster, red-faced and breathless from the walk to the restaurant. Her waitressing outfit, a tight white shirt and a short black skirt, was sexy as hell. If she had been serving Josh, he would have tipped her bigtime.

'Again the metro was delayed, I suppose, Corinna?' said Hilde.

Corinna shrugged.

'That orange line train from Sherbrooke is pretty unreliable, eh?' said Josh, hoping this entrée would cement their bond as bohemian Plateau dwellers united against suburbanites such as Hilde but Corinna merely shrugged again.

'That shirt: is it not a little tight for you?' Hilde continued, fingering Corinna's sleeve, her lips puckered in disgust as if the shirt was made from the skins of dead babies.

'I think your shirt looks great, Corinna,' said Brad.

127

Josh was stunned that Brad had dared to say the words that were in his own head; the words he was too shy of saying for fear of sounding obvious.

'You know what Max said to me?' said Hilde, examining her perfectly manicured beige-polished nails for imperfections.

'No, but I think we're about to,' said Josh, hoping to win a few points over Brad by being bitchy towards Hilde.

'He said I had the figure of a twenty-five year old.'

'A twenty-five-year-old what?'

'A twenty-five-year-old girl, of course.' Hilde puffed out her impressive chest and smoothed her skirt over her hips.

'Max was a charmer,' said Corinna.

'Who is this Max, anyway?' said Josh. Whoever he was, Josh didn't like the sound of him. He hoped it wasn't another waiter who had yet to arrive.

'The old chef. The one before Assad. He was Russian.' Corinna's voice was neutral but her mention of Max's nationality confirmed his glamour.

'You can never trust a Russian,' said Josh, remembering as he said it that Alexei, the man Henry had left her for, was Russian.


Ibrahim presented them each with a float of thirty-three dollars and thirty-three cents in preparation for the following day.

'I am counting, I am counting,' he said, peeling five dollar bills from a roll with an expression of distaste. 'After payday you will return to me this money and bring in your own float.'

Assad held them behind for half an hour and slowly ran through the menu:

'Garlic bread – that's bread with garlic . . . Onion soup – that's soup with onions . . . Hamburger with fries – that's . . .'

'This is kinda self-explanatory, Assad,' said Josh.

'Yes,' Corinna suddenly stood up. 'I'm really sorry, Assad, but I have to be somewhere at seven.'

Josh watched her leave, his disappointment cut with apprehensive curiosity about her seven o'clock appointment. He had hoped they might return to the Plateau together and laugh about their co-workers on the way.

'The look he gave you when you left – he was really mad,' Brad told Corinna the following day, but Assad smiled at Corinna as broadly as ever and seemed to bear no grudge. He had arrived at work with his shirt unbuttoned to his waist.

'Ooh, Assad, you have your shirt open,' leered Ibrahim. 'Let me see what is in there: I like to see nipples. Nipples – they give me a special feeling . . .'

Josh raised his eyebrows: 'Even Assad's?'

'Big nipples, small nipples, Assad's nipples, any nipples – they all give me that special feeling.'

When Ibrahim had satisfied himself with the sight of Assad's nipples, he took a seat and began to paint his tasseled loafers with instant shoe shine, while waiting for the onslaught of customers.

'Nobody has noticed my new shoes,' he crowed,

stretching out his thin legs. 'I have new shoes. Nobody has said, "Well done".'

'Well done, Abraham,' said Brad.

'Thank you, Bradley. Only Bradley, he sees my shoes.'

Brad bounced up and down, thrilled by Ibrahim's gratitude. 'Oh yeah, I'm really observant; really good at noticing things; I see everything.'

'No Bradley – only Allah sees everything.'


Corinna seemed preoccupied with private troubles but she showed Josh how to carry two dishes of food in one hand and how to clear dirty plates, stacking them on one arm and scraping them clean with the used cutlery. Though she and Hilde obviously loathed each other, they swung between the tables, serving, clearing and setting places with synchronised grace. Josh's presence upset their dynamic like a clog dancer trying to join a pair of prima ballerinas in a *pas de deux*.

Business was slow but Assad and Eddie still panicked and sent out the wrong order more than once.

'These are chicken legs. I asked for breast not legs. Breast! You understand?' Hilde shrieked, slamming the plate back onto the hatch.

Five minutes later, the order bell pinged: 'Here are your breasts, my darling.'

On the way home Brad accompanied Josh and Corinna halfway along the orange line. He sat opposite them, leaning across the aisle to talk above the rattle of the train. 'Hey, guys, we should all go out together some time, how 'bout it? There's some great bars down

Crescent Street. You guys go down there?'

'I tend to go out on the Plateau mostly but, yeah, I used to frequent La Rue du Croissant in a former life,' said Corinna.

'"La Rue du Croissant". You're funny. Hey, Winny's has a happy hour between five and seven. They should call it 'happy two hours' not 'happy hour' huh?' Brad laughed immoderately.

At Square Victoria he jumped out. As the train pulled away he waved through the window. Corinna and Josh raised half-hearted hands.

'Is it preferable to be a happy fool or a miserable sage?' said Josh.

'Don't be mean. Brad's a sweetheart,' said Corinna.

'So are you planning to accompany him to "La Rue du Croissant" for the "happy two hours" at the "Sir Winston Churchill"?'

'Why not? It might be fun. Re-living my teens, re-living the time when I was still young and full of hope.'

'How old are you now, Corinna – twenty-one, twenty-two? You can't be that jaded yet?' Josh knew she was older than this but he needed to accrue more points on the charm-o-meter.

'I'm twenty-four but I feel about a hundred and four, I'm so tired these days. This year has been so exhausting and awful, what with the fire and . . . everything else.' It was clear that Henry stood for 'everything else'. Around the time Henry had left her, their apartment on Clark Street had been destroyed by a fire, started accidentally by the next-door-neighbour's kid. This was how she had ended up house-sitting for Josh's sister.

'Yeah, you've had a really rough ride these last few

months but, you know, things will get better,' said Josh. Hopefully, her rough ride would end up in his direction.

Corinna sighed. 'I suppose. But sometimes I feel this city is sapping the life out of me, making me so cynical. People like Brad, straight off the boat, they're so innocent, so kind of . . . *green*.'

'Yeah, well . . . that's the big shitty for you,' said Josh.


By Tuesday, word had spread around the industrial estate and sceptical secretaries from the offices round-about had turned up to see if Royalmount 2000 was any better under its new management. Everyone was run off their feet. Ibrahim fluttered around getting in the way. Eventually he took responsibility for the coffees, placing them on the counter with his ubiqui-tous 'Welcome'. There wasn't enough cutlery so Suhil spent the whole time scowling behind the sink in the dining room in order to keep up with demand.

'It makes a wonderful impression, does it not?' said Hilde, 'It looks like we have a fucking terrorist to do the washing up.' Josh tried to imagine his own mother using such language but couldn't. Neither could he imagine her wearing such short skirts.

Corinna had turned up with her eyes dusted in silver glitter, like a beautiful alien.

'This *maquillage*, what is it?' sniffed Ibrahim, 'It is suitable for the discotheque but it is unsuitable for Royalmount 2000.'

'To be obvious is never to be attractive. The less is

always the more,' said Hilde, delightedly jumping on Ibrahim's bandwagon, 'A little mascara, a little lipstick, a little eyeshadow in a natural colour. You should try to be more chic, Corinna, more class.'

'Hilde wouldn't know class if it jumped up and bit her on the ass,' Josh muttered to Corinna as they stood at the serving hatch.

'I think your glitter is really pretty, Corinna,' said Brad.

Sometimes Josh wished he had no brain. Self-knowledge made you self-conscious; unable to say the things simple people said.


No one wanted to drink at the Royalmount 2000 bar so Brad was assigned to delivering take-outs on foot. He was a cheery presence, always eager to please. When Corinna dropped a stack of sugar sachets, he picked them up for her with such charming alacrity that Josh noticed her blush.

'The restaurant looks pretty good now, eh?' he enthused. 'And Abraham seems like a really nice boss, eh?'

Ibrahim was not so complimentary about Brad: 'That boy, he is too slow. He is very stupid.'

Frequently, Josh warmed to the sight of Ibrahim observing Brad with pursed lips. In a crappy job there was nothing better than Schadenfreude to keep your spirits up.

When the shift was over Ibrahim requested all the thirty-three dollars and thirty-three cents floats back and insisted they would have to start using their own money. There was an uproar of outraged clamouring from everyone but Brad.

'No way, Ibrahim. Only after payday, like you said. Only after payday. Come on, Ibrahim.'

Squirming on his seat, he finally agreed: 'OK, OK. No problem. After payday you will return to me the money.' He spread his hands. 'Welcome.'

On the metro home, Corinna sat between Josh and Brad and shook her head defeatedly as Josh raged over the shittiness of Ibrahim. She had been waitressing too long to be surprised by Ibrahim, and she seemed too ground down to care. Brad nodded sympathetically at Josh and suggested reasons for Ibrahim's shittiness: he was under pressure; he was short of money; he was new to the restaurant game.

'You're so patient, Brad,' sighed Corinna, as if she herself was exhausted by the amount of effort Brad expended in being patient, 'How do you manage to be so positive all the time?'

'I just try to focus on the good things about people and that stops me from feeling angry.'

'Jeez. The Dalai Lama of the Royalmount 2000,' muttered Josh.

Corinna shook her head. 'You're so cynical, Josh. If more people took a leaf from Brad's book, the world would be a better place.'

'What is this book? *The Tao of Brad*? Gimme a break.'

Brad smiled placidly as if part of his brain was missing. Corinna turned to him, 'Well, I'm going to try to be nicer from now on.'

'I think you're nice enough already, Corinna,' said Brad.

Josh rolled his eyes. Who was this guy? Forrest Gump? He decided to introduce a little light Hilde-bashing into the conversation, in the hope it would win brownie points with Corinna.

'Hey, Hilde was telling me about her underwear today. She said the Bay had a load of "lingerie" on special and she was going to buy an all-in-one body stocking.'

'Oh God, she told me about that too,' said Corinna.

Josh puffed out his lips and his chest in a parody of Hilde, ''The smooth line unter mein clothes it makes and unter mein crotch the tiny buttons hold it together.' I said to her, "Hey, Hilde, that's a little more informa-tion than I needed".'

Corinna laughed. 'She told me I ought to buy an all-in-one body stocking to hold in my stomach, seeing as I didn't have "the power of the will" to stop eating junk food.'

'"The power of the will"! Ha! I like that! What is she? Fucking Friedrich Nietzsche? Sounds so fucking fascist. I bet Hilde was in the Hitler Youth.' Josh grinned at Corinna, pleased to have her back on his track and to have dropped in about a million cultural references that were way over Brad's head. Corinna had been easily diverted from the *Tao of Brad* but Josh thought it politic not to point this out.

Brad brought the conversation back down to his level with a bump. 'Hey guys, you wanna head down to "La Rue du Croissant" tonight?'

Josh waited for Corinna's refusal, which would be his cue to say no too. Instead, she smiled and said, 'Yes, that would be nice. I could do with a drink. Tell me where and when?'

Brad almost bounced off his seat in excitement. 'Five p.m.? Winny's? Then we can get two hours of happy hour in.'

Josh turned up fashionably late to find Corinna and Brad lolling in a booth, halfway towards being very happy. On the table in front of them was a regiment of empty shot glasses and the dirty smiles of half a dozen crushed lemon segments.

'You wanna slam?' Brad waved a glass at the barman, who was buttoned into a shiny regulation waistcoat like all the other half-wit geeks who worked in the place. 'Hey Mister Barman! Tequila!'

'Actually, I'll just have a Boréale,' said Josh, when the geek came over. Then, very deliberately, sliding his eyes towards Corinna, he added, 'Make it a Blonde.' Unfortunately, she was too busy giggling with Brad to notice, so he wasn't able to reel out his 'Gentlemen Prefer Blondes' line either.

'So, Corinna, how's it going at my sister's?' he asked, when they were all set up with their drinks, casually tossing in their prior acquaintance to exclude Brad.

'It's fine. Simpkin's keeping me company.' Her voice was non-committal. She drew her finger through the spilt salt on the table.

'You haven't started talking to him, have you?'

'I have actually. I'm turning into one of those crazy old cat ladies.'

'You and my sister both.' Jess was out in Alberta, having been employed by some local council to paint murals all over a town called Legal. 'She called me last week, said she was so bored she went to bed at nine most nights and the most interesting things that had happened to her were in her dreams.'

'Isn't that always the way, wherever you are?' Corinna slouched her head against her hand; the happy-hour magic was wearing off.

'Er . . . I guess. Anyway, Jess must be really bored if she's resorted to calling me.'

'Your sister's great,' said Corinna, as if Josh had said otherwise.

'Yeah.'

'Slam?' Brad raised his shot glass and, in unison, he and Corinna licked salt off the back of their hands, downed the tequila, slammed their glasses, bit the lemon and laughed. Josh quietly sipped his beer and forced a smile.

The bar was filling up with college kids and tourists, squawking and shrieking in out-of-town accents. As the lights lowered for the evening crowd, the music was turned up so Josh found he was battling to hear himself or anyone else speak. He decided to insti-gate another 'Who the fuck does Hilde think she is?' conversation.

'You know what she said to me the other day?' he yelled.

'No?'

'She said to me –' He adopted Hilde's preening posture and angular voice. '– she said: "It is so funny, Joshua – ven I voz your age my boyfriends vere all old enough to be my father. Now, they could be my sons. Men my age, they do not have the energy that I have.

They are old men viz their pipe und their slipper." And then she put her hand on my leg and she said, "These old men, Joshua, these grand-vaters, they cannot satisfy me".'

'She put her hand on your leg?' Brad was wide-eyed. 'No way!'

'Way.'

'She wants you, man.' Brad nodded earnestly.

'Jeez. You gotta be kidding! She's old enough to be my grandmother, let alone my mom.'

'She was really pretty back in her day,' said Corinna.

'How do you know?'

'She once showed me this photograph of herself dressed up as a mermaid.'

Brad suddenly leapt to his feet and punched the air in time with the drumbeat thumping out of the speaker above them. His placid features warped into a snarling frown. 'Buddy, you're a boy. Make a big noise. Playin' in the street. Gonna be a big man some day. You got mud on yo' face. Big disgrace. Kickin' your can all over the place . . . We will . . . we will ROCK you' . . . This is my favourite song EVER!' He hurled himself into the scrum of people upon the dancefloor.

'Brad digs Queen. What a surprise.' Josh's smile was for real – now, at last, he had Corinna to himself. 'So, what were you saying about Hilde? She used to dress up as a mermaid? What was she, in the circus or some-thing? Carnival freak show?'

'– she had a job in this swank hotel – somewhere downtown, I don't think it exists any more – and it had a swimming pool in the middle of the restaurant. She used to have to glide up and down in it all evening, while everybody was eating. She was . . . you know: the glamour . . .'

'How the mighty have fallen.' Josh slugged his beer and leaned back contentedly to watch Brad wield an air guitar amid a circle of high-school girls.

'Why are you so negative about everyone all the time, Josh?'

'Huh?'

Josh turned to Corinna but she had slipped out of her seat and was swaying towards the dancefloor.

'We will . . . we will ROCK you!' Brad greeted her arrival like a demented gorilla – flinging his hands above his head and hopping from side to side. Josh slammed his empty beer glass on the table and realised, on closer inspection, he had wrecked the love-heart Corinna had drawn through the salt. Who had she been thinking of when she drew that? Not him for sure. She thought he was negative. She preferred the company of happy brainless fools. Josh picked up his coat.

The next day neither Brad nor Corinna turned up for work. Josh teetered on a mental high-wire with horrific images either side of Brad fucking Corinna like a dirty farm-boy and Corinna squealing like a stuck pig in terrified pleasure. The backdrop to these horrific images was his sister's 2½ on Rue St Dominique, as he had never seen the dunghill where Brad lived. He wasn't able to concentrate too much on the horror though as the restaurant was screamingly busy without Corinna and Brad's help. Hilde charged back and forth across the restaurant floor, screeching, 'I am in the juice. Totally I am in the fucking juice.' Josh was still trying to perfect the art of carrying two plates in one hand so he wasn't able to rescue her from this metaphorical juice.

Hilde banged out orders to Assad and Eddie with machine-gun rapidity.

'What the hell is this? Tell me what it is, Eddie?' Hilde yelled, flinging a plate of underdone chicken brochettes back through the hatch. 'You are trying to give everyone the fucking food poisoning? We are not in fucking Bombay now.'

Eddie stared at her impassively.

'Don't just stand there like the fucking idiot of the village, Eddie. *Mein Gott*!'

'Stop bloody shouting at me, woman. And stop bloody calling me Eddie.'

'I thought that is your fucking name. Assad tells me your name is Eddie.'

'His name's Salaam,' snapped Assad, as he tossed the brochettes back onto the flaming grill.

'Why do you tell me the name wrong? You think I can read the fucking minds? How is it I am supposed to know . . . ?'

'Because Eddie is easier for you bloody Canadians to say.'

'I am not Canadian. I am German.'

When the lunch rush was over and both Josh and Hilde had collapsed to calculate their takings, Ibrahim sidled up to them with an offering of burnt pizza that had been rejected by a customer: 'Welcome.'

'Too kind you are, Ibrahim,' snapped Hilde.

Ibrahim folded himself into a chair at an adjoining table and motioned with his cigarette to the half-empty cup of coffee upon it: 'To whom this coffee?'

'This is mine this morning I pour. I do not have the time to finish.'

'You sleep well, Hilde? You enjoy life?'

'When I am far away from you, yes.'

But Ibrahim did not hear her. He had launched into one of his impromptu lectures: 'Did you know that I am named after Ibrahim, the first prophet in all the religions? . . . And did you know, Islam is the biggest religion in the world? It has over one billion believers . . .'

'Such a great shame this is,' muttered Hilde.

Ibrahim ignored her and turned to Josh. 'To where do you think Bradley and Corinna are?'

'I have no idea.' Josh crunched on a crust of pizza so hard it grazed the roof of his mouth. 'Fuck.' He paused. An idea had come to him. '*Actually*, Ibrahim, I think it might be something to do with what happened last night.'

'*Y-e-e-s?*'

'We all went out together on Crescent Street – Corinna, Brad and I –'

'*Y-e-e-s?*'

'And, uh, well, Brad was getting Corinna totally loaded on tequila.'

'He wanted to make his wicked way with her.' Ibrahim smiled nastily. 'I know the type of man he is.'

'Yeah.' Weren't they all that type of man, given half a chance? Ibrahim especially. Although, since he didn't drink, to have his wicked way with her he would have to knock Corinna out with a combination of instant-shoeshine fumes and cheap aftershave.

'I don't think Brad's a reliable kind of person,' Josh added. 'He likes a drink. I wouldn't trust him running my bar. All that stock you've got there. Whose to say he doesn't . . . you know . . .' Josh allowed the idea to crystallise in Ibrahim's mind.

'*Y-e-e-s*. I will keep my eye on that boy when he return.' Ibrahim stroked his big moustache and gazed meditatively towards the bar. 'If I didn't have the need of them I would fire them both *immédiatement*.'

Josh gulped. 'No! Don't fire Corinna. She really needs the money. She's been having a really bad time. Her apartment burnt down, she's staying at my sister's, she's kind of at a really vulnerable point right now . . . and I think Brad took advantage of that. It's not Corinna's fault.'

Ibrahim stared at Josh through narrowed eyes and smiled.

The next day Brad and Corinna turned up separately looking pale and subdued. They barely glanced at one another, let alone exchanged words. Clearly, they had done the wild thing, made the beast with two backs; this was obviously post-coital embarrassment. Josh seethed with jealous rage. While Brad was off delivering take-outs, he snuck into the bar, opened two bottles of Molson, emptied the contents down the sink and left the empty bottles by the ice bucket.

*

The next day, Corinna still looked like someone had broken all her toys. Brad was back to his obliviously cheery self, treating Josh like his best buddy. Josh went into the bar and emptied two bottles of Hi-Dry into the sink. As he was coming out of the bar he bumped into Hilde. Ever since he had failed to respond with lust to her all-in-one bodystocking information, she had barely spoken to him. She stood, one arm akimbo on her hip, the other arm stacked with dirty plates and fixed him with cold eyes.

'What is it you are doing in there, Joshua? In the bar, there are no customers. Here is where we need your help.'

'Yeah, right. I'm coming. I'll be right there, Hilde.'

The next day, Corinna called in sick. After a few frantic calls on his cellphone, Ibrahim drafted in Ayesha, a friend of his daughter, as an emergency replacement. She was Algerian and she spoke French, Arabic and very bad English. Josh was surprised to find out she was only seventeen, for her face lacked the innocence of youth and her manner was brusque and worldly. She had broad shoulders and she walked and sat like a man, with her legs apart.

'Ayesha's not as pretty as Corinna, eh?' said Brad, man-to-man, as he and Josh tucked into pizzaghettis – a hybrid comprising pizza dolloped with spaghetti bolognese. Ayesha was on the other side of the room talking to Ibrahim in Arabic.

Josh gritted his teeth. How could Brad be so blatant? He might as well shout it out to the whole restaurant:

'Hey listen up, guys – me and Corinna are getting it on.'

'Don't get me wrong,' Brad continued, 'Ayesha seems like a nice person – not as, you know, er . . . high-strung as Corinna, but she's really not as pretty as Corinna, is she?'

'High-strung?' Josh frowned at Brad. What the hell did he know about concepts such as 'high-strung'? Back where he was from they were too inbred to be high-strung.

'Yeah, that's what I reckon. She's high-strung. Kinda difficult. Kinda weird.'

Josh leaned forward. 'Difficult? Weird? In what way? When?'

Backing off like a cornered dog, Brad stammered, 'Well, uh, I don't know . . . why are you asking me so many questions?'

Josh leaned back, took a deep breath, and assumed an easygoing nonchalance. 'I'm not. Don't worry about it.' He glanced over at Ayesha who was laughing at some Arabic joke with Ibrahim. Her laugh was kind of dirty and he liked the way she threw her head back and showed all her teeth. 'I know what you're saying about Corinna,' he mused, 'But Ayesha's got a certain *je ne sais quoi.*'

Brad turned down his mouth in puzzlement. 'I don't know 'bout that *juh nuh say* stuff. She looks kind of greasy to me.'


Ayesha accompanied Josh back to the metro and told him about her husband who earned his living by singing Algerian folk songs at weddings.

'You got a husband already?' said Josh.

'*Ouais, je suis jeune, c'est vrai, mais je suis vieille de coeur.*'

'I know what you mean. I feel pretty old in my heart too.'

A red Jaguar whizzed past. 'My friend has one of those,' said Ayesha, 'Jag-u-ar. It cost him ninety thousand dollars.'

'Cool.'

They took the orange line together – Ayesha explained she was going all the way to Mont Royal to visit her mother. '*Mes parents – ils sont divorcés.* My father is in Paris. One time I work in Paris in my uncle's restaurant.'

'Paris, wow, I'd love to go there. It's a cool city, eh?' said Josh.

'*Oui, là c'est beau. Mais, ici c'est mieux pour vivre.*'

*

After several tokes of a fat joint, which he smoked hanging out of his bedroom window for fear of his parents, Josh felt relaxed enough to call his sister's number and speak to Corinna.

'What's happened, Corinna? Where were you today? Were you sick?'

'Not exactly. I don't know. I just couldn't face coming in. I think Ibrahim's planning to fire me.' Her voice sounded dull and congested.

'He's not going to sack you. You're his prize waitress. You add glamour to the place. He likes that.' Josh smirked at his own smoothness. 'You never know – he might even ask you to dress up as a mermaid. You've got mermaid hair.'

There was a frosty silence followed by the flick of a lighter and a sharp inhalation. Josh imagined Corinna reclining, smoke escaping from her lips, her wait-ressing skirt riding up her thighs. The realisation that she probably wasn't wearing her waitressing skirt since she hadn't been at work that day didn't distract him. He forced himself to concentrate on maintaining the conversation. Her silence had been a little too long for comfort.

'Are you OK, Corinna? You sound kind of down.'

'I am kind of down.'

'Why? What's wrong?'

'You wouldn't understand.'

'Yes I would! Try me.'

'It's that restaurant. Working with people like Hilde. Every time I look at her I see myself in thirty years time.'

'What are you talking about? You're nothing like Hilde. She's just a terrible haggard old whore. Washed-up, harping on about her former glories, still thinking she's some kind of sex bomb. Like some broken-down cabaret singer from the Weimar Republic.'

'Yeah. Exactly . . . Look, I'd better go.'

'Er . . . uh . . . hey . . . wait a moment . . .' Josh flailed desperately to stop Corinna hanging up.

'Yes?'

'Corinna, if you want to meet up some time – you know, outside of work, not on Crescent Street – you've got my number, right?'

'Right.'

'Right.'

The line clicked and she was gone. Josh lay back on his bed and put his hand down his pants. Corinna and Ayesha slid into his mind simultaneously, Eastern and Western devil women swirling around like the opening credits of a James Bond movie. Ayesha squatted over his face, her body veiled in a diaphanous belly dancer's outfit. Corinna was dressed up as a French maid and unzipping his flies with as much decorum as she might use to shake a linen napkin out onto on a diner's lap if she worked somewhere classier than the Royalmount 2000.

*

The next day Corinna called in sick again. Josh emptied two bottles of Fifty into the sink while Brad was out doing deliveries. As he trudged towards the metro, on the way home, he was startled by someone jumping on his back: 'Aaah! Oh, it's you.' It was Brad.

'How you doing?' A cocktail swizzle stick was stuck in the side of Brad's mouth.

'Fine.' Josh couldn't think of anything more to say. A flash car shot past.

'Hey – check out that new Toyota!' shouted Brad.

At the station, Brad slid down the elevator hand-rail to the bridge above the railtrack.

When Josh caught up with him they leant over the platform bridge and looked at the tracks. A soot-black-ened mouse scurried into view, stopped, then scurried away again.

'I'm going towards Côte-Vertu,' said Josh. He had

an appointment with a coke supplier from the West Island, Mátyás – some kind of Eastern European heavy. Russian, no doubt.

'Hang on. I just want to talk to you . . .' Brad shifted the swizzle stick to the other side of his mouth.

'What about?' Josh went cold. Had Brad cottoned onto the empty-beer-bottle scam? Was he about to drop the happy-hick routine and push him over the bridge?

'You know you were asking me yesterday all those questions about Corinna? And I said she was kinda difficult and weird.'

'*Yeah?*'

'Well, it was to do with that night we went out. I never told you what happened after you went home . . .'

'What?' Jesus Christ! The guy really had zero sensitivity. Josh braced himself for a detailed frat-boy tour of Corinna's fleshly attractions.

'Yeah, Corinna really lost it after you left. I mean, she was pretty drunk when you showed up. But after you left we carried on drinking. Switched from slammers to sambuca – you know that shooter where you light the liquor and it's got like a whole coffee bean in the bottom of the glass – ?'

'I know it.'

'– so anyway, there we are lighting and knocking back these sambucas. And then Corinna's suddenly like, "Uh . . . I don't feel too good, Brad".'

'And?'

'So, I said, "Shall we go outside? Get a little fresh air?" and she's like, "Actually, I think I wanna go home".'

'So, you went home? The home of who?' Josh wondered if Ibrahim's syntax was invading his brain.

'Well, we ended up going to mine 'cos it's nearer but before that, oh man, it was horrible. As I'm hauling her up the steps out of Winny's, she suddenly just goes bleeeurgh – all over the wall – like just total projectile vomiting. Phewee! It was *really* gross. The guy on the door was like, "What the fuck? This chick is barred". And I'm like thinking, "Damn it, I hope that doesn't mean I'm barred too." 'Cos I love Winny's. It's like my favourite bar on Crescent Street. The door guy was even trying to get her to give him some money towards cleaning. But Corinna was just out on the street barfing like a mad dog in the snow. So I gave the guy twenty bucks and then I *literally* had to drag her back to my apartment – we couldn't get a cab 'cos no cabbie wanted to take her – and when we got back to my apartment she barfed all up the stairs and then *walked* through it . . . man, I tell you my apartment smells *bad* and the landlord's trying to screw me for extra money to get the place professionally cleaned, get rid of the smell, you know. I tell ya, Corinna has cost me a *lot* of money. She just collapsed like a sack o' potatoes on the couch – I brought her a bucket – and in the morning, I go into the lounge room and she's nowhere to be seen. Couch is empty. Bathroom's empty. Kitchen's empty. She's upped and gone and all there is left is this bucket full of puke. Not even a note nor nothing. Damn. What a night. She's barely spoken to me since. Hasn't even said sorry.'

'Jeez!' Josh tried to contain his joy.

'I know.' Brad nodded seriously.

'Doesn't sound that weird though – I mean, she was drunk, she threw up. These things happen.'

149

A rush of warm air and a rattling from the depths of the tunnel announced the impending train.

'Yeah, but the thing was, all the time I was dragging her out of Winny's and back to mine, she was going on and on, all this crazy stuff –' Brad's voice grew louder and louder over the accelerating rattle of the train.

'What sort of crazy stuff?'

'Crazy stuff, I can't really remember – 'bout how she was all washed-up, getting old, her life was going down the plughole, nobody was ever gonna love her, she was gonna end up all alone a broken-down old whore like Hilde – crazy loser stuff really. Kinda negative and off-putting to tell you the truth. She's not the kinda girl I thought she was. High-strung, like I said. Probably be more fun to hang out with Ayesha and all her *juh nuh say* whatnot. Anyway, I gotta go –'

The train to Henri-Bourassa pulled in. Brad slid down the elevator hand-rail onto the platform and bounded into the carriage.

\*

The next day Corinna turned up looking pale and crushed but even more beautiful in Josh's eyes. Suffering seemed to suit her. She barely acknowledged him though, barely acknowledged any of them, just drifted about the tables as if she was underwater. After the shift was over, she sat alone and picked at a tuna salad. Josh ended up sitting with Brad and eating left-over lasagne. Hilde sat with Ibrahim and Ayesha on the other side of the room.

'I walked for miles today,' said Brad.

Josh forked up his lasagne and nodded vaguely.

Brad gestured out of the window with his knife: 'All the way up there. All the way up to Kraft –'

'– as in Kraft cheese?'

'Yeah, the Kraft factory, but they do all the other stuff as well. All the other Kraft products.'

'Maybe we could get some free cheese slices.'

'Yeah, I love Kraft cheese.' Leaning in conspiratorially, Brad whispered, 'Between you and me, I stopped at this garage for about fifteen minutes.' His blue eyes were shining, anxious to tell more.

'Oh yeah?'

'Yeah. Checked out this really cool Honda Accord. Electric windows, CD system, everything . . .'

'So you were driving around in it, delivering the food?'

'Nooo. I didn't get to drive it.'

He opened up his hamburger and said, admiringly, 'Assad really gives you a lot in these hamburgers. Two burgers, cheese, three slices of bacon – boom, boom, boom . . .'

Before he had finished his paean to Assad's hamburgers, Ibrahim slid over and insinuated himself into their conversation: 'You like beer, Bradley?'

Thought processes moved across Brad's face like the slow shadow of a cloud across an empty field: 'Yeah.'

'Molson? Hi-Dry? Fifty?'

'Yeah.'

'I thought so.'

'What?'

'Two bottles. Empty. On the bar. I say to myself, "To whom these bottles?"'

'It wasn't me, Abraham.'

'Tuesday I find them. Wednesday I find them. Thursday I find them. Today, I want to find out to whom these bottles.'

Josh realised he was inadvertently holding his breath. In the corner of his eye he saw Corinna glance up; she had surfaced from her underwater trance.

'It wasn't me, Abraham,' Brad stuttered. 'I've been out doing deliveries. And, I mean, you'd have to be pretty stupid to steal some beer, drink it and leave two empty bottles on the counter like that.'

'I know.' Ibrahim smiled and began rubbing his hands together. 'I know you are very stupid, Bradley, but not that stupid.' He swiveled to face Josh. The lasagne in Josh's stomach flipped over. Josh suddenly felt very cold.

'Joshua, I know what it is you have done. I know to whom those empty beer bottles belong. I know to whom you were pretending they belong. You were playing a trick on Bradley, pretending to him these bottles belong. But I know the truth. You know why?'

Josh stared at Ibrahim open-mouthed and shook his head. All eyes were upon him. He couldn't see the expression on Corinna's face but he guessed it was a mixture of dismay and disgust.

'The reason why, Joshua, is that, like Allah, I see everything.'

'Oh . . . *OK*. So . . . uh . . . what does that mean?'

'It means you are fired.'

Ibrahim smiled again and spread his hands in a gesture that included everyone in the room but Josh. 'Welcome.'

# Learning Butterfly

While Sean was homeless he picked up women for their domestic bliss. He gained intimate knowledge of more than a few beds, his breakfasts ranged from pancakes to pineapple juice and because he raided their bathroom cabinets, he frequently smelt of girlish scents. It was an exhausting and sometimes perilous method of finding accommodation: amatory duties prevented him from getting a good night's sleep and once he was caught by a woman's husband returning from the graveyard shift at the Fairmount Bagel Bakery. That particular domestic bliss had cost him a black eye and a broken tooth.

The nights he failed to score he slept on a bench at Chez Nanigans, the pub where he worked. The situation was tough but Sean was better equipped to survive it than most because in his head he was a cordon bleu chef with a downtown apartment and devastating Irish charm rather than an untrained pub cook with nowhere to live and thinning hair.

Sean had never been big on the truth. He didn't know why other people were so keen on it because, like most habitual fibbers, he never believed anything he heard. His own lies were as smooth as a pint of Guinness.

He had no home because he had no money to pay the rent. He had no money because over the winter he'd blown it all on coke, cabs and unsuccessful jaunts to the Casino de Montréal. When he crashed at Chez Nanigans he had to knock himself out with noggins of hard liquor before he could sleep. Though he wouldn't admit it to himself, let alone anyone else, the place spooked him at night. The creaks and drips of the barrels and taps were amplified by the stone floor and the windows were the kind at which white faces loomed. Once, while wafting into a whisky doze, a steady tapping on the glass awoke him and he was horrified to see Crazy Davy's rolling-eyed stare.

'What the fuck are you doing, frightening me there like a cream-faced loon?'

Davy frowned with incomprehension and said hopefully, '*Donne-moi un Bleu?*'

'Fuck off out of here, can't you see we're closed, yer fuckin eejit?' Then, momentarily chastened by Davy's crestfallen face, he shooed him away with two bottles of Boréale Noire (the type nobody bought) and the ingratiating warning, 'This is between you and me, Davy. *Entre nous, ouais?* Don't tell anyone you saw me here now, eh?'

Davy, so accustomed to being ignored, was pathetically thrilled to be entrusted with a secret. Sean was thankful only someone as insignificant as Davy had seen him. No one else knew about his shameful living arrangements, though he worried that Zoë had her suspicions. When she found his toothbrush while cleaning the men's toilets, he had to pretend it belonged to Bobby, their boss.

'But Bobby's never in. Why would he leave his toothbrush here?'

'It's one of many. Bobby takes a toothbrush with him wherever he goes. He must have accidentally left that one there. He's got a fetish for cleaning his teeth. It's sort of like an obsessive compulsive disorder.'

'Right. Whatever you say, Sean.'

He and Zoë had enjoyed a brief fling earlier in the year – or at least, he had enjoyed it; she had griped throughout that he never spent any money on her and never invited her back to his place. He had been quite smitten – Zoë was funny and sparky and, though no one would have believed him, he really did appreciate her fine mind as much as her fine body. Sean was far from educated but he was quick-witted and he liked quick-witted women, though Zoë had been a little too smartass at times and, occasionally, he was niggled by her knowledge of a certain one of his little deficiencies. It was true what they said: knowledge *was* power.

As the snow thawed their ardour cooled. Sean wondered if the pub's decline had speeded the decline of their relationship. Chez Nanigans became more and more dismal as the drinkers disappeared and the taps dried up. Zoë seemed to associate its atmosphere of failure with Sean. She had worked there from the beginning – lending her services as a gofer when the pub was still a construction site. When it opened, Bobby rewarded her loyalty by making her a waitress, then a barmaid, then head barmaid and finally, when he could no longer face being caught by his creditors, acting manager.

Zoë had been the queen bee of the bar during the glory days when it was crammed with bohemians from the Plateau and there were monthly *vernissages* for her artist friends. She had nursed dreams of turning it into a salon where intellectuals would discuss Jean Genet and Jean Rhys. Zoë's reading matter tended towards the European and the dissolute. As she once said to no one in particular: 'I only want to read novels that feature cocktails, coffee and cigarettes.'

'You're gonna have to dig long and hard to find any intellectuals in this goddamn backwater,' Bobby had jeered. Hailing from San Francisco – 'the place it's at' – he had the misfortune to marry a Montrealer called Evangeline, who refused to relocate to the state he still affectionately referred to as 'Cali'. He was a rotund chancer with a misleadingly cherubic countenance, whom Zoë nicknamed Bobby the Buddha but Sean persisted in calling 'Blobby'.

Though it might sound fun on paper, living in a pub was no picnic even for a borderline alcoholic like Sean. There was no relaxation, no ease – just a constant fug of aching frowstiness on top of his usual hangover. After back-wrenching nights on the bench, he would shave as best he could over the greasy basin in the men's toilets, sighting sections of his chin in the mirror on the front of the hand-drier. Generally, he wore the clothes he'd slept in – his small wardrobe was stowed in a cupboard in the kitchen and consequently smelt of stale fries and industrial dishwasher fluid. The rare occasions he could be bothered, he washed them at a launderette near UQAM. It was a good place for meeting university girls. Luckily, his head-to-toe black style, which didn't show up the dirt, was already well

established. (Zoë: 'You an existentialist or something?'
Sean: 'Or something.')

Breakfast was leftover Irish stew slugged down with
a jug of coffee. Coffee was the only successful venture
in pub living; there were huge tins of the stuff in the
dwindling stockroom and Sean kept a pot constantly
on the go. He dipped into it throughout the morning,
adding progressively more whisky or rum to his mug
until he was drinking neat liquor. The dusty hour
before opening time he spent slumped at the bar,
scouring the small ads for ways to make money and
for a sign from his long-lost father.

Sean never contemplated revealing his real back-
ground. The story that he had been born and bred in
Dublin and had worked his way around the world as
a chef was far more cheering, to him and his listeners,
than the reality of his childhood. His lilting brogue
was a sham too. He believed it made him more attractive and plausible; Canadians were more likely to give
a foreigner, especially an Irishman, the benefit of the
doubt.


By the spring, Chez Nanigans was seriously winding
down. Since Bobby had cancelled the Guinness order,
it could barely be described as an Irish pub. In fact, it
could barely be described as a pub seeing as there were
only things like Midori and Blue Curaçao left and a few
barrels of Boréale Noire, which customers shunned
even when it was reduced to one dollar a pint. Leila
was long gone – Sean blearily regretted her departure,
mainly because he'd never got round to screwing her.

He and Zoë were left in charge, opening when they had the energy and skiving when they hadn't. Sean would open a can of soup and make his famously awful Irish stew if pushed, though Zoë had stopped chalking up the lunch menu. Instead, she copied out quotes from whatever weighty tome she was ploughing through. For a while the menu board read, '*Longtemps, je me suis couché de bonne heure*', which left the red-eyed regulars somewhat nonplussed.

His affair with Zoë was over by this point and though she had never complained when they were up close and personal, now they weren't she took to making unsubtle hints about his body odour. She would sniff the air and demand to know if the punters could smell something strange. As the clientele was reduced to empty afternoon drifters with similarly questionable personal hygiene, they never could. Eventually, she deposited a can of Right Guard on the kitchen counter and Sean began going to the lido in Parc Laurier to use the showers.

The lido presented a feast of tanned bodies, gently sweating, like salamis on a deli counter. Of all the girls in all the countries Sean had been to – and he had truthfully been to a few – Montreal girls were definitely the sexiest. There was nothing tomboyish about the things they wore and nothing was left to the imagination. In their stringy bikinis, they primped and preened and slathered each other with sweet-smelling cream. They whinnied with laughter at private jokes, flicked their hair and rolled their smooth bronzed haunches around the fenced enclosure, like prize show jumpers.

Sean went to the lido nearly every afternoon, with

a towel and a newspaper rolled under his arm. After a utilitarian shiver under the shower, he bagged the same spot, in the corner opposite the springboard. He liked to watch people dive. He got to see the good techniques; the smooth slide and the contained splash; the slick dolphin actions. He worked out the way they were done.

He didn't bother to infiltrate the groups of girls. Partly, because he felt awkward. The outdoors was not his natural arena and the lido left him naked and defenceless, with nowhere to exert authority. Sean needed the props of pubs to shine: pool tables, dart boards, cigarettes and alcohol. In a dim smoky bar, he was charm personified. He knew how to operate; it was his turf. At the lido, he was just another pale, scrawny loser with acne scars on his back. And anyway, it was easier to chat up a loner.

There was one girl who always came to the lido alone. Sean saw her most afternoons on the opposite side of the springboard. Her hair gleamed like a halo and her cleavage was deep and inviting. She spent most of the time reading and the rest trying to dive. He had seen her faltering over the deep end, blinking into the lassos of white light before splattering onto the surface of the water. Over and over, she fumbled through the same manoeuvres, hauling herself out of the water with exaggerated sighs. After several attempts she would return to her book with streaming eyes.

Sean hadn't yet found an opportunity to talk to her. Her self-contained calm was difficult to interrupt. She did not demand attention, unlike the other girls who shrieked and pranced and made a performance out of everything from buying an ice-cream to drying their toes. When diving, she only took the plunge if she thought no one was looking.

It was as she was tip-toeing towards the pool one afternoon that Sean removed his sunglasses and stared straight at her. His eyes were nice, that much he knew – it was the one feature girls always commented on. He smiled and she smiled back. Her face was friendly and open – when he got to know her better, he would describe it as *honest*. After she had sloppily belly-flopped and was teetering on the edge once again, he called out, 'Hey sweetheart, tuck your head down between your arms.'

'Excuse me?' She swivelled, pulling at her swimsuit nervously. 'I'm sorry, were you talking to me?'

'Yes, I was just saying, you should tuck your head right down, so your arms form a line with your shoulders.'

'Really?'

'Yes, your head's too upright.'

'Is it?'

'Yes. Do this.' Sean demonstrated the movement.

'You're probably right. I really don't know what I'm doing.' She followed his instructions and dropped like a shot pigeon from a telegraph wire. She emerged dripping and gasping with an eager, 'How was that?'

'Better . . . but you need to get a bit more bounce in your toes as you dive in. You need to push yourself off the edge.'

She tried again but he discerned no difference in her technique.

'No, you need to exaggerate the movement. Really

point your toes and pretend you're on the springboard. In fact, why don't you have a go from the springboard?' Sean was hitting his stride now.

'Oh no, no way. I mean, I get totally freaked out just diving from the side. There's no way I'm going to get up on the springboard.'

'Ah go on, it's not that high . . .'

'Nope, I'm too chicken.' She raised her arms, pointed her fingers, bounced on her toes and disappeared into the water without a splash.

'That was brilliant!' he called.

'Thank you.' He expected her to try again but she simply raised her hand in gratitude and padded back to her towel, dripping a trail of neat footprints. Sean replaced his shades and observed her covertly as she applied sun lotion to her legs and opened her book. When he next looked up, she had disappeared. An old woman with improbably blonde hair was performing pelvic thrust exercises in the spot where she'd been.


The next day, fired with anticipation, Sean arrived at the pool early. A long queue of frazzled mothers with squalling kids looped out from the turnstile and by the time he got inside, the place was crammed and the old woman was lying in the girl's usual place. The mercury in the thermometer outside the shower block glinted at thirty-five degrees. The empty sky throbbed with heat and the sunshine ricocheted around the clean lines of the poolside, creating a headache of dazzling planes and angles. Sean sweltered on his square of concrete, until his newspaper was crisp and yellow and the harsh geometry of the lido had softened in the hazy light of evening. The girl did not show up. Back at the pub, he was overcome by a sweaty dizziness which forced him to lie on the cold stone floor for an hour. No one came in, so he didn't have to explain himself.

*

'The thing you've got to work on now is your legs. Your leg position is all wrong.'

Natalie, for that was her name, was kneeling beside Sean, nodding seriously at his pearls of wisdom.

'What you've got to do is kick out and straighten those legs as you dive. At the moment they're all bent up like this –' he motioned with his hand. 'But what you want is more of this –' he swooped his hand through the air. 'Got it?'

'I think so.'

'OK, let's go.'

She pitched herself into the pool without preamble, trying to do as he'd said. She was less hesitant than before, and not just in her diving: that afternoon he had been startled by her sudden shadow looming over him. 'Hello there. Would you like to give me another lesson today?'

'Oh, uh, sure, yes, sure . . . hello again.' He squinted up at her hourglass silhouette, shielding his eyes from the sun.

'Are you going to get in yourself or will you just watch me?' There was something knowing in her tone but as he couldn't see her expression and she didn't seem like the knowing type he hoped she was just being flirtatious.

'I'll just watch you for the moment, darling,' he said, and he was sure she sashayed slightly for his benefit as she made her way to the edge of the pool, but again it could have been wishful thinking: she seemed too innocent and straightforward for such coquetries.

'Well, I really think you've got it,' he called out, once she had dived five times in succession. 'I'm going to get a drink. You want anything?'

'I'd love a cherry popsicle. Would you get me one?'

'Sure I would.'

Her directness charmed him. When he returned she had spread her towel next to his and was sitting on it with her arms around her knees.

'So, what brings you here every day?' he began.

'I like to come before I go to work. I love swimming. It's so relaxing.'

'What do you do?'

'I'm a barmaid at the Cock and Bull. On Ste. Catherine.'

'I know it – Irish pub – same as the place where I work.' He told her about Chez Nanigans but unsurprisingly she hadn't heard of it. 'They got any vacancies for a real Irishman at the Cock and Bull? I'm a cordon bleu chef.'

Girls generally raised a sarcastic eyebrow at lines like these but Natalie said straightforwardly, 'Are you really? I don't think there's any vacancies at the Cock and Bull. They only serve food in the evenings – Chinese. I guess you're a bit overqualified for that.'

He found himself blushing: something that rarely

happened. 'Oh, I'm sure I'm not,' he muttered with a shrug.

'How long have you been in Canada?'

'Um . . . not long . . . three months . . .'

'Were you living in Ireland before?'

'No . . . well . . . yeah . . .' Uncomfortably, he reeled off his fictional curriculum vitae; it was so well rehearsed he had it off-pat – born and bred in Dublin, a year in Paris, three years in London, six months in Sydney, six in Toronto, three in Montreal, with various forays to other foreign lands in between. Natalie listened with encouraging nods and smiles, which made him feel even more uneasy.

'You're so well travelled. Me, I've never been anywhere.' Her tongue chased a drop of red ice as it melted down her arm.

'Are you from Montreal?'

'Longueuil.' She wrinkled her nose. 'Do you know it?'

Sean shook his head.

'It's awful. Total suburbia. Totally boring. Couldn't wait to get away but, as you can see, I didn't get very far. I'd love to go to work in London. What's it like?'

'Ah, it's one of the best cities in the world. So historic: Big Ben, Westminster Abbey, Trafalgar Square . . . um . . . Madame Tussaud's. You just feel like you're in the middle of all this, you know . . . history.' Sean was warming to his theme. 'Yeah, London's great. Place I used to work was on Leicester Square – right in the centre . . .' He always said this because Leicester Square was one place he had honestly been and it was always best to base a lie in truth. He rambled on for a while about the crowds, the pubs, the lights, the life.

'You sound like you miss it.'

'I do, all the time. I've got this friend who sends me over these, like, *care* packages. You know, with pots of Marmite, Worcester sauce, marmalade, Branston Pickle . . . er –' he racked his brains for a few other Brit clichés.'– PG Tips, Colman's Mustard, Heinz Baked Beans . . .'

'You can get those here – I've seen them at the Bay, in the food hall.'

'Oh really? I'll have to check it out.'

Before the lido shut, Natalie swam a few slow laps of the pool with her eyes closed against the lowering sun. The water had turned from blue to gold and there were only a few kids left in the shallow end, trying to ride the back of an inflatable crocodile. Natalie urged Sean to join her but he pretended he had an ear infection. They ambled home together, through the quiet back streets where kids played football in the road and the leaves from the lime trees twirled down on the warm breeze. The sound of televisions and the smell of cooking drifted out through open doors. Natalie noticed things Sean would have passed by – purple passion flowers climbing over a red-brick wall; a white cat, which she stopped to stroke, perched on the end of a gatepost; a boy on a Chopper bike like the one she'd had as a kid in Longueuil. When they got to the touristy stretch of St Denis, where the terrasses were filled with chattering drinkers beneath yellow parasols, she stopped and said, 'I'd better say goodbye here.'

They were standing outside a tall house the colour of strawberry ice-cream.

'Is this where you live? The pink house?'

'Yes.'

'You got roommates?'

'No, I live alone – I've got a 1½. Well, they call it a 1½, but it's more like just a room with a bathroom attached. It's pretty scummy.'

'It looks nice from the outside.'

'You can't judge a book by its cover.'

'I couldn't agree more.'

They danced tentatively around a social kiss.

'Right . . . I guess I'll see you tomorrow,' said Sean.

'I would invite you in but I've got to change and get to work in about half an hour, so . . .'

'That's alright.'

'I'll see you tomorrow. Hopefully.'

He watched her bound up the steps, turn and wave like a happy child before going in.

*

'Now, I don't want to see any bent legs this time. Pointy toes, head tucked in, little bit of a bounce and straight in smooth. Let's see you do it.' Sean demonstrated the action from the safety of his towel. Natalie copied him over the water. Her dive was superb, the best yet. He counted five seconds, ten seconds, fifteen, twenty . . . when he feared she'd hit her head on the bottom she erupted from the water with a triumphant 'Ta da!'

'Jesus, you frightened the life out of me, Natalie. I thought you weren't coming up.'

'What would you have done?'

'I'd've told the lifeguard.'

'You wouldn't have jumped in and saved me?'

'Oh, yeah . . . course I would.'

She wrapped herself in a towel and sat beside him with her arms wrapped round her legs and her feet placed neatly together. Her toenails were painted blue. They matched the colour of the cloudless sky. She surveyed the dancing rainbow of swimmers and sunbathers with a smile. Next to her Sean felt wholly comfortable. He could think of nothing to say but it didn't matter. It was enough just to stare at her breasts from behind the safety of his shades.

'How are your ears?' she asked suddenly.

'Eh?' He frowned. She pointed to her ears. 'Oh, my *ears* . . . yeah, well, it's an ongoing problem really. My inner ear, it's damaged – I used to be in a band – standing next to the speakers, you know, the noise messed up my ears.' Her wholesomeness prevented him from saying 'fucked up'.

'What sort of band?'

'Heavy metal – you know, pretty terrible head-banging stuff – I had long hair back then.'

'What did you play?'

'Bass.' He always said he played bass: it sounded deep and manly and the word itself had a rugged simplicity that he liked.

'What were you called?'

'Um . . .' His eyes alighted on the old woman doing her pelvic thrusts. 'The Peroxide Prunes.'

'I'm sure there was another band with a name a bit like that . . . to do with prunes . . .'

'Yeah, well, we weren't very original.'

'My dad used to be in a band.'

'Yeah?'

'Yes. Back in the sixties. They were quite big. Well, I mean, not *that* big but they supported some famous bands.'

'Like who?'

'Yeah, like The Who actually. Jefferson Airplane, Janis Joplin, Jimi Hendrix . . .'

'Really? Cool.' He shifted a little so their thighs were touching. He could smell the sweetness of suntan lotion on her skin. A bead of sweat slid down her neck and between her breasts. He imagined how he could lick it up the way she had licked the popsicle up her arm the day before. Awkwardly, he shifted again to conceal the stirring in his crotch and tried to concentrate on what she was saying. She was still talking about her father.

'. . . yeah, Dad introduced me to all that music when I was really little.'

'And your dad lives in Longueuil?'

'No, in Montreal. My parents are divorced. My dad left my mum when I was five – he wasn't into being a family man. He just wanted to party with the band, be free . . .' She slid her eyes sideways to Sean. '. . . he paid for it though.'

'How do you mean?'

'He lives in a kind of hostel now. Sort of sheltered accommodation for people with mental problems. Too much acid. He fried his brains.'

Her deadpan simplicity stunned him. It would have been so easy for her to make something up.

'Do you see much of him?'

'Every few weeks we meet up. We didn't see each other a lot when I was growing up – he was always on the road somewhere, on tour. But since I left home and moved into the city, I got back in touch with him. I take him out to dinner or we go to the movies. It's pretty hard though – his mind wanders a lot, it's difficult to follow what he's saying. And he drinks too much, even though he's not supposed to.'

'Yeah, we got a . . . does your dad still play music?'

'He's still got his guitar but . . . what were you going to say before?'

'Nothing, nothing important.' Sean had been about to tell her about Chez Nanigans' resident musical nutcase but he thought better of it.

'So what about your family?'

'They're all over in Dublin. My dad's a lawyer but he's retired now. And my mum was in the music biz too, as a matter of fact: used to be quite a well known country singer . . .'

'Really? . . . Tell me more . . .'

But he couldn't. The story he was about to tell suddenly seemed futile and also somehow conceited, seeing as her family was such a disaster zone. What was the point of getting to know someone if they didn't really know you? The revelation struck him with dizzying clarity. Like a diver facing a sheer drop from the highest board, he took the plunge and said:

'Actually, it's not true. I don't know why I said that before there. My parents aren't really in Dublin. My mum isn't a singer and my dad isn't a lawyer.'

'Oh? What is . . .'

'He's in prison in Manitoba.'

'In prison!'

'Yeah.'

'My God! What for?'

Sean ran his fingers through his hair. If he told her the truth she would be disgusted. The phrases 'armed robber', 'money launderer', 'international jewel thief', 'Soviet double-agent', 'Columbian cocaine smuggler' buzzed through his head: cool, cowboyish kinds of criminals. Unfortunately, none of their crimes were the one for which his father was doing time.

'You don't have to tell me if you don't want.'

'I do want to,' he said quietly. For some reason, inexplicable to himself, this was true.

'OK. Tell me. I won't be shocked.'

'Yes you will.'

'So what if I am? What does it matter?'

'You won't want to see me again.'

'I will.' She looked at him and the honesty of her gaze blew him away.

'How do you know?'

'Because I like you.'

'Do you?' The thrill of what she had said and the way she was looking at him filled his heart with instant sunshine. 'My dad was caught having sex with a fifteen-year-old boy in a public toilet,' he blurted, spoiling the sunshine with a huge black cloud. He looked at Natalie, expecting to see disgust, but instead there was merely concern and disappointment in her calm, clear face.

'I guess you're horrified,' he said.

'Do I look horrified?'

'No.'

'I'm not horrified.'

'I haven't seen him for three years,' said Sean. 'He won't let me visit him.'

'Do you want to visit him?'

'Sort of. He's got nobody else. And he's my only family now. We hadn't seen each other for years before he went to prison though.'

'Why not?'

'Because I was so embarrassed by him. He left my mother for a twenty-one-year-old bloke when I was fourteen. Everyone at school knew why. They all thought I was gay too. I got bullied all the time . . . I was so fucking ashamed of him.' The swearword had slipped out unintentionally in the heat of the moment.

'I know what it's like to feel ashamed of your own father.'

'I guess you do . . .' said Sean, cringing when he saw Natalie flinch. 'I'm sorry, I shouldn't have said that.'

'It's OK. It's true. So are you going to get in touch with him, your dad?'

'I wrote to him once but he never replied. When he got sent down he told me he'd put an advert in the *Globe and Mail* when he got let out but even when he does get let out I can't afford to go to Winnipeg. I've got no money. I've got no money and I've got nowhere to live either – I'm sleeping in the bar where I work. That's why I come here every day: to have a wash. So yes, I'm a total fucking loser in every way. Perhaps, I should go . . .' He began to gather his clothes together. Natalie touched his shoulder and he halted. Her finger-nails were like blue pearls.

'Don't go. What about your mother? She's not a country singer . . .'

'No. She was a big Johnny Cash fan but she wasn't a country singer. She worked in a factory in Laval and she was an alcoholic. She's dead now. She died on New Year's Day when I was fifteen, the year after my dad left. Great new year that was. She'd been drinking Black Velvet in some bar in Little Burgundy – you know what Black Velvet is? Vodka, champagne and Guinness: lethal. Anyway, as she was driving back along Acadie there was a snowstorm and she lost control of the car. She skidded onto the other side of the road and crashed into a truck coming the other way. Died instantly.' Images of that night rushed back like a speeded-up film: the party in Patrick Dooley's parents' house, drinking jungle juice, copping a feel of Veronica McAuley, the police lights making the snow glow blue outside their apartment, throwing up into a drift of whiteness when he heard the news. It was strange how the trivia of significant days got burned into your memory. For some reason he always recalled how Veronica McAuley had been wearing panties with FRIDAY written across the front, even though it had been a Saturday. It struck him as sacrilegious to remember a thing like that from the day his mother died.

Natalie was nodding, encouraging him to continue.

He dragged his fingers through his hair and said, 'So my Auntie Maureen took me in after Mum died. In Longueuil, in fact. I know it quite well. I was a bit naughty, a bit wild. I got too much for her. She had to put me in a foster home. The manager of the home was a fucking pervert. Used to do stuff to me – I thought it was 'cos he knew about my dad, thought I was gay too –' He glanced at Natalie. 'I'm not gay, by the way –'

Natalie merely nodded.

'– so, yeah, I quit school when I was sixteen and went to catering college but I dropped out and went to work as a tree-planter in BC. And I'm not a cordon bleu chef – I only got as far as basic sauces. And I've never been to Sydney. I have been to London once, but only as a tourist. I never worked there. I've never been to Paris and, you've guessed it, I've never been to Dublin either but I did spend a month with my cousins in Limerick when I was eighteen, which is where I picked up the accent. That's the truth.'

Natalie stared at him.

Sean shifted. 'Yeah, I know what you're thinking: what a fucking eejit.'

'No . . . no, I'm not thinking that.' She looked at her feet as if searching for the answer in the blue squares of her nails. Finally, she said, 'I'm sorry you felt you had to lie to me.'

'Don't worry, love, you're not the first.'

She stood up and let her towel drop to the ground. 'I'm going for a dip. I won't ask you if you want to come because I know you can't swim.' Her tone was sad rather than cross. He watched her make a slow stately circuit of the pool and wondered if he should pack up his things and leave. Clearly, she wanted him to go. But, as he began to roll up his towel, she beckoned him in: 'Come on, I'll teach you how to swim.'

They spent a happy half hour thrashing about in the shallow end. Sean was a long way from anything more advanced than doggy-paddle but he when he lay back with his ears submerged and his eyes on the sky, he understood why Natalie loved swimming. The world disappeared into lilac-tinged light and the sound of blood sluicing through your head. When you sunk your head under, you saw bodies floating silently through the bubbles and shards of sun slicing the turquoise water like a stained-glass window.

'Come on, kick those legs,' shouted Natalie, 'I'll have you learning butterfly in no time.'


As they walked downtown his heart and step was buoyant; he would never have guessed that lies were like ballast weighing you down. He recalled his mother, who used to come home at Saturday teatime after confession, shrug off her best coat, unwrap her smart scarf, kick off her good shoes and pour herself a large whisky mac, before sighing, 'Well, I'm glad I got all that off my chest. I can start all over again now.'

'Are you working tonight, Natalie?' he asked.

'No, I'm not.'

'Would you like to come for a drink at my pub? It's not the greatest place but . . .'

'I'd love to.'


It took several moments for their eyes to adjust to the gloom after the brightness of the street. Zoë was lounging behind the bar with her Proust, one arm draped over the Guinness tap.

'Hey, it's about time you turned up. I've been really . . .'

Before she could finish, a clumsy figure had materialised from the shadows and was lumbering towards them with outstretched arms: Crazy Davy, his face lit up with so much joy that he almost didn't look crazy any more. 'Natalie! *Ma chérie. Ma fille. Ma chère fille!*'

Natalie beamed and flung her arms around him. For a moment her delicate features were reflected in his ravaged face. They hugged for several minutes while Zoë and Sean looked on in shock.

Eventually Natalie extracted herself from her father's embrace and turned to Sean. 'Is there anything else I should know?' she asked.

Sean permitted his arm to slide around her waist.

'You'll find out soon enough,' muttered Zoë.

# Double Take

The bathroom was quiet. Very quiet and enclosed. Sweat ran down Corinna's brow and dripped into her eye. She didn't know if it was down to the hot water or the heat outside. Even when night fell, the air stayed humid and billowed against the skin like damp chiffon.

Since moving out of Henry's she had slumped into a torpor, spending too long choosing her groceries, too long walking back from work, too long in the bath. Henry had kept her occupied.

When she wasn't slowly wasting time, Corinna was reading. Too much. Books subsumed her these days – she sank into fictitious worlds completely, floating through her real life like a somnambulist, floundering when she reached a final page.

The day before, on the metro, she had finished *A Handful of Dust* too quickly and, without another book to hand, had no choice but to turn it over and start again.

On Friday night she had lingered in the second-hand bookstore on St Laurent, reading a third of *A Thief's Diary* without buying it, vaguely hoping to be picked up by an intellectual. No intellectuals had been forthcoming and at closing time the owner switched off the lights and turned her out onto the street like a

cat. The punks loitering outside Bar St Laurent eyed
her with contempt.

Corinna pulled the chain of the plug with her big toe
and waited for the water to drain away before she got
out of the bath. She wiped a circle of condensation
from the mirror so she could look at her face. The heat
suited her. It cast a dew over her skin, made it ripe and
tender. Henry was missing out. That day, an Indian
woman on the metro had leaned in close and whispered, 'I read faces, you know: you have a good face,
a strong face.' Before Corinna could reply the train
stopped at Champ-de-Mars and the woman jumped
out. She had been quite beautiful herself which made
the compliment all the more flattering.

The scent from Henry's gardenia hit her afresh – it
got stronger at night. She felt justified in stealing it,
having nursed the plant back to health after Henry
allowed it to wither over the winter. And, of course,
it was one of the few things that had survived the
fire. In May, following her mother's advice, she had
driven a rusty nail deep into its soil so it could absorb
the iron. Surprisingly, it worked: the shrivelled leaves
became green and shiny, and the pale, consumptive
buds swelled. When the first pink flower unfurled in
Jess's apartment she considered wearing it in her hair
but that kind of confident whimsicality belonged to
her old self, so she didn't. Since the fire, since Henry,
she had changed. Henry had been too busy for plants

despite his frequent pronouncements that he was a country boy. For him 'country' was shorthand for 'real' – strengths of character were put down to a rural upbringing; weaknesses were ascribed to the city. To Corinna, Henry looked far more at home amid slick urban bustle than he had ever done on his parents' farm.

He had broken the news to her on a Saturday evening. She sneezed for half an hour straight, as if the truth had provoked an allergic reaction. They both cried all night and had tear-stained sex on a borrowed sofa which made her cry even more. The following morning, pale and weak, her body craving iron like the gardenia, she tottered to Moishes for the biggest steak on the menu, followed by four pints of Guinness in Le Bifteck. It was the first time she had sat in a bar alone but she felt too blank for embarrassment. Borrowing the barmaid's pen she tried to write a poem on a beer mat about her first breakfast with Henry, when she had licked a drip of honey all the way up his arm.

Since leaving, she had seen him twice; once in the Jewish bakery on St Laurent where he was buying two slices of baked cheesecake and once on the stairs at Concordia. The second time she hardly recognised him because his hair was cropped short and his eyes were hidden by wraparound shades. She tried to match his breezy tone and was enthusiastic when he demanded her opinion of his newly pierced nose. They skirted around meaningful topics and parted with promises to meet soon; promises that Corinna knew would never come to pass.

Leaving her wrapper on the floor where it had fallen, she stepped into the living-room. It doubled as the bedroom and was literally a step from the bathroom – the apartment was only ten paces from end to end, the second-storey of a duplex on the corner of St Dominique and Duluth. The goods entrance of Segal's supermarket was next door. Every morning she was awakened by the roar of lorries unloading, after a night broken by Simpkin's incessant scratching in his litter tray. Simpkin was a half-blind, one-eared stray cat that Jess had rescued from a life of freedom in the alleys of the Plateau. His litter tray was hidden behind a curtain in an alcove off her studio but Simpkin regularly distributed its contents throughout the apartment, as if to express his discontent at being confined to a 2½ without a fire escape.

Simpkin and Corinna's relationship veered between love and hate – hate when his scratching became so frantic that the flying dust threatened to asphyxiate her; love when she felt the need to touch something living and warm. Sometimes she had an urge to toss him over the balcony but she resisted it. The cat was part of the deal: Jess had allowed her to house-sit for the summer so long as Corinna looked after him.

Jess was way out west painting murals in Legal, Alberta – a name that had provoked some mirth among her friends. She was lodging with a family of religious maniacs. Corinna had received a few strained phone calls:

'Corinna, can you talk?'

'Jess! How's it going in *Legal*?'

'Oh, you know . . . it's fine. How's Simpkin?'

'Same as ever, scratching his little heart out . . . How's it really going?'

'Like I said – fine. How's it going with you?'

'OK. I guess.'

'Well, gotta press on.'

'Yeah.'

Corinna admired Jess's stoicism. She was like a man that way, buckling down and pressing on without complaint, without mooning around and gazing out the window at people who were having more fun.

There was nothing on TV. Corinna stepped into the kitchen and opened the fridge. It contained a bagel and a bowl of fruit salad. She was addicted to fruit salad. Every day she came home laden with mangos, nectarines, strawberries and grapes. 'Got yourself some fruits, eh?' shouted Jimmy, who owned the *dépanneur* on the corner of Clark. He said it every time she saw him, ever since she'd rushed in there one afternoon, demanding fruit. 'Fruits!' he shrieked in his exaggerated Jamaican twang. 'Ain't no fruits in 'ere.'

The fruit salad gone, Corinna sawed the bagel in half and placed it in the toaster oven. She'd bought the oven for fifteen dollars from a junkshop on Mont Royal, along with a saucepan and a wooden spoon. The only cooking implements in Jess's kitchen were a beer opener and a knife and fork. Jess existed on art and fresh air, eating when she had to in cafés.

Corinna was able to survive on the all-day breakfasts at work, but sometimes a little variety was necessary. Since the fire and the break-up with Henry, food loomed large in her mind. She craved sweet things – baklavas from the Lebanese kebab place, custard tarts from the Portuguese bakery, lemon sorbet from Ripples ice-cream parlour, where they issued loyalty cards guaranteeing a free ice-cream for every ten you bought.

At work she spooned squares of jello into her mouth when no one was looking or sneaked a few inches of the one-inch cake slices they served for dessert. The week before on her day off, cycling around the rich, quiet streets of Westmount, she had been overwhelmed by hunger. Her stomach felt concave with emptiness and she was forced to pedal weakly down the side of the Mountain to the Indian buffet on Duluth, where she ate two helpings of every single dish. Her hunger was disconcerting.

She ate the bagel with peanut butter, slumped naked on the futon, with the radio on for company.

'Simpkin, come to me, come and say hello,' she urged, patting the spot next to her. The cat stalked off to the balcony with his nose in the air.

'God, I'm bored, Simpkin. Are you bored?' Corinna was surprised by the sound of her own voice, she used it so seldom these days. Sometimes the only things she said for twenty-four hours were 'Can I take your order?' and 'How would you like your eggs?'

That evening, Sergei, the Bulgarian delivery driver, had offered a lift home and, to his delight, she had accepted – just for the chance of some conversation.

He careered along the Décarie Expressway at full tilt, filling her in on life back in Sofia, where his father once owned five restaurants and three nightclubs.

'I came to Canada, fearing for my life,' he declared, waiting for Corinna to ask why.

'Why?' asked Corinna.

'Because the Mafia, they kill my father. They club him to death the day before New Year's Eve. With baseball bats.'

'Why?'

'Because he owe them so much money. They set my car on fire – I knew I was the next. So I escape.'

Corinna arranged her features in an expression of sympathy.

Each time they passed an expensive car, Sergei glanced at her and said, 'You like that? . . . That's what I'm going to buy next.'

Corinna rearranged her expression.

'You can drop me here,' she said, when they reached Sherbrooke.

'I can take you to your house.'

She shook her head.

'Why don't you call me, Corinna? I give you my number two weeks ago and you didn't call.'

Corinna gave a hollow laugh. As she got out, he said, 'I'm going to be crying tonight because you didn't call me . . .'

Sergei's Mafia stories and promises of flash cars could never overcome the fact he was too bald, too over-weight and, most of all, too desperate. If he looked like Max, the new chef, it would be a different story. Max, whose cheekbones made up for his bad teeth; Max who had read all of Dostoevsky; Max who declaimed his woes while he cooked:

'Give me eggs, easy over,' Corinna would shout

through the hatch.

'Give me a kiss,' Max would wink, then: 'Why nobody love me? Nobody care about me. Nobody nice to me . . .'

His girlfriend, Natalya, the other waitress, would swoop in and shout at him in Russian, shooting icy stares at Corinna.

The voices on the radio were discussing something dull about money. Corinna turned the dial to a Francophone station that she sometimes listened to in the hope it would improve her French. She'd slowly come to the conclusion it was dedicated to religious programmes from the preponderance of words such as '*catéchisme*', '*sacré*' and '*Dieu*'. She dressed in her new post-inferno clothes, listening to a discussion about La Mère Teresa and looking down at a man walking past on the street below, licking an ice-cream with a basket of pears propped on one shoulder. He looked so casual and content that it pinpointed her restlessness. Back in the bathroom, she examined her face once again in the now-clear mirror. The bloom on her skin was still apparent and it seemed a waste not to show it off. Decisively, she pulled the light cord, carried Simpkin kicking in from the balcony, locked the windows and grabbed her wallet from the kitchen table.

Out on St Laurent, the bars were beginning to fill up. The air reeked of frites, fried chicken and petrol. Like the gardenia, the smell of the city grew stronger at night. Two girls swung past her in matching hipster jeans and crop tops. A boy in the window of La Cabane called out to them. Corinna crossed over and walked up Duluth. She passed a house with sunflowers ten-feet tall and the Café Santropol, both of which reminded her of Esmé, her former next-door neighbour. Since the fire, which destroyed both their duplexes, Corinna had not seen the little girl but the rumours were she was living with her mother in a women's refuge and her slug-like stepfather had slid off back to California. The fire had been a catalyst for chaos in more ways than one. Corinna ended up in Jess's house and Henry ended up with his new lover.

Up on the basketball pitch a few kids were knocking hacky sacks around, long-shadowed in the glare of the floodlights. Esmé was not among them. At Park Avenue, Corinna crossed over and stood between the two lions, trying to make out the face of the Angel in the falling darkness. A couple on a nearby bench frowned at her intrusion into their privacy, so she turned back down to Duluth.

Jimmy was lounging on the steps of his *dépanneur* drinking beer when she passed. He was dressed entirely in white like a louche Ghandi. Corinna stepped over his legs and pushed against the shop door.

'I closin' up now, girl,' he said. 'You want fruits again?'

'No, I need something really sweet.'

'I sweet.' Jimmy grinned.

'I need chocolate.'

'You not getting enough sex. That's what chocolate is – substitute for sex.'

'Is that right?' Corinna put her hands on her hips.

'Me, I never eat no refined sugar . . . only refined sugar I eat is in beer.' He held up the bottle. 'You want some?'

Corinna smiled and allowed him to crack open a bottle from the paper bag at his feet.

'Sit down, girl. Relax.' He gestured to the space next to him on the step. Corinna sat.

And, like every man she'd ever met in Montreal, he told her all about who he was and where he was from; how he was half Indian, half Jamaican and he'd left Kingston fifteen years ago: 'You know, there's a disease in Jamaica,' he said. 'It killing all the cocoa trees. Soon, there gone be no chocolate left.'

'What will we do without chocolate?'

'We gotta start havin' sex instead.' He put his arm around her and chinked his bottle against hers.

She'd seen him on St Laurent with a Chinese woman pushing a pram but for that moment she forgot this and so, apparently, did he.


Back at the apartment she pulled the futon flat into a bed. Simpkin skulked in a corner and yowled when Jimmy tried to stroke him.

'He don' like another man on his territory,' said Jimmy, uncurling his long brown body on the white sheets. He seemed too big for the apartment and his voice was too loud. Briefly, the scenario appalled Corinna but when Jimmy pulled her hand she allowed herself to follow.

*

The sky was violet and fumed with smoke. On the other side of the street an old van was parked. Inside was a boy reading a magazine. A girl ambled up to the open window, passed him a pack of cigarettes and climbed in. Both were nut-brown and loose-limbed in beaten-up old jeans: partners in crime. The boy jumped out, walked away, did a double take and tossed a cigarette back to her before sauntering off with a smile. The girl kicked back with her bare feet on the dash and lit up.

Corinna watched them enviously from her balcony, dressed in her wrapper, drinking the last of Jimmy's beer alone. That double take, the remembered cigarette; that was love.

# Roger's Dream

The car was a 1984 Cadillac Eldorado, white with silver trimmings and a red leather interior so plush it was like a padded cell.

'This is a great car,' said Jason. He was on the passenger side fiddling with the cigarette lighter while Amy tried to coax the engine into life. She talked to the car like it was a stubborn horse refusing to jump a fence – 'Come on, baby, come on, baby, you can do it.'

'Shame it doesn't work.' Jason wound the window down. It was ninety degrees outside and the Cadillac was filled with the sickly smell of a coconut-scented air freshener stuck to the dash. Amy had driven it up from Nashville to Montreal the summer before she met Jason. For a whole winter the car had languished in the snow and now it was stranded on an island of weeds in the yard of Saul's workshop. The back seat was littered with stained Styrofoam cups, empty cigarette packets and pizza boxes. A pink-faced Madonna figurine was stuck to the dashboard and a rosary hung from the rear-view mirror, even though Amy wasn't Catholic. Jason opened the glove box and a pile of country music tapes clattered to the floor, along with a copy of *The Carpetbaggers* by Harold Robbins. The cover showed a still from the film of the book: George

Peppard throttling Carole Baker. On closer inspection Jason realised they were embracing.

He noted the names on a few of the tapes as he threw them back where they belonged: Merle Haggard, Waylon Jennings, Steve Earle, Kenny Rogers. *Kenny Rogers?*

Amy slumped back and lit a cigarette. 'You know, this car was practically my home that summer. I literally lived in it.' She flipped the sun visor down. 'Hey, look at this . . .' She passed Jason the photograph that had been stashed there. In it she smiled out from beneath a white Stetson. She was leaning against the hood of the Cadillac, one hand on her hip, the other splayed out to show off her long pink rhinestone-studded nails.

'I had those nails done when I was in Nashville.'

'Great picture.' Jason smiled: the pose was so typical of Amy. There was a casual defiance to all her gestures. He noticed it the first time he saw her. She was standing at the bar of La Cabane, with her waitressing apron tied over her jeans, drinking soup in rapid spoonfuls. She poured the final drops straight from the bowl into her mouth with a twist of her wrist. He liked the way she did it. When Lazlo introduced them, she frowned. At that time the words 'When I was in Nashville . . .' were always on her lips.

'It won't start, huh?' Saul burst from the doorway of his workshop, leapt down the step and gave the bumper an irritable kick. He was Amy's stepfather, a short, muscle-bound man, who talked in a deep monotone. 'I told you it wouldn't start. You're gonna have to tow it 'cos I can't have it blocking up the yard any more. I'm getting sick of the sight of it – makes the place look like a dump . . .'

'Yeah, yeah,' said Amy.

The previous night they had driven in Jason's van to her parents' place in the Laurentians. Amy had sat, bare feet propped on the dash, eating the poutine that Jason had fetched for her. She grinned at him between mouthfuls and he glowed with satisfaction because he had her to himself for the next three days.

'Mondo-Fritz definitely do the best poutine. The sauce is very . . . *piquante*.' Amy pronounced the word with a flourish. She always dropped French words into conversation as if she couldn't remember the English. It was one of the little affectations Jason indulged without comment, like the way she spelt her name *Aimée*.

Jason started the van and checked the street was clear to pull out. A girl in a bathrobe was sitting on the balcony of an apartment across the road. When he caught her eye she quickly looked away. He wondered what she had been thinking, but as soon as he was on St Laurent, his attention shifted to the people swanning in and out of the swanky bars, and he forgot about her. They bowled past a boy in shiny leather jeans with his arm around a girl in a backless dress.

'Jeez, so many Ginos in this goddamn city,' said Amy.

'Yeah, it's terrible.' Jason turned to watch a girl in a sequined boob-tube totter out of Buano Notte on six-inch platform heels.

St Laurent grew drabber as they headed north for the Pont Viau. Amy pointed out the Turkish bar on Jean-Talon where she had once worked for a night.

'The owner was married to an Eskimo and belonged to the Turkish Mafia.'

'Everyone belongs to the Mafia, according to you.'

'Do they?'

'Yes, you're obsessed by the Mafia.'

'Am I?' Amy considered. 'I guess I am.'

Their first date, they'd gone to the Cock and Bull on Ste. Catherine and she'd spent the evening pointing out members of the Russian Mafia – a heavy-jowled bruiser in a sharp-shouldered suit; a guy with a felt fedora and gold signet rings on every finger; a lounge lizard wearing a toupée and aviator shades who was drinking vodka and Kahlua. They certainly looked the part but Jason wasn't sure if their underworld connections were a figment of Amy's imagination. It seemed unlikely that the Russian Mafia would hang out in a pseudo-Irish pub surrounded by college kids.

Beyond the Pont Viau, the suburbs thinned out and the road grew wide and empty, winding between rocky cliffs and looming firs. The moon glinted in and out of the branches like a dropped coin. Sometimes it glimmered over pools of black water, sometimes it disappeared entirely. The van's headlamps forged a bright tunnel through the darkness, catching the flash of a fox's eyes as it slunk across the road and the ghostly white swoop of an owl overhead.

'Wait till you see the lake. We'll have to go swimming,' said Amy.

At one thirty, Jason stopped at a gas station and filled up the tank. He bought a cup of coffee for himself and a hot chocolate flavoured with After Eights for Amy.

'This was my winter craving, do you remember?' said Amy.

'That's why I bought it for you.'

He had a vivid picture of her on the stoop of the house on Villeneuve in a leopard-skin coat, plucking on her guitar. 'I've just discovered this most delicious drink at that gas station on Park. You have to try it,' she'd said and they'd walked hand in hand through the snow to buy a cup. Her hand had felt so cold he had tried to squeeze some warmth into it and she had yelled in pain.

'You know, I love all-night stores,' she called across the aisles as she stood selecting a doughnut, 'They're one of my favourite things.'

'I know,' said Jason. It was what she'd said in the gas station on Park. They had walked home listing a few more of their favourite things – fireworks and fog, matchbooks and mackerel skies, cocktail parasols and sugar cubes, the smell of old roses and green olives stuffed with pimento. Amy thought of more than Jason – it was as if she'd rehearsed the list many times before.

'Shall we play The Object Game?' Amy asked, as they pulled out of the gas station.

'Oh, OK.' Jason hated The Object Game but he knew Amy would say he was boring if he didn't agree to play. She had taught him the game when they first met but he could never quite play it to her high-faluting level.

'OK. Think of someone.'

'Um . . .' Jason frowned. 'Why don't you think of someone?'

'Because I'm always doing the thinking. I want to do the guessing for a change.'

'Um . . . um . . . OK, I've got someone.'

'Right . . . If they were a pair of shoes, what would they be?'

'Uh. I don't know . . . a pair of flip-flops.'

'What sort of drink are they?'

'Er . . . rum and Coke.'

'Jason! That's so obvious it's my sister. Just because she wears flip-flops and likes rum and Coke . . . you're not supposed to have objects they *like*, you're supposed to have objects that represent what they *are like* . . .'

'Well, those are objects I associate with your sister because she likes them.'

'Yes, but do they actually represent her? You see, if I was going to describe my sister, I would say she was . . .'


Sunrise was still several hours away as they padded through her parents' living room. Saul had built the house out of pine and it still had the tang of sawn wood inside. The solid shadow of a black cat weaved through their legs and bobbed his head against Amy's hand, keening for caresses. 'Herschel, my sweet!' she cried, clutching him picturesquely to her chest before dropping him and leading Jason into her old bedroom.

'What about your mom?' asked Jason as they twisted together on the bottom bed of the bunk Amy had once shared with her sister.

'Momma won't mind.' said Amy, her voice muffled against his armpit.

The night passed in a thin doze for Jason. Herschel scratched intermittently at the door. At dawn, Amy let him in and he tried to sleep on Jason's head before creating a nest for himself between their interwoven legs. His road-drill purrs fell into time with Amy's faintly snoring breath.

Elaine was on the porch smoking a joint when they went down for breakfast. She was thin and quiet with a sad, gentle face. Her feet were clad in faded red sneakers and her hair was long and grey with a centre parting. Jason could tell it had once been blonde like Amy's. She asked him about the journey and left him the rest of the joint while she slowly stirred up a pancake batter. A soft mist clung to the pine trees around the house and rolled across the lawn. Although he couldn't see the lake, the damp air suggested nearby water. Jason gently rocked himself on the swing seat while Amy fumbled through a Chopin *étude* on the old upright piano.

Saul bounded downstairs, clad only in Bermuda shorts. Throughout breakfast he reminisced at length about Montreal delicacies from his youth. 'There still that chocolatier where they sell the nougat down on St Laurent, near Rue Ontario? Really good nougat: freshly made with real pistachios and cut off these huge blocks. Turkish delight too. Best Turkish delight in the town, used to be able to buy it by the pound: so tender it just melted in your mouth and I tell ya, the scent of it was so powerful it was like eating a whole bunch of rosebuds. God, it was delicious. Amy, next time you're down that way see if it's still there, get me some if it is, will ya . . . What you two gonna do today anyway?'

'Not a lot. Might go for a swim.'

'Before you do anything, you gotta do something about the Cadillac. I saw Roger last week and he said he'd take it, so I told him you'd be round some time soon, he said he'd pay a hundred bucks for it, gonna use it for parts I think. You know Roger that's got the scrapyard on the way out to Morin Heights, Elaine, you know Roger don't you . . .'

Elaine's grey eyes glazed into the middle distance as she silently flipped pancakes onto their plates and opened a can of maple syrup.

'So, who is this Roger?' asked Jason, as they tied the Cadillac to the tow bar of the van.

'Just some guy that Saul knows. French.'

'Is he in the Mafia?'

'He could be. You never know.'

Amy steered the Cadillac while Jason towed it away, chasing the mirages of water that shimmered along the hot road.

The scrapyard was in the middle of nowhere at the end of a dirt track. Rusted carcasses of cars were piled high on every side and a corrugated iron shack stood tip-tilted at the far end. A black dog shot out as they pulled in and circled the truck barking. A man appeared from the shack and shouted at the dog.

'Salut,' he said, as Amy walked over to him. Jason trailed in her wake, watching the sway of her hips.

'Saul, he say you will come. I am Roger.' He pronounced his name the French way and held out an oil-blackened hand to them both. Three of his fingers were stumps.

'You remember me?' he asked, but Amy said she didn't. 'I remember you when you very little.' He held his hand up to his knee. 'You grow big, eh?'

He ran his stumpy fingers through his matted hair and grinned, his teeth shining in his ink-black beard. Though he was middle-aged, his body was thin and wiry as a teenager and his skin was the colour of chestnuts. He wore a grimy purple T-shirt with sawn-off sleeves and a palm tree on the front. A gold ring glinted in one ear. Jason felt colourless and stiff with city manners in comparison. Although he would never be able to explain it exactly, Jason knew Roger was part of a world that Amy would be intrigued to dip into, if only for that morning. The only worlds Jason could show her were the ones she already knew.

From the get-go Roger addressed only Amy and the pair descended into rapid Joual that he couldn't follow. He sidled off awkwardly to inspect the battered indy cars dumped around the yard, all painted with extravagant orange flames. From time to time he glanced over to see Amy smiling as Roger twinkled at her with his gypsy eyes. She looked coolly crumpled in her oldest jeans and her faded Willie Nelson T-shirt. In her head at that precise moment she was probably the heroine of some white-trash country song that he didn't know the words to. That was the trouble with Amy, and also what he loved: she was always soaring off to some imaginary place he couldn't quite reach.

'So what's up?' he said, finally, wandering over to

where the two were giggling at some private Québécois joke.

'Roger's gonna give me a hundred bucks for the car.'

'Yes, maybe I swap the Cadillac body with another car and I could use it for races,' pondered Roger, scratching his beard. 'Yes – Roger, 'e 'ave a dream . . .'

He smiled and twinkled some more at Amy.

'I gotta have a memento of the thing,' said Amy. She spoke to Roger in French and he went into the shack and returned with a screwdriver. He and Jason watched while she prised off the number plate and the silver Cadillac sign.

'Beautiful car,' said Jason, for want of anything else to say.

'*Oui, belle, très belle,*' said Roger.


'Come by next time you're 'ere,' he called, once they were in the van, after he'd licked his remaining fore-finger and counted ten greasy ten-dollar notes into Amy's hand. 'Maybe you will see me race in your old car.'

'I'd love to,' shouted Amy.

On the drive back Amy kept chuckling to herself. Finally, she said, 'If Roger was a drink what kind of drink do you think he would be?'

'I don't know.' Jason kept his eyes on the road.

'A broken cup of hot black tar.'

'What are you talking about? You can't drink tar.'

'Oh Jason, don't be so literal.'

Thunder rumbled faintly in the distance like someone moving giant furniture. Jason thought about pointing out that thunder was one of his favourite things but Amy was glaring out the window so irritably he decided not to bother and the rest of the journey passed in silence.

They found Elaine in the kitchen pounding basil leaves with a pestle.

'Did you sort out the car?'

'Yeah, we towed it to Roger's.'

'Oh yeah?'

'Yeah, "Roger, 'e 'ave a dream,"' said Amy. 'He asked after you actually.'

'Did he?' Elaine blushed and laughed.

Overhead, the clouds cracked open.

'Guess we won't be able to go for a swim now,' said Jason.


For the rest of the afternoon he lay on the couch with Herschel on his lap and read Amy's copy of *The Trial*. He found it heavy going. From time to time he went to the porch and watched the rain falling very hard and straight. Amy sprawled on the hearthrug and wrote copiously in her notebook, shielding the page with her arm. When Jason asked what she was writing, she said it was a short story. She snapped the notebook shut when he tried to read over her shoulder.

'Not about "Roger" by any chance, is it?'

'No,' said Amy, but Jason didn't believe her.


That night she was cool and distant and eventually climbed onto the top bunk, saying she felt too cramped beside him. For a long time Jason lay awake, listening to the rain drumming on the roof. He was awoken from a claustrophobic dream by her hot breath on his face.

'Guess what?'

'What?'

'It's stopped raining.'

'So?'

'Let's go for a swim . . .'

'What? Now?'

'Oh please, come on. Swimming at night, it's one of my favourite things. Please . . .'

So, reluctantly, he followed her out across the sodden grass, down through the dripping trees to where the lake stretched out, silent and glittering and smooth. Like charred paper, the sky was greying at the edges with the coming dawn and ducks were beginning to stir among the reeds. Amy tore off her clothes and stumbled into the shallows. Her body was pale and delicate as a moth and she slid into the water with a shriek. Jason swam after her into the black depths and their laughter rippled out with the waves they made.

'Tell me, is there anywhere you'd rather be?' demanded Amy. Jason watched as she arched her neck until her head was immersed then flicked back up with a gasp and clasping her against him, he had to admit that there wasn't.

# Taste of Love

The café was on Ste. Catherine opposite the Cock and Bull pub. It was cramped and smoky and the floor was strewn with crumbs and dust. A big man with a ginger beard and a dirty sweater slowly prepared the food which customers ordered from menus stuck to the tabletops. A small man with a gentle face and lame right leg took the orders and operated the big silver espresso machine with casual deftness. Both men wore yellow baseball caps with La Croissanterie embroidered in blue letters across the front.

It took a while for customers to notice the care the two men took with their food: the glass filled to just below the rim with juice that had been shaken for ten seconds; the precise alignment of the napkin upon the saucer beneath the bowl into which the soup was poured; the crisp baguette lined with a satisfying patchwork of cheese and ham. When regulars came in their drink specifications were remembered wordlessly and the poor and lonely were allowed to linger with just one coffee. For these reasons La Croissanterie was a favourite with the cognoscenti of the city; the people who appreciated time and thought over glamour and excitement. Every year its downbeat charm won the café a Taste of Love award from *Le Miroir* – the pink heart-shaped certificates were framed and hung around the plastic pine walls.

For the regulars La Croissanterie was an extension of their apartments, an extra living room where they could stare into space, cushioned by comforting bustle, acknowledged and yet anonymous. Magdi, the small man, wondered about them but he was too respectful of their privacy to pry. When business was slack, Artur, the big man, would squeeze into the corner table with a Coke and quiz whoever was to hand without listening to their answers. From these interrogations, Magdi learned that Steve, the guy who made the 'A-OK' signs, was a born-again Christian; Jagjit and Harjit, who sat opposite each other in silence for hours, were cousins; Mátyás, the Hungarian in the felt fedora, had 'business interests' on the West Island; Pierre studied philosophy at Concordia; and bald, glassy-eyed Silvio, whose size equalled Artur's, was a former cruise ship singer with unspecified psychological problems.

At the end of the day Silvio swept the floor in return for a chef salad with no cucumbers. He had a horror of cucumbers and melons and anything else hard on the outside and watery within. Salads were his only sustenance: he blamed his medication for his weight. His pills kept him placid for the most part but occasionally his eyes twitched and his legs jiggled and he had to be calmed with soft words and a cup of *verveine*. Magdi monitored Silvio covertly at all times lest he break into 'Somewhere Over the Rainbow' and scare off the other customers.

On Thursdays and Fridays, Magdi's sister, Maryam, came to help behind the counter. Though Magdi found her annoying he had to admit she was good with

Silvio. When he was agitated she would curl her thin arm around his mountainous shoulders and make him breathe in time with her. His unnerving stare did not unnerve her and she had no fear of his darting fingers.

During break times, if Silvio wasn't there, she loudly divulged the information she had elicited from him. A recent titbit had been: 'Of course you know that Silvio goes cruising along Rue Beaudry on Saturday nights.'

'Cruising!' Artur had shrieked, as if he knew the meaning of the word.

'And it is not the kind of cruising that ships make . . .'

'I don't know what you mean by this "cruising" and neither should you, Maryam, you're a married woman.'

'Well, Magdi: he picks up young men, takes them to a public toilet and he has then sexual relations with them in their anuses.' This had been followed by a triumphant suck from her banana milkshake.

'Maryam, I think it is now the time for us to make muffins.'

To make muffins, Magdi measured out flour and sugar with an old jam tin, poured in milk and eggs and churned the mixture with a repetitive sweep. He enjoyed the way it coalesced into something different from its constituent parts. He had a chemistry degree and it pleased him to see materials change: thin cream becoming thick, egg whites becoming foam, dough becoming twice its size. His hands were surprisingly strong and he enjoyed using them, though he wished it was for something more manly than muffin-making. In Alexandria he had been a laboratory technician. In Montreal he ran a café because no one took him seriously.

*

For a long time, homesickness had been a sharp ache just below Magdi's heart. One day, with a guilty jolt, he realised the ache had disappeared without him noticing. Cursing his fickleness, he tried in vain to bring it back.

Then, one July afternoon, five years after he had emigrated, while standing on the corner of Ste. Catherine and St Mathieu waiting to cross the road, he was suddenly, unexpectedly, back in Egypt. His eyes blurred with tears and he felt so dizzy he had to lean against a lamp-post. Workmen were digging a drain as cars honked at a turning truck and the doors of a kebab shop swung open; the heat, meat, noise and shit was a symphony to Alexandria crashing over him.

After that, he learned to let memories flood back spontaneously with the smell of strong cigarettes and petrol, the slant of sunbeams on a dusty staircase or the sound of a man watching baseball on a TV in his front yard. These instances gave him a glimpse of something grander and more important than the present. He had an urge to write them down but was always disappointed by the way words failed to capture their essence. Maryam once discovered a napkin scribbled with Magdi's musings and translated them aloud to the customers at hand: '"*Dust it dance like shiny . . . little things . . . particles . . . molecules . . . in the air that is hot . . .*" Magdi, what is this? A shopping list?'

'Of course it is not.' Magdi snatched the napkin away and used it to wipe up a coffee spill.

*

Mostly Magdi plodded through his days with steadfast practicality. He wasn't following his chosen career or living in his chosen city but he wasn't bitter. He took a mild pride in his café's success and he enjoyed its gentle rhythms: for breakfast he ate a croissant with jam; for lunch he ate a croissant with cheese; every other day he made muffins; every Friday he made vanilla biscuits; twice a week he made spanakopita and every morning he made soup. He preferred not to delegate these tasks to Artur or Maryam because their inefficiencies irritated him.

'Slowly, slowly, squeezy, squeezy,' he warned, when he showed Maryam how to drain defrosted spinach for the spanakopita. Maryam plucked feebly with her jewelled fingers.

'No, no, you're not squeezing fast enough. Your hands are too small . . .'

'Oh, you squeeze it then. I can't be bothered.'

Magdi plunged into the seaweedy mulch with secret relish.

Artur's big hands were competent at spinach squeezing but hopeless at slicing and arranging meat.

'You must do it neatly so all the pieces look the same, then put it on the plate round and round,' Magdi explained, forcing the ham through the monstrous steel cutter and fanning the slices into a spiral like a deck of pink cards.

'Why does it matter how we put it? The customers don't care.'

'If we lose these details, Artur, we lose everything. It is this that shows the touch of love.'

'"Touch of Love"? You mean, "Taste of Love".'

'Taste of Love, Touch of Love: it is all the same.'

For Magdi the touch of love was as elusive as his feelings for Alexandria. Women in Montreal were so brash and worldly, they had no time for a quaint little Egyptian. Maryam, who married a Greek trucker a year after arriving in Montreal, had once paraded her husband's single female relatives for Magdi's delectation but none had lasted beyond a strained first date so she had given up. Though his face was fine-cut and handsome, his lame leg, the result of childhood polio, made Magdi shy. As a young man he had frequented the narrow alleys near the docks, where the whores lounged in the sun, stretching their limbs like cats. Thinking back to those afternoons in their ramshackle perfumed boudoirs where flies circled in the shuttered gloom, made him hot with shame.

*

'Magdi, come over here. We need a hot chocolate.'

'Artur, I am occupied with the meat.'

Magdi was lost in peaceful concentration, passing the ham back and forth across the blade, dropping stray slivers into his mouth and letting them dissolve on his tongue like communion wafers.

'Magdi. This woman wants you to make her chocolate.'

'Lady . . .' murmured Magdi. Artur, who was Armenian, always forgot the subtle niceties of the English language.

The woman stood at the counter with her purse and smiled at Magdi.

'I came in here the other day and yours was the best I've ever tasted. Chocolatey. Not too sugary.'

'Thank you. I will try to make it the same.' Magdi heaped cocoa, sugar and milk into a cup and shot a jet of steam through it. He watched the woman settle herself at a table, crossing her legs in an attempt at elegance, and tried, unsuccessfully, to remember her previous visit. She was in her forties, short and plump, with a pleasant, forgettable face. He set the cup on a coaster on a saucer on the counter, heaved himself around the counter and limped over to place it before her. She asked him for a vanilla biscuit and when he returned she said, 'It's the combination of bitter and sweet I like.'

'I understand.' Magdi returned to his slicing but glanced at the woman from time to time. He could see from the way she dipped the biscuit, let it draw up the chocolate and took a sip with each bite that she was as careful with the arrangement of her senses as he was.

'I think she will come back again,' said Artur, when the woman left.

*

Artur was right. The woman came back nearly every day. Her order never varied. The days she didn't come, Magdi missed her. He never said so but somehow Artur and Silvio guessed. They always clamoured to welcome her.

'You are here again. Thank God. Magdi has been waiting.'

'He's been crying for you, darling, crying.'

Magdi lurked behind the espresso machine fiddling intently with the taps and handles.

'He plays hard to get but really he is very happy to see you.' Silvio's lunacy allowed him to be direct. As did Artur's social ineptitude: 'What is your name? Where you live? What job you do? Are you married? Do you have some children? Why you did never come to La Croissanterie before?'

The answers were: Barbara, on Tupper St, secretary, no, no and because she had only just moved into the area.

Magdi always took her cup over personally so they could exchange pleasantries. She had an unassuming manner that he liked but he supposed it was this that made her unmemorable at first. Even once he knew her, he would have found it difficult to describe her face except to say that it was nice.


'I can't wait to see this Barbara lady,' shrilled Maryam. 'It is about time you got married and settled down, Magdi.'

'She only comes in for hot chocolate. She has said nothing about marriage.'

'It is on her mind. I know it is on her mind.'

When Barbara came in, Maryam expounded the virtues of her brother: 'Look see, he is smart, he is clever, he has a business, he is clean and polite, he is good with his hands.'

Barbara blushed and said she was sure Magdi was a very nice man.

'Very nice. He is very nice. I do not say this just because he is my brother, but because it is the truth.'

That day business was slow so, at six thirty, Magdi let the rest of the staff leave, so he could have some peace. He had perfected the art of staring into space for hours, an art that North Americans had forgotten. He lit his second cigarette of the day (the first he smoked after breakfast) and, after a while, picked up the copy of *Lucky* by Jackie Collins, which was shelved inside the defunct dumb waiter along with *The Story of American Hunting and Firearms*, *How to Win at Bridge in Ten Easy Steps*, *The Curse of the Giant Hogweed* and *Look Young, Live Longer* by Gaylord Hauser. Magdi had no idea where the books came from but he sometimes read them when he had done with the *Montreal Gazette*. Infuriatingly, a copy of *The Carpetbaggers* by Harold Robbins had been stolen from the dumb waiter when he was on the final chapter.

'Are you enjoying that? I found it a real good read.'

Magdi jumped to find Barbara in the doorway.

'Yes . . . it is . . . quite . . . amusing.' He snapped the book shut. 'The pleasure of you two times in one day. It is too much for me!' He threw his hands in the air and she laughed.

'Sorry, to disturb you . . . I was just passing and I saw you sitting here. Are you closing up soon?'

'No . . . I mean . . . I might be. Would you like a cup of chocolate?'

'No, that's OK.' Barbara looked different: Magdi

guessed she was wearing make up. When she moved closer he was swamped by sweet perfume.

'Coffee, tea, another kind of drink?'

'No, no . . .'

'Well . . .'

'Actually I came in to ask a favour. Don't feel you have to say yes.'

'What is it?' A flickbook of potential favours leafed through Magdi's mind. Inexplicably, he could hear his heart beating.

'Well, it's kind of silly but the tap in my kitchen is leaking and the dripping is keeping me awake at night. It's only a little noise but I find myself listening out for it when I'm in bed and, I tell you, it's like Chinese water torture . . .'

'. . . Chinese water torture . . .'

'Yes . . . so . . .'

'So you would like me to fix your tap? Of course, it would be my pleasure.'

'. . . your sister said you were very practical . . .'

'. . . good with my hands . . .'

'. . . and I've got a washer and a spanner and . . .'


Magdi twirled the Open sign to Closed and locked the door of La Croissanterie. He was glad Barbara lived nearby, as he felt awkward being outside the café with her. Inside, he felt safe – he was the owner, she was the customer; the rules were understood. Here in the street, he couldn't think of anything to say and he was embarrassed by the fact she had to slow her pace to match his.

'Feels like thunder, doesn't it?' Barbara held out her hands to test for raindrops. There were none but the sky was foreboding and the air still and expectant. Litter whirlpooled around the street. 'Do you like thunder?' she asked.

'I like the smell of the air after it.'

'So do I.'

Silence fell again and Magdi found himself wishing a storm would break just to create some distracting noise.

'Here we are!' said Barbara, after ten minutes, once they'd reached a long narrow street of tall Victorian-style houses. 'My place is right at the end.'

Her place was at the top of a rickety redbrick town-house that had been divided into apartments. There was no elevator. Effortfully, Magdi lugged his leg up the steep stairs.

'This is it,' she said, as she unlocked the door. Magdi wiped his boots unnecessarily on the Welcome mat and stepped inside. The apartment was hot and dark and decorated throughout with whimsical wallpaper: Superman in the hallway, *trompe l'oeil* beach views in the living room and leaping dolphins in the bathroom. The effect was oppressive. Every horizontal surface was crammed with holiday souvenirs: straw donkeys, sombreros, snowstorms containing Eiffel Towers, Big Bens and Taj Mahals, dolls dressed as cowboys, bull-fighters and dairymaids. Magdi found them tasteless so he made no comment.

'I bet you're thinking, "Oh my God",' said Barbara.

'You have a lot of things,' said Magdi, to deflect her from what he was thinking.

'They remind me of all my trips.'

211

'You have been to many places?'

'Many places. I spend all my money on vacations.'

'You are very lucky.'

'Shall I show you the tap?'

She took him into the kitchen. From the window other people's kitchens could be seen across an enclosed courtyard. There was a pigeon huddled on every sill, burbling in the setting sun. The pigeon outside Barbara's window rolled its tiny baleful eyes, flared up its wings and flapped away. Magdi's heart fluttered at the shock of the movement.

Against a backdrop of anthropomorphic vegetables, Barbara fixed the dinner while Magdi fixed the tap. It was a simple task, which he suspected she could have done herself. Still, she professed her profound gratitude once he was finished, and pressed him into a chair with a glass of wine. It required much self control for Magdi to stop himself from criticising her onion-chopping technique, her failure to tenderise the steak and her cardinal sin of slicing rather than tearing the lettuce.

'Is the big guy with the red hair your son?' asked Barbara, finally, when it became apparent that Magdi was not going to start the conversation.

'My son? No! Artur is Armenian.' Magdi hoped she wasn't going to be so ignorant as to ask where Armenia was.

'The other guy is kinda funny, isn't he?'

'You mean Silvio? Unfortunately he is mad. Also he is homosexual.' Internally, Magdi winced. His nerves were making him idiotic. The word 'sexual' buzzed in the air like a trapped wasp.

212

'Actually my brother suffers from mental-health problems,' said Barbara. Magdi breathed a sigh of relief as they steered the conversation to safer ground.

When they had finished eating, Barbara made coffee and brought it to the table with cups and a bowl of sugar cubes. Magdi was impressed to see sugar cubes in a domestic setting and relieved the coffee wasn't instant.

'I hope this will be up to your standard, seeing as you're a coffee connoisseur,' said Barbara.

'I do not doubt it will be delicious,' said Magdi.

She noticed his puzzlement as she touched the edge of a sugar cube against the surface of the coffee for a second before dropping it into the cup. 'Don't you ever do that?' she laughed, 'I like the way it soaks up – like blotting paper.' He took a cube and tried, agreeing that it was quite pleasing, the change of matter from solid to sludge.

Silence fell, broken only by the rumbling of the pigeons.

'That noise . . .' said Magdi, cocking his head, 'In Alexandria I hear it all the time when I lie in bed.'

'Takes you back?'

'Yes. It makes me feel sad.'

'I understand.' She recounted her experience at the lido the weekend before, when the smell of an old bottle of suncream had transported her back to the best summer of her life.

'I started crying there and then. It was lucky I was wearing my sunglasses, otherwise everyone would have thought I was really strange.'

'What happened that summer? Why was it the best?'

'Oh, I don't know. It just was,' said Barbara, looking down at her coffee dregs. Sadness made her look pretty. Magdi's insides turned to honey and he wondered if this was the taste of love.

'Is there anything else you would like me to do?' he asked. 'Anything else that needs fixing?'

'Well . . . there is my shower curtain: it keeps falling down.' She led him into the bathroom where the dolphins dipped and swerved. The shower curtain contained a shoal of rubber goldfish, trapped between sheets of clear plastic.

'I'll leave you to it,' she said, passing him a screwdriver and some screws, 'Come and find me when you're done.'

Magdi removed his shoes and stood in the bath to work. The task took two minutes but he spent a while examining the labels on her surprisingly expensive-looking lotions and potions. He was suddenly nervous about returning to her. Her invitation was loaded with expectation and he feared she would be appalled by his clumsiness. In the mirror, he considered his reflection, first with his cap on, then with it off. Using a little water, he dampened his hair where it had been flattened by the cap. A muffled call summoned him from the bathroom. With shoes in one hand and the cap in the other, he ventured out.

The kitchen was empty. The hallway was dark. The living room door was ajar and a crack of light cut a diagonal across the linoleum. Soft music and the sweet scent he had smelled on Barbara earlier wafted into the hall.

'I'm in here,' came a voice.

There she was, nestled on the sofa in front of a tropical sunset. Her eyes reflected the flames of the candles, which were grouped like a shrine on top of the wide-screen television.

'Candles,' said Magdi, for want of anything better to say.

'I love candles, don't you? The light is so soft and flattering and romantic.'

There was a forced gaiety to Barbara's tone. Magdi wondered if she was drunk. He perched on the furthest end of the sofa, clutching his shoes and cap like a life raft.

The singer on the stereo was declaring over and over that he needed 'sexual feeling' or at least that was what it sounded like. Magdi tensed with embarrassment, praying for the song to end.

'Do you like Marvin Gaye?' asked Barbara.

'What! I'm not gay.'

Barbara gave a tinkling laugh and suddenly seemed to be sitting closer. 'You misunderstand me. That's not what I said.'

Magdi recoiled as he turned to face her. Her perfume, clearly recently re-sprayed, was overwhelming. Flecks of fresh lipstick grazed her teeth like blood. The wistful delicacy had been replaced by a brashness reminiscent of the Alexandrian whores. The taste of honey, the taste of love, curdled into bitterness.

# Finding Freya

The old neighbourhood had grown a little shinier, Elaine noticed – the paintwork on the houses was fresh and tasteful, there were bijou cafés brimming with bright young things and the rotting family groceries had been replaced by boutiques selling sweet-smelling fripperies.

'The people that live here now throw out real quality furniture,' her ex-husband Joey told her, when she rang him at the studio to say she was coming over. 'I found a beautiful carved-oak armoire the other day – Maureen's going to distress it.'

'I bet she is,' Elaine replied and they laughed. They shared an unspoken subtext that his second wife Maureen was slightly ridiculous.

'Remember those pallets we used to sleep on?'

'Of course I remember – my back hasn't been the same since.'

In those days the cast-offs had been proper trash. She and Joey furnished their attic flat with empty tea crates, shelves made from planks balanced on bricks, stolen cuttings planted in olive-oil cans and candles shoved into their many empty wine bottles. Joey saved the corks and used them to tile the tiny bathroom. Elaine recalled reading the smudgy crests of far-off vineyards while she soaked in the tub. Leaving the cork bathroom had pained Joey: 'A real labour of love that was. Gonna take me years to collect that many corks again.'

'I shouldn't think it'll take you that long,' said Elaine.

She wondered if he was still collecting them now. Or if his boundless creativity had alighted on some other junky craftwork. Last thing she knew he was making mobiles out of old cutlery. Freya had brought one home at Christmas. Saul hung it grudgingly out on the porch where it tinkled in the breeze.

'Maureen's got these hung up everywhere,' Freya told them. 'They really jangle on your nerves after a while.'

Maureen had called two days previously. Elaine had been prone on the couch leafing through her brother's latest exhibition catalogue. The phone jolted her out of a reverie about a painting of a dwarf and an angel.

'Elaine! I'm so glad I caught you,' she began breath-lessly.

'Maureen! Is everything alright?'

'Well, actually, no . . . everything is not alright . . . It's Freya . . .'

Something was wrong with Freya – she was never home, when she was home she was asleep, she never ate, she looked ill, she was surly, her grades were going down, she'd been seen on St Laurent with *a black man* – Maureen hissed the words. Elaine could picture Maureen's round brown eyes growing even rounder. When she failed to respond Maureen quickly qualified that there was nothing wrong with black men, *per se*, but this one had looked far too old for a young girl to be hanging out with.

'I'll drive down and talk to her,' said Elaine, deciding as she said this that she would talk to Joey first, find out his side of the story.

'Would you, Elaine? I'd appreciate that. I mean, there's only so much I can say to her.' She left the words *as her stepmother* unsaid.

Maureen's appearance on the scene had upset Freya the most out of Elaine's three daughters. Both Skye and Amy stoically shrugged off the arrival of Maureen but Freya railed against her constantly. Ironically, it was Freya who wound up spending most time with Maureen, moving into the apartment she shared with Joey and their boys on St Viateur, to attend a media course at Dawson College. 'The woman is a nightmare,' she moaned, 'She talks all the time and she never says anything interesting. She's constantly nagging me. She listens to Kenny Rogers. All the time . . .'

Joey's studio was the last bastion of the counter culture on Laurier. The words HOT STUFF were still emblazoned on the front wall in psychedelic letters and the old hub caps painted with peace signs still decorated the big barn doors. Joey had hung them there twenty years ago, when Glory Hole Glass first opened. At the launch party he disappeared with a sculptress who'd changed her name from Jenny Smith to Jenny Sunshine, leaving Elaine, who was in her vegetarian phase, to tend the spit-roast pig. Jenny Sunshine had been one of many clouds on the horizon.

Elaine squeezed quietly between the gap in the doors. Joey was rolling a red-hot globule of glass.

She waited until he'd blown the globule into a filmy balloon, teased it into a tall vase and dappled it with slivers of silver and gold leaf which would glisten like the rainbow in a soap bubble once the glass was cold. It still fascinated her to watch Joey blow glass, the same way she liked to see Saul fashion a dove-tail joint. 'You always were attracted to artisans,' her mother said, on learning Elaine's second husband-to-be was a carpenter. Mrs Kleinmann had hoped her son would become a doctor and her daughter would marry one. Ralph and Elaine had disappointed her on both counts.

When the vase was finished, Joey prepared coffee. His hands, which were like slabs of meat, were clumsy with domestic tasks. Elaine noticed he stored his coffee beans in the red-and-gold tin with the Russian writing she'd bought from a thrift store on Mont Royal when they were married. He ground them in the wooden grinder with the brass-handled drawer they'd been given as a wedding present. She recalled how his bulky frame used to suggest, like an aura, the way he would plump out in middle-age. Years of drinking and Maureen's stodgy Irish cooking were catching up with him; he lumbered around the studio as if his body was a beer barrel being inched across a bar-room floor.

'Ah, Freya's fine. She's been a bit distant lately, haven't seen much of her but she's just a normal kid, growing up, finding her independence; Maureen's over-reacting,' said Joey, when Elaine explained the reason for her visit. He held up a glass ornament shaped like a pirouetting foot, 'Like it?'

'So you're doing feet now, are you?' said Elaine

absently, unreassured by what he'd just said.

'Yeah, feet and hands. I can charge more for this kind of thing 'cos it looks like Art.'

'You doing much engraving?'

'Yeah, I've got a commission from Janet – you remember Janet from Bagels Etc? Well, I did their store window and now she wants me to soundproof her bedroom – all glass panels engraved with naked women.'

'Really? Soundproofed?'

'Yeah, I said to her, "Janet – what are you going to be doing in here, that you need it soundproofed?"'

'What did she say?'

'"Never you mind, Joey."' He guffawed.

Elaine picked up a glass paperweight shaped like a female torso. She wouldn't have been surprised if Janet had been next in line after Jenny Sunshine. At the time people complimented Elaine on her dignity in the face of Joey's infidelities, not realising she was like a wrung-out rag, too limp to care. She'd fled to Montreal after the debacle in California, encouraged by her school friend, Pamela, who was living there. She had swapped one commune for another, though Pamela's contained only women. It was lucky Elaine didn't have sons.

When Skye was six month's old, Joey had impregnated Pia, a new recruit to the San Francisco commune. Pia was a seventeen-year-old runaway from New York, half-Italian, half-gypsy. She was lush and sweet and when her stomach swelled she looked more than ever like an over-ripe fig. It was bad enough for Elaine knowing Joey had been unfaithful but seeing Pia growing bigger week by week while she struggled with a new baby and a toddler was unbearable. *Sharing* was a principle tenet of the commune's philosophy but there were limits. Elaine did a midnight flit in their battered old camper van; Amy throwing up into a plastic bag for most of the journey while Skye wailed inconsolably. Three months later, Joey turned up penitently at the door of the women's commune on Rue de la Gauchetière, and was pelted with eggs and tomatoes from the upper floor. He had hitched in grain trucks and cattle lorries all the way from the West Coast. Too worn out to hitch back and liking the laid-back vibe of the city, he stuck around, finding himself a job at a glassworks in Rosemont. Elaine did another midnight flit to rejoin him in his Clark Street attic and a year later she was pregnant with Freya. Pamela and the other women never forgave her for returning to the enemy but, in truth, she had grown weary of their wholemeal seriousness and the fact that someone else had always used the last Tampax.

'I think I should see what's going on with Freya, though, don't you?' said Elaine, raking her teaspoon through a pile of sparkling glass dust.

'Sure, if you can find her,' said Joey.

'What time do her classes finish?'

Joey shrugged: 'God knows. I don't even know if she goes to them.'

Elaine frowned at his lassitude but he was too busy admiring the vase he had just made to notice. 'Well, I'll just have to go down to Dawson and hang about there then, see if I run into her,' she said, putting down the teaspoon and gathering up her bag.

The students circling the staircase at the college sported clothes that were not dissimilar to those Elaine and Joey had worn during their first years in Montreal. They were good-looking kids with the blithe confidence of the late teens, yet to be unsettled by life's knockbacks. When Elaine enquired whether they knew Freya Johnson on the media course, they said no, but directed her politely to the relevant department. The media students were instantly recognisable by their self-conscious funkiness – most had a piercing or tattoo, like tagged and branded cattle.

'Freya? She hasn't been in for a few days,' one of the girls told her.

'Have you any idea where she might be?' Elaine found it hard to focus on anything but the two-inch spike through the girl's lower lip. Did it hurt? Did she have problems eating? How was she able to kiss anyone? What a shame to spoil such a pretty face . . . Elaine stopped herself. Sometimes she feared she was turning into her mother . . .

'She often goes to Carré St Louis when it's hot.'

'Carré St Louis?'

'Yeah – on the Plateau.'

'I know where it is . . . Thank you so much for your help.'

'Can I give her a message?'

'No, no . . .'

'Is she OK?'

'Oh yes . . .' Elaine scurried away with alarm ringing in her ears. The crumpled consternation in the girl's face worried her. Why wasn't Freya at college? And why was she hanging around in a public park like a bum? When the girls were small Elaine had sometimes taken them to play in Carré St Louis but she'd stopped when Amy found a hypodermic needle in the fountain. The area was rougher in those days; the drug dealers and prostitutes, or chippies as they were known, more brazen. Since the Plateau had been spruced up for the tourists, the seamier side of the city had been squeezed out to the east.

She took the metro to Sherbrooke. On the windy concourse a violinist was vigorously sawing his way through the Spring section of Vivaldi's *Four Seasons*. He was middle-aged but raffishly handsome and Elaine liked the intensity of his playing. She tossed him a dollar and was rewarded with a wink, which made her smile all the way to the square. It was a long time since anyone had winked at her. As a young woman she had fizzled with the continual frisson of men's gazes. In Montreal the scent of sexuality was as much a part of the air as oxygen. Perhaps because it was poor, or perhaps because it was full of people from hot countries – Morocco, Algeria, Haiti, Egypt and the Ivory Coast – it wasn't like a normal northern city. And the Québécois themselves were unrestrained, unrefined, good-time people.

'Peasant stock, that's what Québeckers come from,' Mrs Kleinmann pronounced, when Elaine said she was settling there. After visiting the city, she declared it 'a hick town with local colour'. The Kleinmann's came from Chicago, where base instincts were kept in check.

As a young woman, the sexual braggadocio of

Montreal had alternately exhilarated and exhausted Elaine. Sometimes, she had hated being undressed by a dozen hot eyes on the way to the *dépanneur* but more often it had buoyed her up. When she had been married to Joey, it was what she needed.

Elaine wondered when she had sunk from public consumption – it must have been a gradual retreat; with the birth of each daughter and when she started wearing clothes which hid rather than hugged her figure. 'It's a relief not to care about men anymore,' she'd told Amy. 'The menopause is very freeing.' Amy had looked embarrassed and doubtful. But it was – her mind was clearer, less swamped by sudden sluices of hormones. She could concentrate on simple pleasures like gardening and cooking; she hadn't felt so much like her own true self since she was a child.

As she crossed St Denis into Carré St Louis, an unkempt man in dungarees approached her: '*Madame, voudriez-vous acheter mes poèmes?*'

'*Je ne parle pas français,*' Elaine lied automatically.

'Would you like to buy a book of my poems, Madam?' The man was English. He pressed a thin photocopied booklet into her hand. The poems were interspersed with garish drawings of celestial landscapes. 'I've translated them into French and English. Take whichever you prefer.'

'How much are they?'

'Whatever your heart sees fit, whatever you can afford.'

Elaine fumbled in her purse for a two-dollar piece.

'Enjoy!' said the man, as she hurried away, stuffing the booklet into her bag.

She scanned the grass, which was scattered with sun-bathers; mostly office workers with their uncomfortable clothes rucked up or removed. There were a few vagrants beached on ragged blankets drinking from bottles wrapped in brown paper bags, remonstrating with each other and their filthy dogs. Freya was not among them, nor was she with the guitar-strumming kids congregated near the fountain. The water erupting from the cupids' embrace was shot with rainbows as it arched through the sunlight. Someone had sprayed *Vive Le Québec Libre*! in red paint along the fountain's stone base. How soulless to spoil such elegance. Carré St Louis had been a stylish address when the villas bordering the square were first built. It was becoming chic again, judging from the expensive drapes and polished floors glinting through the ground-floor windows. When Elaine used to push Freya's pram beneath the cottonwood trees the place had been overrun with squats, the gingerbread gables painted bright colours, with hippies sprawled on the stoops in their ragamuffin finery, playing bongos and smoking dope.

Back then Leonard Cohen had lived in Carré St Louis, though not in a squat: he was far too reclusive for that. Elaine had been a huge Cohen fan, had even considered calling her first two daughters Suzanne and Marianne until Joey shouted her down. He had wanted to name their children Jackson, Willem and Rothko, despite the fact they were all girls and, as Elaine pointed out, Rothko is a surname. (Joey: 'Yeah, but the name Mark is so boring.') Eventually, he had agreed to feminised versions of French Surrealists for their middle names: Amy Marcella, Freya Andrée and Skye Renée.

Mrs Kleinmann had been appalled: 'Elaine, I despair of you. Why not nice normal Jewish names like Judith or Sarah or Rachel?'

'Because, Mother, that would be a waste of a name opportunity.'

Elaine had been dreaming up baby names since childhood and deplored her own and her brother's. She had no idea how her mother could have held them as babies and exclaimed, 'Yes! Elaine . . . Ralph. How charming! How pretty!'

Her daughters reveled in their unusual names now, though they had each passed through phases of wishing to be called something more normal, like Mandy or Kelly. For a time Amy had signed herself Ami with a heart instead of a dot over the 'i'.

As Freya was nowhere to be seen, Elaine decided to call in on Amy or Aimée as she had taken to calling herself lately. Her eldest daughter lived in a shared apartment on Rue de Bullion, round the corner from the Carré.

Amy's boyfriend, Jason, answered the door.

'Hello, Mrs . . .' he faltered, evidently unsure of her married name.

'Mrs Kominsky but call me Elaine, please. Is Amy in?'

'She's actually asleep but come in. I can wake her.'

She followed him up a dark stairway into a shady lounge where Amy was curled on a red velvet chaise longue with her back to the room. The light was filtered green by a profusion of tropical plants which blocked the window. In the centre of the coffee table stood a vase of calla lilies, curling brown at the edges like burnt paper. Elaine guessed this was Amy's touch – she had a flair for homeliness. Cigarette packets, lighters, cups and dirty plates surrounded the vase.

'Aim, your mom's here,' said Jason, nudging Amy's shoulder.

'Huh? What time is it?' Amy rose and stretched. 'Momma! What are you doing here?'

'I was just passing.'

Elaine explained the reason for her visit while Amy bustled in and out of her bedroom, brushing her hair, applying lipstick, changing her loose jeans and T-shirt for a tighter outfit suitable for work, which was where she had to be in an hour. Jason made coffee in an old enamel pot and brought it in on a tray with cups and saucers and a jug of milk: Amy's influence, no doubt. Elaine had always found Jason somewhat evasive but she supposed he might just be shy. Amy certainly seemed the dominant force in their relation-ship, but then Amy was the dominant force in most of her relations, romantic or not. Elaine wondered if she was getting bored of Jason. The pair had visited a few weeks before and she'd got the distinct impression they weren't getting on. When they got back from Roger's scrapyard, where Amy had dumped her old Cadillac, Jason had been even quieter than usual. Perhaps some-thing untoward had happened there. She wouldn't have been surprised. Roger was a prime example of unreconstructed Québécois peasantry. Unbeknown to Saul, when she first moved to the Laurentians, Roger had vied for her affections, turning up in his pick-up truck with huge canisters of maple syrup, fresh from his own sugar shack in the middle of the woods. He had taken her there once and they had kept each other warm during a snowstorm, bathed in the sweet tang of burnt sugar and pine wood.

'I don't see that much of Freya,' Amy was saying, swigging at her coffee. 'Our schedules don't really coincide because I'm always working in the evenings and she's at college in the day.'

'I went to Dawson today and her classmates said she hadn't been there for a few days. When was the last time you saw her?'

'Um . . . she came into the bar a couple of weekends ago . . .'

'How did she seem?'

'Oh, you know . . . bitching about Maureen . . . as ever. She seemed a little subdued, I guess.'

'Did she look ill?'

'She looked tired, she definitely looked tired . . .'

'Thin?'

'It's hard to say, I think she may have lost weight but I'm not sure . . . what do you think, Jason?'

'She's always been very slim since I've known her,' said Jason.

'Slim . . . not unhealthy thin?'

'Yeah.'

'Jason's being polite, he wouldn't say. Would you, honey?' Amy squeezed his hand. 'Oh, I forgot! She's got a new job at this place on St Laurent.'

'What kind of place? Why didn't you tell me before?' Sometimes, Elaine caught herself sounding exactly like her mother.

'I'm telling you now,' said Amy. 'Yeah, she's working in this boutique, right down the hill, almost into Chinatown. Selling clothes. She said she could probably get me a discount but I haven't got round to going yet.'

'Do you know the name of it?'

'Jason, can you remember the name . . . ?'

'Tango or samba or something . . .' Jason screwed up his forehead. 'Mojo?'

'Samba! That's what it was . . . Boutique Samba.'


Elaine left with Amy, walking alongside her between the rows of plastic chairs and tables outside the Greek restaurants on Rue Prince Arthur. They were set for the supper rush, their paper tablecloths flapping in the breeze. All had two-for-one deals on lobster, the specialty of the St Lawrence seaboard, which Elaine tried to like, as it had been forbidden during her childhood, but always found overrated. When they reached St Laurent, they kissed and parted, Amy walking up the Boulevard and Elaine walking down. She peered into the plate glass windows at the smart bars where the waitresses looked like models and the drinkers like millionaires. She wondered how anyone could relax in such a place. Their clinicality made them more like dentists' waiting rooms than somewhere to eat or drink.


The quality of the stores on St Laurent went downhill with the slope of the road. Past Sherbrooke, the storefronts were makeshift and raggedy. There was a barbershop-cum-watchmender and a travel agent which specialised in cheap flights to the Middle East. 'GET YOUR PASSPORT PHOTOS DONE HERE' read a sign on the door. The window display was decked out in yellowing black-and-white photographs of Arabs. Their clothes looked outdated and they had solemn, bilious expressions like people in Victorian sepia prints. There were several wholesalers, selling cheap jewellery and electrical equipment, and a Tunisian takeaway called Le Soleil. Boutique Samba was a double-fronted store next to this. Elaine climbed the steps with trepidation. The place looked seedy. The mannequins in the window were decorated in skimpy strips of Lycra. The store comprised two rooms, divided by a dingy corridor which led to a costume warehouse and the upstairs lofts. A dark, stocky man was lounging against the radiator in the corridor, smoking a cigarette. He smiled at Elaine and gestured for her to browse. In the larger of the two rooms, a tall man with midnight skin was behind the till, shooting plastic price tags onto clothes with a gun-shaped implement. Was this the black guy Maureen had been clucking about? He was wearing a white crocheted hat, which resembled something her mother might have used to cover a milk jug circa 1950. Still, he managed to carry it off with panache. He nodded at Elaine as she circled the clothes racks, fingering garments and taking discreet peeks at him. When she had checked her daughter was not in the other room, she approached the man in the corridor and asked him if Freya worked there.

'Freya . . . yes,' he replied slowly with a Middle Eastern accent. 'I send her out just now to Dunkeen Donuts. For coffee.'

'Will she be long?'

'No, not long. She get it there because next door,

I don't like.' He meant the Tunisian takeaway. Elaine
noticed the timbre of his voice was suffused with a
gentle smile, even when he was saying 'I don't like'.

'You are her mother?'

'I am.'

'I can tell – you look like each other, very much.'

The man's liquid brown eyes swished over her. He
was very handsome, very charming. But there was
aggression buried in him, like a dark whirlpool deep
beneath a mountain. Elaine had a finely tuned antenna
for violence. He would be slow to anger but when
roused, he would be vicious.

'Momma! What are you doing here!'

Elaine turned. There was Freya, with a cardboard
tray of Dunkin' Donuts coffee cups. She was wearing a
pink shirt which brought out the colour in her cheeks.
Her brown curls were escaping from her ponytail and
her green eyes were lit with amusement and surprise.
She was bouncing with a secret inner sparkle. It had
been a long time since Elaine had seen her daughter
look so happy.

'Hey, you took your time,' snapped the man.

Elaine's voice rose with relief, 'Freya, darling! How
are you?'

Her daughter's level gaze did not waver. 'I'm fine,
Momma. Absolutely fine.'

The black man appeared and took his coffee, passing
Freya a cigarette in exchange. Freya glanced at her mother
with a flicker of embarrassment but stuck the cigarette
in her mouth and took the man's proffered light.

'I didn't know you smoked, Freya,' said Elaine.

'You don't know everything about me, Momma.'

# Secrets of Voodoo

When the store was empty, Omar and Freya went into the yellow hallway and leaned against the gold-painted radiators for warmth. Sometimes Omar heated pitta bread on them, which they tore into pieces and ate dry. Though not a regular smoker, Freya accepted cigarettes from him out of companionship. Like a gentleman, he always offered her a match and then lit a joss stick to mask the smell of cigarette smoke. He persisted in flicking ash over the floor even after she had just mopped it.

'Don't worry – it doesn't matter,' he soothed in his slow, gentle voice but Freya was irritated nonetheless.

They took turns to buy mint tea and honey cakes from the Tunisian takeaway next door. The cakes were a figure-of-eight made from orange batter deep-fried in oil. The mint cut through their wincing sweetness, though Omar always poured six sachets of sugar into his tea. One day the Tunisians questioned his excessive demand for sugar and he promptly boycotted their shop. He pretended it was for hygiene reasons ('I once saw a mouse in there. I was walking past and I saw a mouse, I swear to you.') but Freya knew better. From then on he insisted they patronise Dunkin' Donuts on Ste. Catherine instead, which was in the middle of the red-light district and always crammed with down-and-outs coughing into their coffees.

Omar was very particular. The broken mirrors in the changing rooms had to be cleaned with vinegar and newspaper rather than paper towels. The splintered floorboards had to be mopped in a precise circular motion with very little water. The shirts had to be folded into exact thirds.

On her first day, he explained his sales technique to Freya in solemn detail: 'It is all psychology. In Iran I was a psychology student so I understand this.'

The customer had to be left to browse but secretly watched to see which garments they liked. After five minutes they should be offered assistance. Once in the changing room, they were to be plied with the items that had originally interested them.

'Flirt with the customer all the time. Make him feel he is looking sexy. This is the most important thing,' said Omar.

'What if the customer is a girl?'

'Make her feel she is sexy too. I flirt with all of them – men and women. If their boyfriend or girlfriend is there don't flirt too much but still make them feel sexy. You think you can do this?'

'I think so.' In truth, she didn't think she could. She had always been astonished by the shameless way her friends batted their eyelids, tossed their hair and held men's gazes for just a fraction longer than necessary. Amy, her sister, liked to play a game called 'Be Sexy With', which involved toying flirtatiously with whatever objects were to hand: teasing the tines of a fork with her tongue; caressing the curves of a pepper grinder; using a napkin as a yashmak. Freya was hopeless at it.

A clean-cut boy in cream Chinos came through the door. Freya watched as he disrupted the display of folded sweaters.

'*Don't stare*,' whispered Omar.

Freya sidled around the shop, tweaking at garments and straightening hangers unnecessarily. When she looked up the boy was still flicking idly through the sweaters.

'I really think that would suit you,' said Freya.

'Which one?' The boy had his hand on a pale pink turtleneck.

'The turtleneck. Maybe not the pink but what about the black?'

'Black?'

'Yes, black turtlenecks – very Left Bank, intellectual, Beatnik, Parisien –' She caught Omar watching her with wry amusement. Too quickly, she blurted: 'I just love men in black turtlenecks. I think they're so understated and sexy.'

'Right . . .' The boy sounded sceptical. 'I was sort of just looking for something warm . . .'

'Something chunky?'

'I guess so.'

'How about this?' Freya shook out a cable-knit jersey the colour and texture of lumpy porridge. 'This will make you look really chunky, really manly – the kind of guy who could build fires.'

'I *can* build fires.'

'You can? Wow. That is *so* attractive. Women really go for men who can build fires. I certainly do . . . Would you like to try this on. I can tell already it's going to suit you.'

'Uh, well, thanks but I gotta go . . .' The boy edged out of the door.

When he was gone Omar hove into view waggling his finger, 'You must be cool, cool. Too excited, you lose us customers. Canadian girls, perhaps they are no good at flirting?'


In retrospect, Freya could pinpoint the exact moment when Omar began to desire her.

He had been bragging about his former life as a professional boxer, the champion of the Isfahan heavy-weight league.

'Everybody was crazy about boxing. We used to get up at five in the morning to watch Mohammed Ali on TV.'

He showed her how he would rub his nose before each fight to make it soft so it never got broken, and then put up his fists, his face set with dark determina-tion.

'I can imagine you were pretty good,' said Freya.

'I was. The best.' He grinned.

'I can punch.'

'I bet you can't. Most girls they don't know how.'

'I'm not most girls.'

'OK. Punch me.' Omar squared up to her, puffing his chest out.

Freya slammed her right fist into his shoulder with impressive force and at that instant she saw a fire flare in his brown eyes.

'You remind me of my wife. I show her how to make punches and sometimes she comes at me and won't stop. I say 'Stop, stop, stop' but she keeps on coming at me.'

After this Omar became more suggestive.

Freya brought in her favourite hipster pants, which had been ruined by photographic fluid at college, in the hope that Misteva, the drag queen who made all the store's clothes, could fashion another pair. Omar held the pants in the air and slowly unzipped the flies, locking his eyes with Freya's throughout.

'They're a really good fit,' she said.

'Yes I can see.'

Once she caught him observing her while she devoured a submarine sandwich and another time as she luxuriated in the heat of the radiator on her back.

'You like that, do you?' he had said on each occasion, and she guessed he divined some evidence of sensuality in these gestures. She started using her friends' pretty tricks, lowering her lashes coyly, throwing back her head when she laughed at his jokes and catching his admiring gaze a little too deliberately. The way he could be so easily manipulated was intoxicating. Each weekend she vowed she would not encourage him but the long empty hours left nothing to do but flirt. Her learning curve in the art of flirting was steep and from being a complete ingénue, she became a past master.

One afternoon, while they were lounging on the old red velvet cinema seats at the back of the hallway, she pulled off her sweater and accidentally snapped her necklace, scattering beads everywhere.

'Here – let me help you.' Omar's fingers darted between her thighs where some of the beads had fallen.

'Omar! Stop it!' Freya leapt up, thrilled and shocked, strewing more beads to the ground. On hands and knees, he helped her search for sparkles among the ash. She found most of them because he spent more time looking down her shirt than on the floor. He cupped the beads in his clammy palm for her to pick out and restring on the remaining thread. After a few concentrated minutes he tipped the beads into his crotch.

'I am not picking them out of there!' She pushed him away.

He chuckled. 'OK, OK – I will give them to you one by one.'

Freya had met Omar's wife once, a well-spoken English woman named Annabel, who had come in with their four-year-old daughter, Aliyah.

'She likes to check out the girls I take on,' Omar explained.

Annabel had chatted with Freya while Omar, as was his habit, withdrew into the toilet with the sports section from the *Montreal Gazette*. His bowels couldn't move without reading the sports section and he became distressed if it was mislaid.

'I don't want you to feel that I'm being nosey but in the past Omar has taken on these awful girls who are completely surly to the customers and very rude to me,' Annabel had said. 'Sometimes I just wonder what they're up to.'

Freya smiled and nodded sympathetically.

After she had gone, Omar said, 'I think my wife likes

you,' which clearly meant Annabel didn't consider her a threat.

'You can bet your bottom dollar that if Omar starts an affair with you, his wife'll blame you, not him,' her sister Amy said, crossing her arms and nodding sagely. 'That's the way it always works – it's psychology.' Amy was an expert on older men – she was on the verge of having an affair with her boss, Ruey, and was obsessed with some grizzled old mechanic up near their mother's place.

Freya was guiltily delighted that Amy thought an affair with Omar was even possible. 'Give him one signal and he'll leap,' said Amy.

'Do you really think so?'

Amy's pronouncement made the possibility more real. The only drawback was Annabel. Freya spent hours wrangling over the problem, drawing up columns of pros and cons in her diary. Annabel was the main con. If she hadn't met the woman she could have pushed her out of her mind. She knew it was unsisterly to steal another woman's man. Freya was a feminist: she had read the first chapter of *The Female Eunuch*, after being pruriently intrigued by its cover on her stepmother's bookshelf.

'That book was my bible in the seventies,' Maureen declared. 'Germaine Greer opened our eyes like you wouldn't believe.'

'Shut up and cook the dinner,' said Joey.

*

One weekday evening Freya went to collect her wages. As usual Omar had been unable to pay her at the weekend. Freya found him slumped in semi-darkness on a beanbag in the side room, working his way through a box of dates.

'In the slums in Iran there are people who eat just one date a day. That is all they have to eat,' he said. 'A man can live on one date a day. It has everything he needs to live.'

'He'd still be pretty hungry though, eh?'

Omar laughed. Digging in his pocket, he held out her wages in one hand and an extra ten dollars in the other: 'Will you go and get me some beer? And some for you too.'

'Omar, I have to go.' She reached out for her money but he pulled it away.

'Go where? Where do you have to go?'

His warm brown eyes froze over. She couldn't remember where she had to go. The way he was looking at her was no longer like flirting.

'Are you scared, Freya?'

'Scared? What of?'

'I think you are scared of being alone with me.'

'Don't be so silly, Omar. I spend every weekend alone with you.'

'Tonight you seem scared.'

'I'm not. Omar, please can I have my wages?' She grabbed at the thin wad of notes but he whisked them out of reach.

'Only if you will have a beer with me.'

'I'll have one beer with you and then I've gotta go. OK?'

He placed the money in her cold nervous hand and folded her fingers over it. His hands felt hot and moist and he was smiling with satisfaction. She knew he was watching her as she tripped down the steps and across the road to the Indian store. This was where she bought the submarine sandwiches, assembled with agonizing slowness by the tall Indian man, and where Omar sent her for change if customers wanted to pay for clothes with anything bigger than a fifty.

'Business – good?' asked the tall Indian, nodding towards Boutique Samba as he wrapped two bottles of Boréale Rousse in a paper bag.

'Not bad,' said Freya.

'Omar – good?'

'A bit naughty.'

'One date a day,' said Omar, when she returned. His eyes had melted again, his old slow smile was back in place. He held a date aloft before popping it into his mouth. 'Iran is a very hard place.'

'Is that why you left?'

'Yes. It was becoming too hard.'

'In what way?'

'In many ways.'

He told her how things changed after the Shah was overthrown; how he was arrested time and again for drinking, for partying, for having fun. Then Iran went to war against Iraq and he was called up to fight.

'I told them: I don't want to be killed and I don't want to kill people.' He said it with a sweet simplicity as if he was talking of an ice-cream flavour he didn't particularly care for. He explained how he saved up his money for a fake passport and a one-way ticket to

Istanbul. At the airport the immigration official mistook him for a long-lost friend and waved him through without question. For five months he hid with Iranian contacts in Istanbul before the Turkish police caught up with them.

'They wanted to torture us,' he said, still smiling benevolently.

'Torture! Oh my God! Really?'

'Yes. Really.'

'Why?'

'Because we were illegal. We weren't supposed to be there.'

'What did they do? What kind of torture?'

'They wanted to take off all our clothes and tie us up and put water and electric on our fingers and balls and give us an electric shock. I was so scared. They did it to all my friends but not me.'

'Why not you?'

'I talked to them, the policemen. I made them like me. I was lucky.'

Freya stared at him in horror. Omar's face remained serene.

'God, I can't believe that this kind of thing goes on.'

'Not everywhere is nice like Canada.'

The tortured friends were deported back to Iran but he managed to stay in Turkey and escape to Rhodes, smuggled in the bottom of a fisherman's boat. For six months he picked olives on a farm on the island. But Greece was too poor. He wanted to make money. He bought a Canadian passport for two thousand dollars and flew to Montreal via Prague.

'I could not speak English or French but I had this Canadian passport. It was crazy. The only kind of work I could do when I got here was in a factory and I lived in one room with six other Iranians. We had one mattress and we took it in turns to sleep on it. We went out drinking all night and dancing and meeting girls. Those first few months in this city were the worst times but they were also the best.'

His charm had saved his life. Sitting alone with him in the darkness, Freya felt her skin prickle with fear.

'Maybe I should go.'

'No, stay here. I will buy you another beer.'

'Well, uh, I don't know . . .'

'Please. I like talking to you, Freya. You are a good listener.'

'OK, I'll stay for one more.'

He dashed to the Indian store with uncharacteristic haste and returned with two beers and two samosas. She gobbled them down and rose to leave.

'No, don't go.' Omar jumped up, knocking over a beer bottle, and clasped her against his chest. 'I want you to stay.'

'Omar, stop it . . .' His clumsiness was embarrassing.

'I just want to kiss you.'

She made to kiss his cheek but he forced his lips onto hers. He tasted of smoke and spices. Their noses clashed and she wrestled free from his heavy arms.

'Omar, what about your wife?'

'In Iran we have a saying: "One rose and then the spring still comes".'

'What does that mean?'

'"One rose and then the spring still comes."'

'I don't understand.'

'It means a man can have another woman but go back to his wife and she don't know and it is all OK.'

'Yeah, well, maybe that's the case in Iran but in Canada it would be more like, "One rose and then the shit hits the fan".'

The next time she saw him a froideur hung between them like the frozen mist on the street outside. He remained on the beanbag all afternoon with a bag of almonds, watching the hockey game on an old teak-framed TV, which he had placed in the window with a mannequin wearing hotpants on top. Freya loitered in the doorway, mesmerised by the loops and swerves of the skaters.

'I bet I can guess your star sign,' she said, trying to instigate some of their old bonhomie.

'What?'

'Your star sign: I bet I can guess it.'

'Go on.'

'Taurus.'

'How did you know?'

'Certain star signs I can sense. Taurus is one of them. Strong, stocky, solid, sensual . . .'

'. . . yes, that's me . . .'

'. . . stubborn, greedy, can at times tend towards laziness . . .'

'Have you cleaned the mirrors?'

'Yes.'

'The floor?'

'I did it this morning.'

'You know, Freya, you got to make more sales. You're not selling enough.'

'It's pretty difficult when there's no customers.'

'I think you got one now.'

A boy in a baseball cap and baggy pants mooched in with an off-hand 'Salut'. Omar shoved Freya towards him, hissing, '*Flirt, flirt.*'

The boy was unmoved by her entreaties to buy a pair of pants identical to the ones he had on.

'They look really sexy. The girls will love them.'

'Actually, I'm gay.'

'The boys will love them as well,' Freya blustered, 'Boys or girls. They'll both love 'em.'

'Salut . . .' The boy left with a dismissive wave.

'You make a sale?' called Omar, when the boy had gone.

'No.'

'Why not?'

'He was gay.'

'Oh.'

'Yes.'

'Maybe I need to get a boy instead of you.'

'Whatever.'

'You know I got a new partner to help run the shop?'

'Oh yeah? Business partner?'

'Yes. His name is Dick. He is from Haiti.'

'Dick? What kind of a name is that?'

'I don't know. His name.'

It was some time before she met Dick. He sprang up the steps as she was leaving one Saturday evening and towered over her in a seal-fur coat that matched his strange grey eyes. She noted the silver ring on his little finger as she shook his hand.

'Hey girl. I like your style,' he said, looking her up and down.

'Yours ain't bad either.' She flushed at how sassy she'd become.

'You the weekend girl, eh? Omar tell me about you.'

'Yeah. You must be Dick.'

'That's my streetname.'

'Interesting.'

The next day she discovered his actual name was Deck, short for Dechelan Robillard and he had a little boy called Fabrice, whose mother was a six-foot stripper.

The following weekend Omar was absent and Deck came in to mind the store. He was dressed entirely in black with a white crochet hat over his dreadlocks. Though the temperature had dropped to minus thirteen and it was snowing, he sent Freya out to drum-up business with flyers advertising a twenty-five percent sale. She stood outside St Laurent metro paralysed with cold.

When all the flyers were gone she returned to find Deck sprawled on one of the old cinema seats smoking. His dark angular figure was thrown into sharp relief by the red and the yellow.

'I'd love to take a photo of you.' She looked through squared fingers at him. 'I could use you in my project for school. It's all about Montreal As A Melting Pot Of Multiculturalism.'

'No.'

'Why not?'

'*Parce que'est mon image*. Nobody can have my image.'

'What are you talking about?'

'My image is part of Boutique Samba. The trademark. I want to open more stores in Montreal, then Toronto, Vancouver, move into America and one day Samba will be like Nike or Coca-Cola . . .'

'A global brand. World domination.'

'*Exactement*. That's why I need to keep my image just for me.'

'Right.'

There was a pause. Deck blew two smoke rings. Freya watched them float like miniature halos, then wobble, expand and disintegrate.

'Can I have a cigarette?'

'No. *C'est ma dernière*.' He showed her the last in the pack.

'If you were a gentleman you'd give it to me.'

'If you were a lady you wouldn't ask for it . . . Anyway I'm not a gentleman.' He produced a quarter. 'Here's twenty-five cents – you can go and buy one from the guy over there.'

'The Indian?'

'*Ouais*.'

'He sells single cigarettes?'

'If he know you.'

'He knows me.'

'Go on then. *Vas-y*.' He shooed her away.

'You're too kind.'

The Indian man gave her *une seule clope* from a

pack of Du Maurier's when she laid twenty-five cents on the counter.

'Business – good?' he asked.

'Not bad.'

'Deck – good?'

'No.'

Back in the store, the boy with the birthmark from the loft upstairs was talking to Deck. From the way he spoke French she could tell he wasn't Québécois. He broke off ice-cold chunks of chocolate for them from a large bag he had in his hand. Freya took alternate tastes of it and the cigarette. When the boy had gone Deck said, *'Le chocolat – c'est aphrodisiaque.'*

*'Tout est aphrodisiaque pour les hommes,'* said Freya, *'Le chocolat, le vin, les fruits de mer . . . les légumes, les fruits, les épiciers indiens, les viandes* halal . . .' These last she read from the sign outside the Indian store.

*'C'est quoi, la plus grande peur des gens?'* said Deck, gazing philosophically at his spirals of smoke.

'I don't know. What is peoples' biggest fear?'

*'Devinez.'*

'I don't know. *Je ne sais pas. Dites-le-moi.'*

*'La peur de l'amour – ça, c'est la plus grande peur des gens.'*

'The fear of love? No. *Non. Ce n'est pas ça. C'est la peur d'être seul.* The fear of being alone.'

*'Mais on naît seul. On meurt seul donc ce n'est pas une peur.'*

'People still fear being alone even though they are born and die alone.'

'Being alone – I do not fear it. *Je n'en ai pas peur, moi.'*

*

Although it was a Saturday night the snow had smoth-
ered the sounds of the city, making it unnaturally quiet
as Freya trudged up St Laurent at the end of the day.
Her hat was pulled over her ears, so she only noticed
someone was behind her when she looked around to
cross Sherbrooke.

'Hey, girl, you goin' home?' said Deck. 'You wanna
share a cab?'

'I thought you wanted to be alone.'

'No. I don't mean that when I was talking about
being alone. I mean I don't have no fear of being
alone. Let's share a cab.'

'I don't have any money. Omar didn't pay me yet.'

'I pay.' He hailed a cab.

They sat in silence and peered out at the fairy-lit
streets as the cab trawled through the slush. Deck
wound down the window and lit up his last cigarette.
The cab passed the turn-off to St Dominique, where
Freya lived, but she didn't ask the driver to stop. At
Parc La Fontaine, Deck handed the driver a ten dollar
bill.

'So, we are here,' said Deck, when they were out on
the sidewalk.

Freya waited for him to offer her a cup of coffee or
some such euphemism, but he simply assumed she
was following him as he unlocked the door to his
apartment block.

'I used to live in a five thousand square foot loft,'
he warned, as they climbed up three flights of stairs to
his 2½, which overlooked the ice-rink in the park. A

few skaters were still wheeling around, illuminated by strings of white lights that had been flung through the trees like giant pearl necklaces.

He poured two glasses of beer and they sat opposite each other in the tiny living room – him on the brown velour couch and her on the green chaise longue. His face merged into the darkness and, though he appeared to be half-asleep, she could tell he was looking at her. She realised she was holding her breath.

'What happened to the five thousand square foot loft?'

'Oh. I moved out. I needed a change.'

'You like change?'

'Yeah.'

'You're a Gemini?'

'How you know?'

'I'm a Gemini. I can sense other Geminis.'

'How?'

'The way you said you needed a change – typical Gemini. I can sense Taureans too. Certain star signs I can sense.'

'I was born on a Wednesday on the 21 June. I was my mother's middle child born on the middle of the week in the middle of the year.'

'What time?'

'Ten in the morning.'

'Shame it wasn't twelve.'

'Yes.'

The way he looked at her made her stomach lurch. To avoid his eye, she wandered over to the window. Propped on the sill were several framed photographs of a woman in a blue wig, poised carefully on a chair with her long hands reaching down her long legs to her ankles.

'Is this your girlfriend?'

'Not my girlfriend: the mother of my boy.' His voice was tetchy.

'She's a stripper, right?'

'Yes, that's what she is. I don't judge. It's her money. I don't take it.'

It seemed best to abandon the subject. 'Can I have a cigarette?' Freya asked.

'I don't have no more. You know that. Stop being nervous.'

'I am nervous.'

'Why?'

'Because you're a stranger.'

'I can't do nothing to you – you know where I live, you know where I work.' He held out his hand. With half a second's hesitation she allowed him to pull her towards him onto the couch. She was acutely aware of the stink of her T-shirt, an orange one she'd borrowed from her brother because she liked the colour.

'I'm sorry about my shirt. It's dirty.'

'I know. I smelt it.'

It didn't seem to put him off. His skin felt like moist rubber and his body was as tightly sprung as an elastic band. Around his neck, a large gold cross flashed against his night-time chest. So. This is it. This is it. This is it, was all Freya thought as she watched car lights swoop across the ceiling and smelt the hot musk of his body. When it was over, he dropped the used condom onto the floor, and they lay and watched a girl on TV figure-skating to 'Heart of Glass'. Freya took a sit-up bath in the tiny tub and sang the tune to herself. The only personal effects in the bathroom were a razor, some Dax hair oil and a wind-up plastic frog, which obviously belonged to Fabrice. The minimalism of Deck's existence was very stylish.

When Freya returned to the living room, the condom was gone and Deck was fully dressed and had changed channels to a film about a young boy at a Catholic school.

'*C'est comme à l'école.*'

'In Haiti?'

'Yeah.'

'Tell me about Haiti.'

Reluctantly, he told her a few things – about the mangos, his grandparents' farm and his near-death experience at the age of eleven.

'I was run over by a truck. It went right over me. I was underneath it. No injuries at all.'

'Was it voodoo?'

'No. Of course not. It was just good luck.'

'What is voodoo?'

'*"Voodoo" – c'est le pouvoir.* Power. *Tu as le "voodoo".*'

'I do?'

'*Bien sûr.*'

'But I want to know what voodoo *really* is.'

'*C'est le catholicisme.*'

'Surely it's more than that – you know magic and stuff.'

He considered for a moment: 'Voodoo means black.'

'Is that why you can't tell me? Because I'm white?'

'That's right.'

He put his hat on and drew himself into the corner

of the couch so that no part of them was touching any more. Freya extracted his long spidery hand. Her hand lay in sharp relief against his – the image illustrated perfectly 'Montreal As A Melting Pot Of Multiculturalism' but it seemed best not to broach the subject of photographs again. She felt frustrated that the colour of her skin forbade her from finding out the secrets of voodoo. If she softened him up a little he might relent though the unresponsive weight of his hand on her knee did not bode well. She twisted the ring on his little finger.

'Who's that?' She pointed to the profile embossed in the silver.

'César.' Irritably, he pulled his hand away.

'Do you want me to go?'

'No, you can stay.' He gestured off-handedly to the chaise longue. After five long minutes lying under her coat, she said, 'Why don't you come over here, Deck? I feel funny sleeping here on my own.'

'I never sleep with anyone who's not my girlfriend.'

'Oh.'

'I am not a person to give affection. That's not the kind of person I am.'

'OK.'

'If you want affection you should go to Omar.'

'Fine.' Freya began to pull on her jeans.

'I have done wrong?' His grey eyes gazed up at her, suddenly penitent.

'No.'

'You didn't like it?'

'I liked it. Makes me wish I'd done it before.'

\*

All the way home, through the tranquil, drifted streets, her smile kept breaking through. Her virginity had weighed her down since the eleventh grade, when she claimed Peter Filbert had taken it at a Hallowe'en party while she was dressed as a victim of *The Texas Chainsaw Massacre*. (He had come as Edward Scissorhands.) The fiction became so firmly entrenched she almost believed it herself. Peter Filbert helpfully moved out to BC in the twelfth grade so he wasn't able to corroborate the facts. Now it really was gone forever. She had lost her virginity before she could legally have a drink. She felt unburdened, weightless, light as a snowflake. She laughed aloud and the people walking past looked at her like she was just another crazy drunk.

Maureen opened the apartment door while she was still scrabbling at the lock.

'Where the hell have you been? Me and your dad have been worried sick.'

Freya stomped past up to her room. Joey's snores rumbled through the apartment. The scent of sex wafted from her clothes as she undressed. When she looked in the mirror she swore she looked more wanton than she had done that morning.

# The Former Miss India of 1979

Several Saturdays in a row, since getting back from Alberta, Jess had gone to La Cabane for a salad. The salad featured salami, peppers, olives, artichokes, green beans, feta cheese and hearts of palm. It was tasty and cheap and if she still felt hungry their frites with pepper sauce were good. The bar was manned by Freddie, who talked at anyone within earshot. Jess didn't mind going to La Cabane alone – she liked the anonymity, feeling like a *flâneur* amid the kaleidoscopic pageant of the Plateau. This was the freedom she had craved while out west, where she had been employed by a local council to paint murals across a small town named Legal. She had lodged with a family of painfully stilted religious maniacs. Mealtimes had been an eternity of squeaking cutlery and nervous coughs, preceded by Grace. She had spent hours wandering between cornfields that stretched into infinity, smoking the cigarettes that were forbidden in her lodgings and wondering what was going on in Montreal. Most evenings she went to bed at nine because there was nothing else to do.

It was way past her former bedtime when Jess arrived at La Cabane that particular Saturday. One woman was eating at a table in the corner and there were only three drinkers at the bar: Raymond, Larry and Gordon. Raymond was a middle-aged Quebecker, who exuded an almost embarrassing virility with his Burt Reynolds moustache, tight white vest and intent way of eating. His shiny Chelsea boots were a foppish anomaly in his otherwise full-blooded machismo.

Larry was a lounge lizard with improbably mahogany hair. He sipped Beefeater gin with soda and lined up the plastic stirrers on the bar to keep track of how many he'd drunk.

Gordon, a whiskery old Newfoundlander, worked unpaid as Freddie's keg man, hauling crates of beer up from the cellar and changing the barrels. In return he was allowed an unending supply of Mick's Red on 'promo'.

'Hey, Jessie.' Freddie was the only person with the cheek to call her this. Raymond, Larry and Gordon merely nodded and continued sucking down their drinks.

'Hey, Fred.' Jess took her usual chair and ordered her usual salad from the scruffy blonde waitress, who slammed down a napkin, a knife, a fork and a basket of bread with stylish haste.

'How's it going?' Freddie wiped the beer taps unnecessarily. He made a big production of his job, was forever emptying near-empty ashtrays, polishing the gleaming bar and re-aligning the spirits so the labels were parallel.

'Oh, you know, same as ever.'

'Knocked off a few masterpieces since last we met?'

'Yeah, right.' Jess was studying fine art at Concordia. She had been working on a new series of paintings but it would be pointless sharing this with Freddie. He liked the image of serving drinks to artists but had no interest in their actual art. Her new idea had popped up earlier in the week, while cycling through Westmount. The neighbourhood's pristine avenues and crescents were lined with modern mansions, each a jumble of marble lions, Doric columns, half-timbered walls, turrets and cupolas. These architectural pretensions struck Jess with a nameless dread that she could only capture in paint. Fizzing with inspiration she cycled higher and higher to Summit Crescent, where the super-rich lived. A red and white Budweiser airship slid into view between the rooftops. For something so huge its silent stealth was unnerving but the sheer silliness of it cheered Jess. She imprinted the image on her memory and freewheeled down to the Plateau where all the action was.

'Hey, wake up. Your salad's here.' Freddie snapped his fingers at Jess as the waitress banged down the plate of salad. 'Oh Christ, look who we got here.' His attention had zipped to a droopy old man who was tottering in with a shabby suitcase. He wore a dirty raincoat and a battered fedora, as if he had just stepped out of the Depression.

'Ten dollars?' The old man held the suitcase aloft.

'Thanks but no thanks, Lester.'

With a shrug, Lester cadged a cigarette from Gordon and shambled out.

'Jeez. Lester. Every day he comes in,' said Freddie, 'And everyday it's something different.'

'Do you remember the time he came in with a bale of hay?' Gordon broke into wheezing laughter. 'Christ knows where he got it from but at the end of the day I went out and he'd dumped it outside the door.'

'I once bought quite a nice chair from him. Paid five bucks for it, fixed it up and it looked good as new.'

'Ruey once bought a vacuum cleaner off him. Gave him twenty bucks. We've still got it. It even works.' Ruey, who was Portuguese, co-owned La Cabane with his brother Amerigo. Gordon leaned into the bar: 'Hey – you seen who's here tonight?'

'Oh yeah.' Freddie glanced at the woman on the corner table and pulled a wry face.

Jess regretted turning round because the woman smiled and beckoned her over.

'No, my dear, it's you I require,' she said, as Jess checked over her shoulder. The woman's voice boomed across the bar as if she was auditioning for a Shakespeare play.

'Now you're for it,' muttered Freddie, 'You better go and see what she wants.'

Close up, the woman was quite beautiful. Her hair was so black it had a peacock sheen when it caught the light, her heavy-lashed eyes were enormous and her smile was like sunshine breaking through a cloud. She looked Indian, so Jess was surprised to see her chugging back a pint of beer. Jess had assumed Indian women were too subservient to drink and certainly too subservient to get drunk.

'My dear, come and sit, come and sit.' The woman had an English accent which, beneath her slurring, was brittle as bone china. 'Is it good, the salad? I had the fried chicken.' She lifted an oily vegetable from Jess's plate into her mouth.

'Hey, that's my artichoke!'

'Delicious it was too. Can I have that olive?' Without waiting for a reply, she snatched it away.

'You're not annoying our customers are you, Kiran?' shouted Freddie.

'No, I'm bloody well not. This sweet lady – pray, what is your name, my dear?'

'Jess.'

'Jessica and I are having *un petite tête-à-tête*. Bring me another beer and one for sweet Jessica.' She snapped out the order, brushing aside Jess's attempts to correct her name. When the beers arrived, she lowered her voice and said, 'Of course he doesn't know who I am, that *bar steward*.'

'Who are you?'

'My dear, *I* am the former Miss India of 1979.'

'Really! 1979. The year I was born.'

'Was it? Oh, 1979 was so long ago but I remember it so well. Standing outside the Grosvenor Hotel, shivering under the stone-grey sky, my lovely gown getting soaked by the never-ending deluge.' Her voice swooned dreamily, as if she was telling a fairy story. 'My father was a very handsome man from India and my mother was a very beautiful woman from Italy.'

'Right.'

Kiran continued as if Jess had not spoken. '– she had strawberry-blonde hair, sky-blue eyes, skin like a ripe peach. She was an air hostess. My father was a pilot. They fell in love, madly, desperately in love. As soon as my father saw my mother he had to possess her. He stole her away from Rome and took her to Delhi.'

'Really.' Jess sensed Kiran had told this story many times before.

'– that was where I spent my childhood, my sister and I . . . But we were taken from my mother . . . She was considered unfit to rear us . . . she was a sweet delicate butterfly, charming and entirely decorative . . . She knew nothing of the world, of the harshness of the world. We were torn away from her. *Torn*. The cruelty.' She fixed Jess with a dramatic stare: 'That can kill a woman – being torn asunder from her children. It killed her. Literally. She drank herself to death.'

'I'm really sorry to hear that.'

From her purse, Kiran produced a black-and-white passport photo of a young wide-eyed girl: 'That was me. I was sixteen when I became Miss India. Observe my charm, my fresh innocent charm . . . I had every advantage . . .'

'You were very attractive.'

'I was a nice-looking girl, entirely adequate for the role that was required of me,' Kiran conceded, snapping up the flame of a gold Zippo and applying it to the end of a Gauloise. 'You know, I was even chosen to be a *Playboy* bunny. Hugh Hefner handpicked me. He saw me in the Grosvenor and he wanted me. Of course he did – what man wouldn't want to possess that fresh innocent girl? But I turned him down, naturally. It was impossible. I was too young. And I knew I had a decadent personality . . .' She exhaled a plume of smoke and flashed an arch smile at Jess. Jess wondered what it was like to have a decadent personality.

A sheaf of other photographs was tossed onto the table – mainly of Kiran's sister, Reena, who had worked in a Hong Kong casino for many years but now lived in Las Vegas. A pair of new sequinned mules were thrust into the air for Jess's approbation. A long rigma-role was related, regarding another pair of more divine shoes, which Kiran failed to purchase because the only sizes left were too large for her dainty feet. Her many charming, successful friends were cited along with her current stop-gap, pin-money job as a waitress at the Three Amigos on Ste. Catherine. With a glazed autom-aton grin, Kiran mimed the way she waited on tables: 'How may I help you? How would you like your steak? Would you like something to drink?'

Jess tried to catch Freddie's eye for moral support but he was tossing a bottle of Absolut from one hand over his shoulder and catching it behind him with his other hand, Tom Cruise *Cocktail* style.

Sighing over her sixteen-year-old self, oblivious to the sniggers from the bar, Kiran said, 'I had so many advantages but I was angry, angry, angry. Abused!'

The word was a challenge, a cue to inquire further but Jess ignored it. Kiran struck her with the same nameless dread as the Westmount mansions. She was corrupt yet mesmerising, international trash, empty at the core. All her glamour had receded to nothing. She sat folded in on herself like a shut fan. 'I'm happy,' she insisted as if Jess had said otherwise, 'Terribly happy. I allow the gods to lead me, my dear – the gods, you know – they know.' She lifted her eyes to the heavens then dropped back to earth.

Jess wondered how she could get away from the woman without seeming rude. Like many drunks Kiran was teetering on a knife-point between friendliness and aggression and one false move could make her cobra fangs lash out with poison.

'Do you have any weed in your possession?' asked Kiran.

'Weed? In my possession?' The conversation had taken an unexpected turn. Was the woman an under-cover cop? Was this whole thing a sting? Jess's nameless dread began to have a name.

'Jessica, if you are fearful that I am a plain-clothes police officer, you are entirely mistaken. I want to buy some marijuana and I thought you might have some, that is all.'

'Erm . . . no. I don't.' The bag of British Columbian skunk in Jess's back pocket felt like it was on fire. She'd bought it from her younger brother that afternoon. Josh, who was a mathematical genius, ran a drug-dealing operation known as The Prescription from their parents' home. From six till eleven each night, he and his friend Phil bicycled around the Plateau responding to calls from a select bunch of clients who had been issued with the coveted Prescription phone number and password. Josh and Phil were the most mild-mannered drug dealers in existence but their business was highly profitable. They supplied Jess with cut-price high-quality grass, which she smoked without ceremony. It was a staple part of her day, like coffee and cigarettes.

'I don't believe you, Jessica.' Kiran ignited her smile. 'I suspect you have some right in your back pocket. You strike me as that kind of girl.'

Jess had two options: create a short, sharp scene ensuring it would be impossible to return to La Cabane again for fear of bumping into Kiran, or be polite, sell the woman some dope and get through the next half hour with both their dignities intact.

'How much do you want?' asked Jess. She had never been one for creating scenes. In any case, she could do with some extra cash.

'How much do you have?'

'I don't know – two grams or so.'

'How much is it worth?'

'Er . . . well . . .' Jess glanced around nervously.

'Shall we repair to the back alley?'

'The back alley?'

'Yes. If you go to the bathroom there is a door which leads out to the alley behind the bar. It is where they deposit their refuse. I will go first and then you will follow me. I'll give you the money and we can have a friendly smoke to seal the deal. Good idea?'

Without waiting for a reply, she was up, slopping beer from her glass but stalking across the bar with a surprisingly assured step. Jess ignored Freddie's raised eyebrows as she picked up her pint glass and followed.

The back alley was dank with trash and puddles of a dubious liquid that could not be rain as there had been a heatwave for the past month. That night, though, clouds obscured the stars and there was a crackling expectation of thunder. Further up the alley three boys played football, darting among the laundry strung between the balconies above.

Kiran was sitting with her knees crossed on the penultimate step of a fire escape, dangling a spangled mule from one foot as if she was perched at a cocktail bar.

Jess pulled out the bag of skunk and passed it to Kiran. Kiran opened the bag, her eyes fixed on Jess all the while, and sniffed the contents luxuriously as if it were a glass of fine wine with a complex bouquet. She smiled broadly; 'Haven't got a clue whether it's any good or not. You could be selling me pizza herbs for all I know.'

If only she had thought of bringing out a bag of oregano with her. Jess cursed inwardly. 'Fifty bucks, the whole bag,' she said, in a clipped tone, like a decisive deal-cutter. How on earth did her brother do all this stuff and keep a straight face? More to the point, how on earth did he do it when he wasn't selling to a greenhorn like Kiran? 'Twenty-five for half a bag.' The price was slightly over the odds and Josh had originally sold it to her at a reduced price so the evening was turning out to be less of a disaster than she had feared.

'You're very masterful, aren't you, Jessica?' said Kiran. She scrabbled in her purse and brought out several crumpled notes and a handful of change, which she heaped messily into Jess's outstretched hands. 'Fifty dollars, the whole lot. Now. Would you like to join me for a joint?'

'Uh . . . well, I'd quite like to go back in and –'

'Oh darling, don't be boring!' Kiran ducked her head and made hurt Bambi eyes at Jess. 'You're not going to snub my invitation, are you? That would be very impolite.'

Jess tried to expel her weary sigh quietly. 'O-K. Go on. Roll one up.'

Kiran was instantly animated. 'Marvellous! Oh, but

unfortunately, I don't have any "papers" with which to roll a joint. *Darling?*'

Wordlessly, Jess handed her a packet of Zig-Zags. She watched as Kiran fumbled with the weed and the papers, giggling girlishly as one paper dissolved in the beer she had spilt on the step and another tore as she pulled it out of the packet. 'As you can see I have always been led into decadence by the will of others and I, myself, am an innocent when it actually comes to instigating the decadence −' she fluttered.

'What you're trying to say is you want me to roll?'

Kiran clasped her hands in front of her chest. 'Oh! Would you?'

Jess nodded. Within two minutes she had rolled a perfect joint which she sealed with one quick lollypop lick.

'The way you did that was most pleasing, darling,' said Kiran, lifting her glass and motioning with her eyes for Jess to copy her. 'To eternal elegance and poise. *Santé.*'

'Cheers.' Jess slugged her beer and patted her shirt pocket for her lighter but Kiran intervened with her Zippo.

'You know, Jessica, you should never toast like that,' she said, the flame glittering in her eyes as Jess inhaled.

'Like what?'

'The way you just did . . .' Kiran mimicked Jess, lifting her drink with averted eyes and a mumbled 'Cheers.'

'How should you toast then?'

'Like this . . . cheers, *santé, pröst, salud, yum sing . . .*' She toasted Jess heartily, with firm eye contact. 'You have to look like you mean it and say it with panache.

Otherwise you may as well not toast at all.'

'OK. Right. I'll endeavour to remember the correct procedure in future.'

Kiran held Jess's gaze for several seconds. Suddenly her thin hand shot out from her folded body and grabbed Jess's chin.

'You have good cheekbones, Jessica, strong cheek-bones.' She turned Jess's face this way and that as if she was considering an antique vase. 'I read faces so I am well versed in these matters. The nose – strong. The forehead is good too. The skin: reasonable. The mouth: adequate. The eyes: a little close together but they have a nice shape. The chin: weak. The rest of the features make up for the chin. However, you have not yet learned the art of making yourself attractive to the opposite sex, or indeed to the same sex.'

Jess jerked her chin away. The pressure of Kiran's touch was still apparent, as wince-inducing as finger-nails on a blackboard. She stood up. 'I need the bathroom.'

Kiran snatched the joint, shooing her away like an insect.


In the bathroom, Jess smoothed her hands over her forehead, her mouth, her chin. There was no mirror in which to check her face. She felt shaken by Kiran's judgment. And angry. It was shocking to hear someone slice through to the truth. Girlish fripperies had always bored her – her clothes were practical, her haircut was serviceable, her face was scrubbed clean – and she scorned the sly confidences and whispered confidences of female company. Or perhaps 'bored' and 'scorned' were the wrong words. Femininity *embarrassed* her. People would laugh if she wore a skirt, painted her lips, accentuated her nicely shaped but close-together eyes with mascara. They would do a double take if she joined in with the college gossip. She knew this refusal to play the game made her an outsider. At college she was not unpopular but she had no close friends. Her brother's drug dealing gave her a certain cachet though she never bragged about him. She went to classes, drew with fierce concentration and socialised minimally in the cafeteria. She was most at ease among men but, instinctively, she knew they found her too straightforward and lacking in coquetry to be sexually viable, though she could never and would never voice this thought the way the former Miss India of 1979 had done. Nevertheless, she couldn't show Kiran she cared. As she washed her hands, Jess plotted a cool escape.

The alley was empty when she returned. She considered sneaking away down the backstreets of St Laurent, before remembering her bar bill.

'Hey, how's your girlfriend?' called Freddie, as she counted out notes for the waitress who dug in her apron for change. Raymond, Larry and Gordon broke into heckling laughter. Kiran was back in the corner, deep in conversation with an Indian man who was selling single red roses wrapped in cellophane for five bucks.

'Are you talking to me?' Jess glared at Freddie.

'Only joking, Jessie.' Freddie beckoned her closer and lowered his voice: 'Seriously though, eh, watch out for that woman.'

'Why, what's the matter with her?'

'Well, apart from the obvious fact that she's totally insane, as you may have realised by now, she comes in here all the time and hits on girls. She even hit on Amy the last time she was in, ain't that right, Ame?'

The waitress put her hands on her hips in mock-annoyance: 'Freddie, what do you mean by "even hit on Amy"? Everyone hits on me.'

'Oh yeah, I forgot that you're totally irresistible to all members of both sexes.

Anyway, Jessie, what I'm trying to tell you is that woman is a lezzer.'

'A lesbian?'

'Yup. Total bunny-boiling, ball-breaking lezzer. She's hitting on you, I swear.'

'I'm sure she's not. But anyway, thanks for your concern.'

As Jess tried to sidle out of the bar unnoticed, Kiran suddenly turned around.

'Hey! You're not leaving are you, Jessica dearest?' she boomed.

'Uh . . . well, I have to get back and do some stuff.'

'Come and meet my friend Moeen.' She clutched the rose-seller's arm.

Reluctantly, Jess allowed Kiran to introduce her to Moeen.

'You want a rose?' he asked, pushing his bucket of roses towards her.

'Er . . . no thanks.'

'I'll buy one for her,' Kiran announced.

'No, no, please don't. I really don't want one.' But Jess's blusterings were ignored as Moeen and Kiran made their transaction in a language that sounded like glugging bottles. As soon as the rose had been bought and presented to Jess, he disappeared.

'One of my oldest friends. A dear, dear friend. We're from the same neighbourhood in Delhi. It is so soothing to speak Urdu with him.'

'Yeah, I'm sure it must be nice – remind you of home.' Jess placed the rose on the table but did not sit down.

'Of course Urdu is only one of the ten languages I have mastered.'

Jess wondered where all the modest people were these days. Only the week before, Freddie had bragged that he was fluent in seven languages. Everyone was so keen to spill their life stories these days and no one ever asked about hers. She looked towards the door. This cool escape was not going according to plan.

'*Namaste*,' said Kiran, bowing her head.

'What's that?'

'"Hello" in Urdu.'

'*Nam-uss-tey*,' Jess repeated.

'Very good.'

'*Kaise hai aap* – "How are you?"'

'*Key-sey-hey-aap*.'

'You're quite a fast learner, Jessica. I'm sure I could teach you many things?' Kiran unwound her body and her smile.

'Alright. How do you say, 'I'll have a chicken tandoori and some pilau rice'?'

'I'm not telling you.' Kiran was suddenly abrupt. 'What was all that ribald hilarity you were having with the *bar steward* just now? I saw you laughing. You were laughing at me, weren't you.' Her huge eyes narrowed.

Jess paused, lit a cigarette and took a serious drag as if she was determined to suck out every drop of nicotine. For her, cigarettes had never been flirtatious props. She decided to give Kiran a dose of her own deliberate shock treatment.

'They think you're trying to pick me up.' Her tone matched Kiran's. 'Are you?'

'Those people.' Kiran flapped a dismissive hand towards the bar. 'Jessica, those people are so utterly tedious.' A toss of her chin lumped Jess among them.

'I should probably go.' Jess shoved her cigarettes into her shirt pocket and picked up the rose. 'It's been nice to meet you.'

Kiran's eyes were as cold as a Montreal winter.

It seemed too curt to leave on that note, too embarrassing; what if they bumped into each other in here again? Apologetically, haltingly, Jess said, 'I guess I'll see you around and vice versa.'


Later that night, sleepless on her unfolded futon, the final scene refused to fade out of her mind's eye. Simpkin, her cat, purred insistently and tried to sit on her head, oblivious to her restlessness. Insomnia was unusual for Jess but dawn was creeping over the east of the city by the time she drifted off.

The next day, she threw the rose in the garbage can

even though it was nowhere near dead. The dislocation she had felt on first returning from Alberta hit her afresh. As before, her apartment no longer seemed her own. Then, it had smelled different and Corinna, her house-sitter, had highlighted Jess's domestic failings by leaving the place immaculate. Now, although the apartment smelled familiar, Jess's efficient solitude had been broken. Her lifestyle – early nights, hard work, food and drink when necessary in cafés – seemed stringent rather than Zen. Her cupboards, which contained nothing but cat food and coffee, seemed pitiful rather than purist. As did the fact she used a penknife to butter bread, uncork wine and wire plugs.

As the days went by, the encounter with Miss India was submerged by normality. Jess went to college, painted, smoked, emptied Simpkin's litter tray, spent money on food, drink, drugs, a screwdriver, a corkscrew and a new set of cutlery. She stopped surreptitiously examining her chin in car windows and shop fronts. She suppressed the worry that she never generated gossip, unlike girls like Corinna.

One afternoon, when the city was well-entrenched in winter, while walking down Ste. Catherine, she passed a restaurant with a cartoon trio of Mexican bandits painted across the window. A jolt of memory made her halt: The Three Amigos, La Cabane, late summer, early autumn, that Indian *Playboy* bunny, the lesbian. Jess peered into the unseasonal, cactus-spiked-tequila-sunrise interior, where Kiran was circling the tables with two plates on each arm and a fixed smile on her elegant face. She looked thinner and more skit-tish than before; clearly the gods had led her off on a tangent. The way Kiran set down the plates and tossed her peacock hair as she stalked back to the kitchens reminded Jess of the disdain with which she had been dismissed all those months ago.

*'I guess I'll see you around and vice versa.'*

Bristling like a cat, the former Miss India of 1979 had drawn back her shoulders with a long intake of breath. The shadow of a sneer curling around her lips, she had replied, 'My dear, I have a terrible memory for faces and I doubt I'd remember you if I ever saw you again.'

# The Life and Soul

The party was in full swing by the time Joey arrived.

'Poppa! I didn't think you were coming,' cried Freya, when he blustered through the door with Maureen, Barney and Jasper in tow.

'New Year's Eve. You think I'm gonna stay home?' He pressed his cold lips to his daughter's hot cheek and began to shed his snow-dusted outer layers.

'We bought Irish whisky,' shouted Maureen. 'Barney and Jasper, you can have one can of beer each and that's it. No spirits. I am not going to be responsible for clearing up your puke at the end of the night, is that understood?'

'Yes, Mom,' chorused the boys before disappearing into the crowd to find some hard liquor.

'Cut them a little slack, Maureen,' said Joey, but his wife had bustled out of earshot. Seeing his chance, he slipped into Freya's bedroom for a joint. His eldest daughter, Amy, was in there with a friend, who was changing out of thermal leggings and snowboots into sheer stockings and high heels.

'Daddy! Louisa's getting changed!'

'Don't mind me.' Joey sunk heavily onto the bed. He caught what he perceived to be a coy glance from beneath Louisa's long, dark lashes. 'I didn't think you modern-day girls wore stockings any more. I thought it was all tights and godawful things like that.'

'Dad-dy,' said Amy, warningly. 'I'm just going to get another drink. You want a top-up?'

'Bring some whisky for Louisa and me,' said Joey.

'Can I have some Coke in mine? I can't drink straight whisky,' twittered Louisa. Joey surmised from the clumsy way she began to buckle the ankle straps of her shoes that she was already drunk.

'Allow me,' he said, leaning forward breathlessly to help her. These days his beer belly was an immovable obstacle and he was often wheezy. Maureen had suggested they both start dieting and reduced the quantity of their evening meals accordingly. She was unaware of his addiction to salami and Swiss-cheese specials from Wilensky's Light Lunch.

'Has anybody ever told you, you have perfect feet?' he asked, caressing Louisa's high arches.

'No, do you think so?' Louisa pointed them this way and that, considering.

'They're perfect. I make glass sculptures of women's feet so I notice this kind of thing. Let me see your hands.'

Louisa's pale, doll-like hands made Joey's look like two thick-cut steaks.

'Beautiful. So finely made,' he said, running his fingers over the tiny wrist bones, which looked like they could be snapped in two.

'What about mine?' demanded a girl who had appeared in the doorway. She thrust out a bare foot with red-painted toenails.

'Well, they're nice clean-looking feet.'

The girl snorted and turned on her heel.

Amy returned with the bottle of whisky Maureen had brought, loaded up their glasses and disappeared.

'To your infinite beauty,' said Joey, holding his glass up to Louisa, who sipped her whisky gingerly and wrinkled her nose.

'I think I'm going to go and dance,' she said, tottering off on her heels.

Joey reclined on Freya's bed like a pasha and took alternate puffs and sips. The room was littered with the frills and furbelows of femininity that he adored: a pink silk counterpane; a red chiffon scarf tinting the light from tasseled lampshade; a dressing table dusted with beads and powders; a hatstand dripping with impractical coats and ridiculous hats; a closet bursting with sequined camisoles, lace gloves, lengths of gold lamé and feather boas.

It had been strange having two boys after fathering four girls. Barney and Jasper (named on his insistence after Barnett Newman and Jasper Johns) were easier to understand but since Freya moved out, Joey missed his glimpses into the perfumed, peachy realm of girls. A woman like Maureen wasn't the same; she was solid and earthy, a big-hearted, practical Irish woman from Newfoundland. She knew how to trap rabbits and fish for lobster, for God's sake. She made Elaine and Pia and all their sweet, sly daughters seem as fey and tricksy as will o' the wisps.

'Papa, why don't you come out and mingle?' said Freya, poking her head around the door.

'All right, I will.' Joey lumbered to his feet. The room skewed so alarmingly he had to grab the hatstand to steady himself. He'd drunk quite a bit at home and the grass from BC had been surprisingly potent.

In the living room, people were moving energetically to rhythmic noise: neither dancing nor music were apt descriptions in Joey's view. He lurched through them into the kitchen where Maureen, who had clearly ditched the diet for the night, was plundering the vast buffet.

'Good spread, huh Joey?' she mumbled through a mouthful of meringue, 'I'm going back into the other room. You coming?'

'No, I'm just going to dig in here.' Joey began to systematically load a plate with a little of everything on the table. It certainly was an impressive feast: tomato quiches criss-crossed with anchovies, a ham dotted with cloves, a whole poached salmon with its staring sightless head still intact, dainty sandwiches, lozenges of pizza, a ripe and pungent brie, unctuous dips made from avocados, blue cheese, chick peas and fish roe, a school of vol-au-vents bedecked with shrimps, a nest of quail's eggs, a pride of chicken drumsticks and a bevy of beautiful desserts: raspberry pavlova, key lime pie, chocolate roulade and apple strudel.

On one corner of the table Freya's roommate, Sandra, who was home on leave from the merchant navy, was arm-wrestling with anyone who would take her on. She was a tough middle-aged Québécois woman, a lesbian Joey suspected, who considered herself the head of this house on St Urbain even though she was away at sea for three months out of every four.

'Hey, Joey, you wanna give it a shot?' she demanded.

'OK, Sandra, but you're probably going to beat me.' Joey settled himself down and grasped her rough, rope-hardened hand. She gave him a good match, clenching her jaw and wincing heavily but he managed to topple her. Their onlookers whooped with delight and sloshed cheap rum into his glass.

'Not bad, Joey. Not bad,' Sandra admitted, slapping him on the back. 'Anybody want to take on Joey here?'

'Ah nah, I'm going to finish my food,' said Joey, lifting his plate aloft and squeezing back into the living room.

Freya's other roommates were scrawny Etienne, a philosophy student, who resembled a nocturnal, underground animal so pale was his skin and so huge were his black saucer eyes, and winsome Sophie whom Joey spotted swaying seductively in front of her boyfriend, Jean-Michel. Jean-Michel was sporting a white vest with orange flames printed along the bottom. This and the fiery tattoos around his biceps, made him look like an indy car. Joey reckoned Jean-Michel was responsible for the sorry welfare types slumped in the corners. Their grimy army fatigues, bad teeth and stunted bodies lent them an oddly mediaeval appearance. They were all Francophones and Joey had an idea they were holding themselves aloof from the Anglos. The rest of the guests were college kids and sailors, hoping for a quick fling before they returned to ship.

To Joey's sodden sentimental mind, his daughters shone like angels amid this motley crew. Amy was resplendent in a beaded dress, the colour of ripe cherries, with her blonde hair twisted into a chignon. She was smooching on the dancefloor with Jason, who was wearing a white Stetson that Joey was sure he'd once seen on Amy. Skye was laughing with her half-brothers; dear sweet Skye in her flares and mirrored smock, still burnished with the tan she'd caught while travelling around India. She had returned a month ago, slender and suddenly worldly, her eyes shining from six months of adventure. Freya was dolled up like something out of *La Dolce Vita* in black pedal-pushers and a red halter-neck with a yellow rose behind her ear. She was talking to Maureen and, to Joey's amazement, smiling warmly. It had been difficult living with them both under the same roof; Freya had a knack for bringing out the fishwife in Maureen and Maureen brought out the bitch in Freya. But since she had moved out, they had reached an amicable truce.

Louisa was dancing with one of the college boys. No rhythm, Joey noted, despite her beautiful feet. Not like the girl with the painted toenails who was gyrating feverishly in the centre of the dancefloor. She was less delicately pretty than Louisa but she possessed a certain robust sensuality. Joey was nothing if not catholic in his appreciation of women. Her backless dress showed off her milky shoulders and she was whipping the skirt up like a flamenco dancer. The tune ended. Jean-Michel took up his guitar and began playing a bass solo. The girl waltzed off, brushing past Joey.

'Hey,' he smiled.

'Hey,' she replied, coolly.

'I was just watching you dance. You're a great dancer.'

She melted immediately: 'You think so?'

'I definitely think so.' Flattery. Worked every time. Joey scanned the bobbing heads but Maureen was nowhere in sight. 'And may I be so bold as to ask your name?'

'Roisin.'

'Roisin – what a beautiful name. Irish, am I right?'

'Yeah – my mother's from St John's.'

Joey had to stop himself saying 'so is my wife'. Instead, he jerked his head towards the bedrooms and suggested they repaired there for a smoke.

'I'm not sure . . .' Roisin demurred.

'Oh come on. I'm perfectly safe. I don't bite.'

'OK.' Roisin smiled. Her teeth were slightly crooked but Joey liked them.

Back in Freya's room, she retrieved the beers she had hidden outside on the snowy windowsill while he skinned up.

'I put it out there to chill, so nobody'd find it,' she explained, cracking open a bottle and passing it to him in exchange for the joint. The way her lips formed a moue as she took a drag was really sexy. He offered her a shrimp vol-au-vent from his unfinished plate but she wrinkled her nose in disgust: 'No, thank you – I can't stand seafood.'

'Really? What a shame. I adore it: shrimp, lobster, oysters, moules, I just can't get enough of them. When I lived in California we had this boat and we used to take it out to the rocks where the moules were and just pick them – all these moules, then pick up a couple of cuties and have a few beers and cook the moules on the beach with garlic butter – mmmm!' He kissed his fingers.

'Sounds like the life,' said Roisin, drawing her feet up onto the bed.

'It was. It was the life.' Joey puffed away contentedly as he thought of those golden summers. He missed the endless heat. Even when the sun went down your skin still held the warmth from the day.

'Is that your daughter out there?' Roisin asked, conversationally.

'Which one?'

'The pretty one that's just got back from India. I was talking to her . . .'

'Oh yeah, Skye, yeah, she's just got back from India. When I went to India – this was twenty years ago – I caught dengue fever and all my body hair fell out. Can you believe it? Luckily it stopped at my neck and I still have a full head of hair and my beard.' What the hell was he saying? When he was stoned his mouth tended to run away with him and all sorts of ludicrous rubbish came out. Roisin's dress had ruched up a little and he found himself smoothing his hand ruminatively along her shin. 'Such smooth skin you have.'

'Please don't do that.' Roisin batted his hand away as if it were a fly and moved to the edge of the bed.

'Excuse me, I'm sorry but you know you girls . . .' His voice trailed off as he lost the thread of what he was going to say.

'Are you OK?' Roisin was asking, but her voice seemed very far away.

'Just tell Amy to bring me some . . .'

He dropped down onto his back and closed his eyes. Some time later he was conscious of Amy standing over him with a glass of pink lemonade. Later still, he was woken by the countdown to midnight. Propped on one elbow, he lay and listened to them shouting ten . . . nine . . . eight . . . seven . . . At the stroke of twelve there was a huge cheer and their voices shambled into a tuneless rendition of 'Auld Lang Syne'. Joey staggered out of the room and from the darkness of the hall, watched the party welcoming in the new year. He observed with an avuncular smile the kids, who had been circling each other hopefully all night, locked in slobbering clinches. Roisin had her mouth clamped onto Etienne's. Louisa was entwined with the college boy. His daughters were embracing their respective beaus. Barney and Jasper had found a couple of cuties. Once upon a time he would have wanted to be among them.

Unnoticed, he opened the door into the street where strangers were hugging each other and crying out 'Happy new year'. The snow was still falling, sparkling golden in the orange light of the streetlamps. It gathered in perfect, crystalline folds on car bonnets and along the tops of walls, like siftings of icing sugar. It looked good enough to eat. Joey swiped a fistful from the gatepost and licked it with the tip of his tongue. The taste made him think of the snow ice-cream he had made as a child by pouring sugar and milk into freshly fallen drifts. He lifted his face to the flakes swirling silently through the frail mesh of bare trees in the front yard.

'Joey! There you are!' Maureen appeared at his side. Her cheeks were flushed with wine and she gathered him into her arms, warming his body with her own. Snow was collecting in the red waves of her hair, which shone as bright and bonny in the streetlight as it had when they had first met. A tired peace overwhelmed him and he felt grateful that she was there and all their years of youthful striving were behind them.

'Happy new year,' she said.

'Happy new year,' he replied, kissing her on the mouth beneath the quiet falling snow.

Many thanks to the Rooinecks Writing Group, my fellow students on the MA in Writing at Warwick University, as well as Chloé Collins, Robert Edric, Mark Etherton, Maureen Freely, August Kleinzahler, Mark Lackie, Jane Rogers and John Salt.

Finally, thanks most of all to my family.

*This book is a work of fiction and, except in the case of historical fact, any resemblance to actual persons, living or dead, is purely coincidental.*

Rowena Macdonald was born on the Isle of Wight, grew up in the West Midlands and studied at the Universities of Sussex and Warwick. While living in Montreal after graduation, she worked as a waitress, bartender, life-model and cleaner. She now lives in east London and works at the House of Commons and Westminster University. Her stories have appeared in anthologies published by Serpent's Tail, Roast Books and the Do-Not Press. She has won several prizes for her short fiction, including two Asham Awards.